HOLLIS HERMAN

W9-DBG-789

NOVELS BY ROBERT CAMPBELL

The Junkyard Dog
The 600-Pound Gorilla
Hip Deep in Alligators
Thinning the Turkey Herd
Cat's Meow
In La-La Land We Trust
Alice in La-La Land
Plugged Nickel
Red Cent

JUICE

ROBERT CAMPBELL

POSEIDON PRESS
NEW YORK   LONDON
TORONTO   SYDNEY   TOKYO

POSEIDON PRESS
Simon & Schuster Building
Rockefeller Center
1230 Avenue of the Americas
New York, New York 10020

This book is a work of fiction. Names, characters, places and incidents are either the product of the author's imagination or are used fictitiously. Any resemblance to actual events or locales or persons, living or dead, is entirely coincidental.

Copyright © 1988 by Robert Campbell
All rights reserved including the right of reproduction in whole or in part in any form.
POSEIDON PRESS is a registered trademark of Simon & Schuster Inc.
POSEIDON PRESS colophon is a trademark of Simon & Schuster Inc.
Designed by Karolina Harris
Manufactured in the United States of America

Library of Congress Cataloging-in-Publication Data

Campbell, R. Wright.
  Juice / Robert Campbell.
    p.   cm.
    I. Title.
PS3553.A4867J85 1988   88-25328
813'.54—dc19   CIP

ISBN 0-671-66524-3

BOMC offers recordings and compact discs, cassettes
and records. For information and catalog write to
BOMR, Camp Hill, PA 17012.

Elizabeth Lopresti

wise soul . . .
kind heart . . .

There was a character hung around Hollywood Park, maybe ten, eleven years ago, by the name of Cholly Englehart, always bet on gray horses and Japanese jockeys. It wouldn't matter if a silver mount with a yellow-skinned slant-eyed midget on his back had three legs, Cholly would've bet the cripple to win.

That's one of the reasons Cholly died broke and ended up hanging in the freezer over at the university medical school with ice tongs in his ear holes. Billy Ray, who wanted to be an actor, was scraping up a stake working nights in the school morgue at the time and saw old Cholly there on the overhead conveyor, naked as a loser of a three-horse parlay gone sour, inside his rubber sack.

Over coffee at the drugstore on the corner of Sunset and Crescent Heights, he told Ham Purdue, Manny Ciglianni and Harold Chomsky all about seeing Cholly without his pants on in such an undignified setting, and how it only goes to show that bettors shouldn't fall in love with specialty items.

"It's like falling in love with a hooker what does it hanging upside down from the jungle bars," Chomsky agreed. "You could enjoy it once but how is she going to keep up the pace over six furlongs?"

"Everybody knows gray blood's weak and Jap jocks are not to be trusted," Purdue said.

"How big was his shlong?" Ciglianni wanted to know.

"Jesus Christ, look at this," Ray said, glancing up from the racing form he was reading even as he carried on the conversation. "Jenny Chicago, going in the fourth."

His three confidants consulted their own forms.

"A bow-wow," Purdue said. "Thirty to one on the morning line."

"An also-ran," Ciglianni agreed.

"A never-was," Chomsky chimed in. "Here's a match, burn your money."

"A black filly with a white blaze on her forehead and two white socks on her front feet," Ray said. "That means running blood. Look at her last three starts."

"Dead last in a field of nine," Purdue said.

"Out of the money and tiring at the finish," Ciglianni added.

"Third in a four-horse race," Chomsky summed it up.

"She's coming up," Ray said triumphantly. "She's ready to make her move."

"It's possible," Purdue said doubtfully.

"It could happen," Ciglianni said, more forcefully.

"It's worth a bet," Chomsky declared.

"So, who wants to go in a pool with me? Two and a half bucks and we eat Italian over to Benito's tonight. With two bottles of guinea red."

It's not recorded in anybody's memory if Jenny Chicago finished in the money, but a buck'll get you ten they ate out of a can that night.

That was a while ago.

Ciglianni's dead. Keeled over with a heart attack last year doing triples with two teenage whores he picked up off the hookers' stroll at Hollywood and Vine. They were from Biloxi, Mississippi, and him dying that way made their reputations. They call themselves the Killer Pussies since then and dress like twins in black leather and knee-high boots.

Chomsky gave up the track, also show business. Actually he'd had an illustrious career as an extra during the late great days of the majors back in the fifties. He was known to work three jobs at the same time, getting a friend at two of the locations to sign him in and making an appearance at least once during the day so the assistant director would remember seeing his face.

Back then Chomsky flew to New York at least once a year for some large athletic event, the World Series, the Super Bowl, a championship fight. He had a deal where a block of seats were reserved for him by this ticket broker. Chomsky went back and scalped them—he had such great contacts—and they split the illegal pie. Sometimes he took a bath but mostly he made a killing.

Everything was angles with old Chomsky. Word on the street and in the coffee shop across the boulevard from the Chinese Theater, which took over as the hangout after the drugstore on Sunset packed it in, was that Chomsky had gone legitimate and was living with his daughter and her husband and three kids back in Lodi, which isn't even in New York but across the river in Jersey. What the hell. Why not? Why shouldn't he live in some place like Lodi, New Jersey? Hollywood isn't Hollywood anymore. And L.A. is still trying to be a city.

Purdue and Ray, twenty-five years younger than the other two cronies, were still around. Still sucking hind tit.

Purdue worked as a grip on the soundstages, hoping to make first hammer before retirement. It was an unlikely hope.

Billy Ray was still waiting to get discovered, driving a hack meanwhile, when he wasn't trying to get an angle on girls in thin dresses standing at bus stops with the sun behind them.

He was married to a woman by the name of Lisa, who had a pocketful of busted dreams of her own, but he still took what he could get, still played the ponies, and still lost the farm nearly each and every time he tried to be a sport. One way or the other.

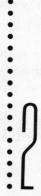

Detective Three Eddie "Panama" Heath had been wearing the same hat of cream-colored straw for ten years. So it really wasn't cream-colored, but only *mostly* cream-colored. He'd knocked it off a skag dealer's head when he broke his nose and, since it fit him just right, never bothered to give it back. What was a man going to do with a panama straw in the slam?

When he strolled along the boulevard in his jeans, white shirt with rolled-up sleeves and denim vest, with the hat shading his eyes from the hot California sun, they didn't call him Eddie and they didn't call him detective. They didn't even call him Heath. They called him Panama. What else?

Wilbur Monk, a Detective Two, had been Panama's police wife for twelve years. The thing is a cop doesn't call his partner his husband, so what you got is two wives.

Monk had another wife, a square wife, a wife who'd borne his two children and kept his house and complained every once in a while about the way Wilbur spent more time with Panama than he did with his own wife and kids. Probably cared more about Panama than he did about his own wife and kids, too.

That wasn't altogether true. Monk cared a lot about his daughter, Hilly, who was in the seventh grade and just starting to fill out in the chest and hips, a late bloomer like her mother. He didn't understand his son, Henry, but he went to watch him play basketball for his high school junior varsity when he could take the time.

What was left between him and Jessie was mostly space. Once in a while she'd put her leg over his and that meant she was feeling needy, but after, and even during, they both lay there staring at the ceiling wondering why they'd lost a half hour of sleep for that.

They never talked about it, but they both knew that as soon as the kids were out of school—five and a half more years—they'd find a way to put even more space between them. Maybe she'd move out, maybe he'd move out, maybe they'd both move out.

Panama and Monk worked out of Hollywood Division most of the time. But they were such a solid team, sometimes they'd be loaned out to Central Bureau or South Bureau. The other cops knew you could deal with them. They weren't personally crooked but they knew what to see and what not to see.

They were parked in an unmarked car every gonnif, pimp and whore on the street knew was a police car, never mind the trademark panama hat. They were waiting for a dealer they'd been tipped was going to make a delivery to the movie rental store in the middle of the block just around the corner from Hollywood Boulevard.

"What are we doing sitting here boiling our balls off for some hinky-dinky little bootleg tape operation?" Monk wanted to know, as if Panama had anything to say about it.

"The film distribution companies are tossing turds at City Hall. How many billion dollars a year you think they're losing with these counterfeits?"

"Who gives a rat's ass?"

"Three, maybe four."

"Pocket change. That's fucking pocket change. What kind of tapes? You think they got any of them toilet-rated goony-poony tunes?"

"They play around copying fuck films they got the guinea mafiosi cutting off their dicks and sticking them you know where."

"No, I don't know where."

"You want me to talk dirty? I won't talk dirty."

"I got to pass the time and forget the heat."

"So what do you want me to talk dirty, make you hotter?"

"Ask Jessica. You talk dirty to Jessica it just chills her out. I'm just like Jessica."

Hoo-hoo Coventry, a black runner for a nickel book, shim-shammed by and slapped the fender of the car.

Monk stuck his head out the window and yelled, "Hoo-hoo, watch who you're fuckin' with."

"Hoo-hoo to you, white meat," the runner yelled back, dipping his hip and doing a half-swivel so Monk could see his grinning face.

Half a dozen hookers on the stroll took up the cry. "Hoo-hoo. Hoo-hoo."

"You know what?" Panama said.

"What?"

"I don't think we do a very good stakeout anymore."

Monk was grinning all over his face. "You saying we're not doing much good sitting here?"

"Paul Newman and Robert Redford would be less conspicuous sitting here than us."

"Newman and Redford wouldn't be sitting here under any circumstances. They'd be out on the golf course or over to the racetrack. Jesus Christ."

"What's the matter now?"

"I was just thinking about the track. Sitting in the grandstand in the shadows with a cold beer in one hand and a ticket on the winner in the other."

"Personal time?" Panama asked.

"Who could begrudge us?"

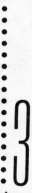

A race caller at any decent track has got to have sandpaper for tonsils. When he growls "They're off!" it's got to send chills up the spine of every horse player in the joint, even the ones in the crapper who got taken short and failed to get a bet down on the race.

When Hetchie MacVee said the magic words, Billy Ray felt a twinge in his pecker. Which also could have been he was getting over a dose of the clap he could've collected in lieu of cab fare some time before when he cabbed a certain whore up the hill to this television star's pad on the top of Mulholland Drive.

Ray elbowed his way to a spot on the rail and leaned his arm against a blonde's tit who was so excited by the two bucks she had riding on a horse with pretty eyes she didn't even feel it.

Ray was a man who took his opportunities where he found them.

She was already jumping up and down and giving him a hard-on when the horses rounded the first turn.

"Lady, they got a long way to go, save your juice for the stretch drive," he mumbled under his breath, giving it everything he had to keep himself from screaming just as loud for his pick, Benny's Boy, running dead last at the quarter pole. Benny's Boy was carrying Ray's hopes, dreams and physical well-being into that long backstretch, also every nickel, dime and quarter Ray had been able to beg, borrow and steal. Because, on the morning of this sun-drenched day, he'd awakened knowing, with the knowing that spills up from the marrow of the bones, that this was his day; his run to glory day; his pay off the shylock and save his ass day; his change of fucking luck day.

"Hey, Panama," Monk said, giving his partner the elbow. "Ain't that your ex-girlfriend's old man up to the rail copping an elbow feel from the bouncy blonde?"

They were sitting seven rows up in the grandstand, close enough to see but not close enough to be sure. Panama put the binoculars they kept in the glove compartment for stakeouts and such up to his eyes and focused in on Billy Ray.

"That's the sucker," Heath said, after two or three seconds.

The horses were rounding the far turn and Benny's Boy was still tying the laces on his running shoes.

"Where the hell are you, Benny's Boy?" Ray pleaded. "That's a fuckin' racetrack you got your hoofs on. It's time to run for home."

"I hear that little asshole spends a lot of time at the track," Monk said. "I hear he's got a respectable record picking winners."

"If I wanted to bet a horse in a two-horse race, I'd go ask Billy Ray who he favored and the one he liked I'd bet against. That's how you pick your winners around Billy Ray," Heath replied.

"Fachrissake, Benny's Boy," Ray prayed on, "at least gimme a kiss if it's your intention to fuck me."

Like the prayer was a red-hot poker shoved up his ass, Benny's Boy remembered that he was racehorse and on a racetrack and some little sonofabitch the size of a monkey was beating his ass unmercifully and his goddam blood was singing and he was passing horses right and left as he charged through the pack going for the wire.

Two strides and a snort too late.

"Look at his face," Heath said. "He just lost his poke."

Benny's Boy finished a respectable second, which was like not finishing at all for a bettor like Ray, who scorned any bet but a bet to win.

Two hundred bucks, two small, two dimes, two C-notes, all blown away. All of a sudden the smell of horseshit wasn't perfume and the screams of the blonde who kept battering him with her tit weren't music.

"I won, I won, I won," she kept chanting like she'd just had the best orgasm of her life.

She was looking him in the eye, wanting to share her excitement with the nearest person. When the nearest person was almost six feet tall, with slick black hair, brown eyes and a solid tan that made him look more than a little like George Hamilton, it couldn't be anything but icing on the cake. She'd won her bet, her pants were hot, and she was ready for a ride to the wire herself and worry about AIDS tomorrow.

"I won, I won, I won," she shrieked, reaching out to give Ray a what-the-hell-ain't-life-grand hug.

"So look at that," Monk said. "Win or lose, that asshole's scoring with the blonde."

"A horse player loses his bet, a sixteen-year-old virgin couldn't coax a hard-on out of him," Heath said. "It's written on the grave of every horse player I ever knew."

The blonde gave Billy Ray breathing room but still held on, looking into his face to see if he was getting the message her groin was tattooing on his groin.

"Why don't you go fuck yourself, lady?" Billy Ray said.

When you're a loser a chance to put somebody down is a godsend. Even a small victory is better than a stick in the eye, and hurting another person takes some of the pain away.

After she'd slain him with a look—so why didn't he fall down and die?—and walked away, Ray immediately regretted his foolish insult. Up on the tote it showed the numbers. Her winning horse paid out twelve-eighty. Even if she'd only had a deuce riding on the banger's nose she might've been good for the loan of a nickel. Enough to at least make a bet on the seventh and eighth, with change left over to call home and tell Lisa he was going to take a double shift.

Now there wasn't even crumbs for the birds in his pockets. He got up on his toes and gave the crowd the eye.

Heath turned his face away.

"What's the matter with you? You hiding from that asshole?" Monk asked.

"That last race busted him. He's looking for somebody to make a touch for a nickel or a dime. I don't want it to be me."

"You're worrying the sonofabitch took your girlfriend away from you is going to come up here and try to borrow a nickel or a dime? You telling me that wimp's got them kind of brass balls?"

"He used to be a friend. He still thinks he's a friend. What am I supposed to do, let him know how much it hurt me him taking Lisa away?"

"It almost fucking *killed* you. You still ain't over it."

"Stick a sock in it, will you?"

"Okay, he ain't looking this way anymore."

Heath lifted his head and watched Billy Ray weighing the crowd.

Ray saw plenty of people he knew, but nobody he could tap for a finnif or a sawbuck.

He did a recon up in the upper stands, inside the clubhouse and through the boxes.

He spotted Eddie Segal, the accountant, and figured it was worth a try.

Eddie Segal had pale hair, pale eyes and a pale face, which was re- markable because he was at the track more than he was in his office. Segal had the kind of face you figured he wasn't a bookie or a dealer, he had to be a shy. It had this kind of innocence which wasn't to be trusted.

"Hullo, Eddie, taking the day?" Ray asked as he sauntered by.

"The day's taking me," Segal said. "How about yourself?"

"I've been spectating."

"You haven't laid a bet?"

"I'm on my way even as we speak."

"You saved your pennies for something in the seventh?"

"The race that's coming up?"

"Seven always comes after six and before eight, Billy Ray. That's the way it's always been and that's the way I expect it'll always be."

Segal stared up at Ray through lashes that didn't seem to be there, sizing up the angle. Was Ray peddling tips? If so, they wouldn't be worth the wind they were written on.

Ray took a quick sneak at his watch.

"Jesus Christ, I got to get in line," he said.

"You got ten minutes," Segal said.

"I'd cut my throat if I didn't get my bet down."

"You know something I don't know?"

"I know something only this many knows," Ray said, and held up both hands with the fingers spread.

"I didn't know you had six fingers on your left hand, Billy," Segal said, grinning in his most seductive way.

"I shouldn't."

"For a friend?"

"Tagalong."

Segal did a quick scan of the form, his eyelids fluttering as he made the calculations. "It doesn't figure, Billy."

"That's why only ten people know it. Eleven."

"What the hell. I'll put a dime on the nag just so I won't be sitting here empty-handed," Segal said.

"Suit yourself," Billy said, and hurried off.

He checked his watch again. He'd taken too long playing the game with Segal. There were only six horses in the race, but he had to make five more stops before the betting windows closed if he was going to have a chance to pick up a little change.

Monk watched Billy Ray making his way here and there, upstairs and downstairs, stopping for a quick conversation one place, then skipping over to another. Monk lost him for a minute now and then. After another minute he'd spot him somewhere else doing another little soft-shoe dance.

"What's he doing?" Monk asked. "What the hell is that Billy Ray doing bouncing around like the ball in a singalong?"

"Scratching backs," Heath said, showing very little interest.

"What?"

"You scratch my back, I'll scratch yours. You give me a tip and the horse wins, I give you a little thank-you note. Maybe five, maybe ten."

"You mean he's touting a different horse in a six-horse race to six different people? Any horse wins, somebody got the winning tip from Ray?"

"That's the game."

"That's so old it does the Charleston."

"Shit, it ain't even legal," Heath said.

"It ain't even smart."

"Anybody takes a tip from a loser like Billy Ray is a hopeless romantic," Heath said, and looked away, because what was a hopeless romantic doing calling somebody else a hopeless romantic? "That's horse players," he added, like it was the eleventh of the commandments.

Billy Ray gave Heart Song to Harry the Preacher, While Away to Jackie Haze, Prince Dark to Dick Miller, Shirley's Song to Connie Dietrich and Chipmunk to Jimmy Murphy, so he had all the horses covered just in time.

"They're off!" Hetchie MacVee grated.

Billy Ray watched the race from the first balcony, out of sight of any of the people he'd rewarded with a tip. If anybody was watching, it would never do for them to see him booting one horse home instead of another, for as far as each and every one of them was concerned Ray had his money riding on the one horse he shared with each one alone. As a matter of fact he would have had his money on Prince Dark, who was a chance at three to one.

The favorite, Shirley's Song, crossed the finish a stride ahead of Tagalong, who'd stumbled and lost the pace coming into the stretch, tried to make it up but couldn't, but still finished in second place.

"You want to stay for the eighth?" Heath asked.

"No, let's get the hell on out of here and beat the crowd."

They got up and started moving toward one of the exits. There were others who had the same idea, but most of the crowd were right-footing, left-footing it, waiting for an angel to whisper the winner of the eighth race into their ear.

Connie Dietrich was gathering up her knitting and her latest boyfriend when Ray got back to her.

"Hey, hullo again," he said.

"Fancy bumping into you again so soon," Connie said, looking at him with her glass eye.

"It's me, Billy Ray," he said.

"Come for thanks?"

"I just wasn't sure you saw it was me," he said.

"Oh, I would've made a bet I'd see you again before the day was through."

"Ain't you staying for the eighth?"

"Nothing I like is running in the eighth and I'm not looking for a tip."

"I only had the one," Ray said, as though he'd given her the family jewels.

She took out a compact as big as the lid on a can of lard and checked her eye shadow, then her lipstick, fingering away some residue from the corners of her mouth with the tip of her pinkie.

"You only had the favorite," she said, snapping the compact shut. "You only had what most of the money in the country had. Anytime you want to cop a present from me, Ray, you bring me a genuine piece of news. I mean an exclusive, a scoop."

"I wasn't sucking around looking for a gratuity," Ray said, acting indignant.

"I'm glad to hear that, because I wasn't thinking of giving you one. Let's go, Rollo. If we hustle, we can maybe beat part of this crowd."

So giving six different people six different tips, knowing that one of the horses had to win and hoping for a little token of appreciation from the lucky punter, hadn't worked. He was still empty.

He was making his way to one of the exit gates thinking that he'd have to work an extra shift after all when he felt a tap on his sleeve and turned around to find Segal walking along just behind him. The accountant smiled one of his white smiles and tucked a twenty into Ray's shirt pocket.

"It wasn't your fault the horse stumbled coming around the turn," he said.

"Hey, I don't want you to pay me off on a loser."

"It wasn't a loser, Billy. I'm a conservative man. I bet two small on the beast to place and show."

Ray patted his pocket and felt good all of a sudden. First he was down and then he was up. It was only a twenty-dollar bill, but fortunes were started with less than that. He turned around to thank Segal, but he wasn't at his shoulder anymore. He was out there somewhere, lost in the crowd.

Ray got crushed up at the gate, then the dam broke and he was through, out in the parking lot and on his way to his cab, which was parked in the ranks ready to pick up a fare for the ride back to town. He could see somebody sitting in the back. He started to trot, running light and easy, dodging, weaving, tapping an arm or a back. "Excuse me." Smiling his blazer, teeth white as milk in his brown face. "Excuse me. Coming through. Pardon me, lady. If only I wasn't married." On top of the world. Twenty bucks in his shirt pocket and a fare waiting for him. Maybe Steven Spielberg. Maybe George Lucas.

Maybe who the hell knew who? Maybe his big break in the back of his cab, waiting to discover him.

"Look at that, will you?" Sam's Man said. His real name was Carmine DiBenedetto, but he had this dog named Sam, a mastiff, something like that, weighed a hundred and ninety pounds, dragged him around every time he took him out to take a leak. So that's why they called Carmine DiBenedetto Sam's Man.

"Look at what?" Manny Machado asked. Machado didn't have a dog.

"Ain't that Panama and his asshole partner, Wilbur Monk? What're they doing hanging around the racetrack, they should be out protecting the citizens?"

"Maybe they're protecting the citizens inside the track."

"I just seen Panama tear up some losing tickets."

"Even cops got to have an outing now and then," Machado said. "Besides, maybe it's their day off."

"I don't give a fuck," Sam's Man said, and stared hard at the back of Heath's head.

When Heath turned around, feeling the eyes, knowing hate when it drifted through the air his way, like any streetwise cop that ever lived long enough to get his gold shield, Sam's Man quickly looked away. Why tempt fate?

When Sam's Man looked up again he couldn't see Heath and Monk anymore but he could see Billy Ray trotting toward them.

"There's Billy Ray. Happy-go-lucky gamoosh, ain't he," Sam's Man said.

"How can he be so happy without he's got a clear conscience?" Machado asked.

"Maybe he had a winning day."

"And maybe the pope's a Jew."

Ray saw the shapes in the back of his cab. Two horse players flush with winnings. Two happy suckers ready to tip him large because they'd won and were full of the milk of human kindness. He got in the front and started to turn around.

"Hey, hey, hey, it's Billy Ray," Sam's Man said.

"Oh, shit," Ray said, twisting around. "What the hell you doing here?"

"You public transportation, you ain't public transportation?" Machado asked.

"Sure, sure. You want Hollywood and Vine?"

"We want a little peace and quiet."

Billy Ray said, "I don't get your meaning," because he was afraid he got their meaning all too well.

"The excitement of the races has got us in a fit," Sam's Man said. "We'll sit someplace out of the way until my heart slows down a little, you don't mind."

"I got to drop the flag," Ray said.

"You drop the flag, I drop my fist on your head," Machado said.

"Well, Christ, I can't just sit here having a conversation while all these horse players are looking for a ride home."

"You got to learn to take it a little easy, Billy Ray," Sam's Man said, "and watch the rest of the world go by."

"Turn around," Machado said.

Ray turned around and stared out the windshield, feeling how Machado scared you with the threat of sudden violence, but Sam's Man terrified you with his pig's smile and a voice that sounded like it was swimming up out of a sea of fat.

He also thought how fast a crowd as big as a racetrack crowd could break out through the gates, hurrying to their cars, walking out to the buses, grabbing up the cabs, leaving acres of empty blacktop behind.

A gamoosh in a plaid corduroy sport jacket stuck his head in the window on the passenger side and said, "You fellas going into Santa Monica, I'll split the fare."

"Hump off," Machado said.

"Hey, the regulations say four can ride to a single destination for the price of one."

"We're going to Sacramento, babe," Sam's Man said, and the way he said it made all the difference.

Ray sat there praying that something big would happen. That a bomb would go off and bring the cops. That a horse would break out of the stables and go running through the crowds inflicting injury everywhere. Anything, so long as all the people wouldn't go away. All of a sudden he had to take a piss. He should have wrung out his sock before leaving the track. He was scared as hell that he was going to shame himself if what he feared was going to happen happened.

When Sam's Man tapped him on the shoulder his bladder almost let go.

"Hey, Billy Ray, pull over there," Sam's Man said.

"Over where?"

"Over by them dumpsters back along the wall."

Ray started the engine and drove off without releasing the handbrake, hoping the liners would heat up and catch fire. He could smell burning rubber.

"Don't be smart," Sam's Man said.

Ray released the brake.

"This is good," Sam's Man said.

There was nobody around. When Ray closed his eyes he could imagine that the sound of traffic from the boulevard was the surf down at State Beach.

"Get out of the car," Sam's Man said.

"You want the cab?" Ray asked.

"You got the two smalls for Puffy, you can stay in the car."

Billy Ray twisted around. "I had the two hundred. Believe me I had the two bills. Then I run into this sonofabitch Eddie Segal. You know Eddie Segal, the accountant? The sonofabitch seduced me."

"It happens."

"He sold me on a dream."

"What was the name of this dream?"

"Tagalong in the seventh. I had the two hundred and twenty over. I was going to bet the twenty." He reached into his shirt pocket and pulled out the double sawbuck. "There, you don't believe me, there's the twenty."

"We believe you."

"I was going to bet the twenty to show. A conservative bet. Maybe I double it at the prices, you understand what I'm saying?"

"This accountant touted you."

"He got me drunk on the idea this Tagalong was certified."

"Accountants shouldn't be gambling. It's bad for their reputations. Who's going to trust an accountant what gambles?"

"There. You got it. He said it wasn't even a gamble. It was a cock-eyed cert. He sold me his insanity."

"You bet the two bills."

"I was temporarily insane. Any court in the country would take that into consideration."

"Get out of the car," Sam's Man said again, in exactly the same tone of voice.

"I'll have it tomorrow."

"That's what you said yesterday and last week. Get out of the car, Billy Ray."

"What the hell for?"

"Because we say so, Billy Ray," Sam's Man said.

Billy Ray got out of the cab. Machado got out of the backseat.

"You need any help, Manny?" Sam's Man asked.

"What are you, insulting me?" Machado replied.

He walked around the hood of the car, up on his toes like a fighter. Ray backed off and put his hands up.

"Put your hands down," Machado said. "Don't make it tough on me."

"Look, what's a week?" Ray pleaded.

Machado threw a hand into Ray's belly. It took him down onto his knees.

"Not the face. For God's sake, not the face," Billy Ray yelled, covering up.

"Drop your hands and look at me," Machado said.

He bent his knees and set himself.

Sam's Man hunched himself forward on the backseat and put his head out the window. "Don't mark his face, Manny. The man's an actor."

"So what do you want me to do?"

Sam's Man thought about it. "Break his wrist."

6

They call it usury, shylocking and loan-sharking. They call it juice. They lend you a hundred and call it a small. They lend you a thousand and call it a bone. It costs a hundred a week vigorish to borrow the bone. You can't pay off a hundred and reduce the principal with another hundred; you've got to pay off the principal in a lump. You borrow a bone, you pay back a bone. If your bill starts mounting because you can't make the interest, there comes the day when the juiceman's collectors make you a visit. Just like Sam's Man and Manny Machado pay Billy Ray a visit and bust his wrist instead of his face because Sam's Man felt generous today.

Sometimes the average working stiff can find another juiceman who'll lend him enough dimes to pay off the first juiceman, interest and principal, with maybe a couple of C-notes left over. What the hell, that's enough to buy a weekend in Las Vegas, a night out with the wife to keep her mouth shut. Let tomorrow worry about tomorrow. That's what's known as stepping into the quicksand. Do it too often and that's what's known as committing suicide.

Sometimes a man's forced to go to a juiceman because he's got a sick wife, a sick mother or a sick kid. Hasn't got the wages to cover it. No charity, social service or government agency ready, willing or able to give any help.

There are times when a friend talks you into a short-term investment certain to pay off ten to one. You got to take a chance in this world if you want to get ahead. Right?

Those two things are called need and greed.

But most of the suckers who go to the juicemen got a habit. You could call it greed, but it's not greed. The habit is a disease and the disease is called gambling.

Juicemen are too smart to lend money to people with habits like booze and skag, though sometimes an alkie or a gow-head in a three-piece suit puts one over on them. It doesn't happen often. And they still have to pay up. Juicemen like to lend money to people with the gambling disease.

Juicemen have no ear for sad songs.

Allan Nadeau, an attorney, had the disease. He and Billy Ray were brothers under the skin. Except Nadeau was a high roller. Wore twelve-hundred-dollar suits, four-hundred-dollar shoes.

Drove a Lamborghini, a hundred twenty-five thousand, drive it away.

Had a house in Brentwood he shared with his wife, two million, turn on the lights.

Owned a hideaway for when he worked late ten miles north of Malibu on the ocean side, eight hundred thousand, here's the key to the door.

Had a suite of offices in Century City.

Everything hocked to the max. Big cash-flow problems.

Divorce, trust work and real estate law were three rivers feeding him, down on his knees sucking up the tailings from all that cash flow.

He put together property deals. Land would become available through a trust after somebody's death. The down payment would come from the purse of a divorcée who suddenly found herself with plenty of cash and property but not much savvy about what to do with it.

Once the land was secured, Nadeau found himself a willing partner ready to match the down dollar for dollar. Earnest money. Formed a corporation. Bought the land for let's say a million. Sold it on paper to the secret partner for let's say three million. Found an appraiser ready to appraise at that figure for a consideration. Took the appraisal to a savings and loan and borrowed construction money two to one. Five million. Built a bunch of condominiums for let's say three million.

Sell them, don't sell them, Nadeau came out. Paid off the divorcée her investment and a nice profit. Paid off the silent partner the same plus another fifty thousand for conspiring to commit an illegal act. Ten thousand to the appraiser. A little here, a little there, tap dancing on his magic little pocket calculator. What did he end up with? One million for the land. Three million for actual construction. Half a million to other participants. Four and a half million, give or take, after incidental expenses. A million in Nadeau's pocket, even if the condos don't sell right away. A million. Some of it on the books, some of it buried under an avalanche of paper.

Not to mention the fees for his services to the trust and the divorcée. A hundred fifty dollars an hour.

It only works in a rising real estate market.

Do one a year you can afford a house in Brentwood, condo on the beach above Malibu, car worth a hundred and a quarter, eat out every night at places that charge three hundred dollars, table for two, bottle of wine, companions at five hundred dollars a night, take off your panties and lay on the bed there by the star-spangled sea.

Nadeau's wife, Helena, beautiful broad, had a disease, too. Cocaine. Two-hundred-dollar-a-day nose. She was one of the few snowbirds who thought she was snowing the snowman *and* the juiceman. She wasn't snowing anybody. The snowman gave her skag on the cuff because he knew he'd have her ass someday. The juiceman knew the husband was good for it. Run a tab, husband and wife, what difference did it make? California was a community-property state, wasn't it?

The three of them, lawyer, dealer and addict, all went to the same shy, Alfonso "Puffy" Pachoulo. Pachoulo was an equal-rights lender.

7

They were sitting around Benito's Pizza Parlor in the back. Pachoulo, Sam's Man, Manny Machado and Iggie Deetch, the bail bondsman. Also Sam, the big dog himself, slobbering on Pachoulo's shoe.

"Look at that. Will you fucking look at that?" Pachoulo said, when his brain finally got the message that he had a wet sock.

"Look at what, Puffy?" Sam's Man asked, the words coming up out of the briny in his belly. He turned this way and that, looking over one shoulder then the other, shifting his great bulk around each time and grunting with the effort.

"Not out the door, fachrissake. Look right down there at my foot. That beast of yours is slobbering all over my shoe. Johnson Murphys, two smalls a pair. You should get a bib for that animal."

Sam's Man jerked on the lead and pulled Sam around. Sam growled, then settled down to drool all over his owner's shoe.

"You owe me a shine," Pachoulo said, going back to his lasagna Milanese.

"You want me to give you the buck now?" Sam's Man asked, in all sincerity.

"A buck. Where the hell you get a decent shine for a buck?"

"So, whatever it costs."

"Don't get smart with me, I'll shove that goddam dog up your keister. You do any good today? You catch up with that sonofabitch Billy Ray?"

Sam's Man took out the twenty they'd taken from Ray and tossed it on the table.

"This is it? This is two smalls?" Pachoulo said.

"He didn't have the two smalls. That's what he had on him."

Pachoulo wiped the last of the tomato sauce off his plate with the folded twenty-dollar bill. "Hey, Sam," he said. "C'mere." Sam raised his head and looked up. Pachoulo reached down with the twenty. Sam smelled it, took it and swallowed it. "That's what I think of Billy Ray's twenty," Pachoulo said.

"You see that?" Deetch said. "That dog eats money. I never seen a dog eat money. I never seen such a thing." He took out his roll and peeled off a dollar bill and held it out to Sam. The dog sniffed it and refused it. "You got a little more of that tomato sauce?" Deetch asked.

"Sam won't touch nothing less than a ten-spot," Sam's Man kidded.

"Five'll get you ten he'll scarf it up if I smear a little butter on it," Deetch said.

He ran the bill through the soft butter and offered it to Sam again. Sam gobbled it down.

"Goddam, I never seen such a thing," Deetch crowed again.

"Hey, Carmine," Pachoulo said, "maybe you got something here. Spread it around your dog eats money. People feed him fives and tens. Every time Sam shits you'll hit the jackpot like you're over to Vegas."

They all laughed.

"So, all right, fun is fun. How about business?" Pachoulo asked. "How about you tell me what you done to Billy Ray to teach him a lesson."

"I had him on his knees," Machado said. "I was going to break his nose, but Sam's Man here said not to."

"Why is that?"

"The asshole's trying to be an actor," Sam's Man said.

"So what did you do?"

"We busted his wrist."

"You know what's your trouble? Your trouble's you're too soft-hearted, Carmine. When's he coughing up the two dimes?"

"Tomorrow. He promised tomorrow."

"It better be tomorrow."

"Oh, it'll be tomorrow. He said he'd get it from his mother."

8

Maggie Ray was always tired. She'd been born tired and it had never gotten any better. Always before, she never knew why she was so exhausted. This time she knew why it was such an effort to get her body out of bed in the morning and drag it through the day. They weren't sure yet, but she could have a cancer.

Not only had she been born tired, but she'd been born without any luck. When she was fifteen and working in the five and dime back in Newark, New Jersey, she got knocked up three times in one year. Since she only got laid three times, she had to come to the conclusion that she was living under a dark star.

She used to say to her friend Jane LaMaster, "If I didn't have any bad luck, I'd have no luck at all."

Well, that wasn't altogether true. Sometimes she got a little good fortune tossed her way in small packages. Like Spooner Ray married her one drunken night when he was on liberty from the destroyer escort come in off the Atlantic for refitting.

That was the fourth time she got laid and the fourth time she got pregnant. Also the last time she saw Spooner Ray after his ship went back to sea.

But at least she had the marriage license, a cheap wedding band, a baby in her belly and the memories of two hot months with Spooner in the furnished room, in her bed, waking in the night with the sheets tangled around her naked arms and legs, reaching over to touch him, bringing him awake and doing it again in the dark, through the long sweaty nights.

Two months after his DE pulled out, word came from the War De-

partment that Seaman First Class John Simon Ray had died while per-
forming his duties on a ship of war on the high seas. Killed not in
action maybe but perished in a war zone all the same.

Later on she discovered, when a shipmate came to call, that her husband had cooked up some raisin snap in a cookpot stashed behind the
boilers, imbibed a glass too much, slipped on the sea-wet deck while
on his way to the crapper and gone overboard never to be seen again.

She had her job at the five and dime and a widow's pension. Enough
to get along even with the baby, her love, her only really lucky strike,
her little ray of sunshine, her little Billy Ray.

"It's nothing, Ma," Ray was saying, waving the cast on his arm like
it weighed no more than an ounce. "I got a day on this picture—"

"Which one was that?" she asked eagerly, having awakened that
morning just knowing that this was going to be a good-news day.

"Well, I don't really remember. It was an independent film they were
shooting over on the back lot on Gower."

"You don't remember the name of the picture?"

"I knew it. It slipped my mind."

"You should remember things like that. I mean I tell Flo and Essie
you were in a picture, they say, 'What picture,' and I say, 'I don't
know,' and they say, 'Oh, yeah, Billy Ray the famous movie actor. I'll
bet we know the name of the movie. *The Invisible Man.*' Then they fall
on the floor laughing. They think I'm a liar. Worse than that, they
think you're a liar."

"So who gives a rat's ass what Flo and Essie think?"

"Don't use that language around your mother. They're the only
friends I got since coming out here to California. I had plenty of friends
back in Newark."

"You also had quinsy throat every winter."

"I never had quinsy, just a little touch of bronchitis. I had plenty of
girlfriends at the five and dime. Out here people ain't so friendly."

"What do you mean, not friendly? People in California are very
friendly. Maybe the friendliest."

"I don't think Californians are very friendly."

"Well maybe *native* Californians aren't very friendly, but I never met
any native Californians. Everybody around here's from somewhere
else. So if the people around here aren't friendly it's because they come
from Newark."

"For God's sake, they couldn't all come from Newark. Newark's big, but it ain't that big."

"You know what I mean."

"Yeah, I know what you mean," she said, reaching out and slapping his cast playfully. "You want me to sign it?"

"What am I, a kid, you're going to sign my cast?"

"Let me sign it."

"Look, Ma, fachrissake, I'm trying to tell you this story."

She folded her hands in her lap and stared at him with eyes that popped out a little, her painted mouth pursed up to show how hard she was listening, her jaws working back and forth slightly like they always did, trying to set her false teeth so they'd be more comfortable. "I'm listening," she said.

"Well, all right. It was this scene in a freight yard, you understand. Me and three other actors—"

"Was this a part you had?"

"What do you mean was it a part? Of course it was a part."

"I mean was it a pretty big part or were you ju—were you a day player?"

"You almost said '*just* a day player,' Ma."

"Slip of the tongue."

"There aren't any small parts, just small actors. Remember that."

She nodded and the curls of her fresh home perm bounced around like springs of copper.

"If you don't want me to tell you what happened."

"I'm dying to hear," she said, very earnestly.

"So, give me a chance, then. These other two *day* players and me were supposed to get on top of this pile of crates."

"That's stunt pay," she said, unable to help herself.

"Maybe so. But what was I supposed to do, say 'I'm not going up there? Get somebody else?' We talked it over, these other two *day* players and me, and we decided to get up there and then, *after* the shot was finished, we'd go the assistant and make him give us an adjustment."

"That was smart."

"You bet your sweet ass."

"Don't say that."

"Well, haven't you got a sweet ass? If you wasn't my mother."

"Stop it, stop it. Don't talk filthy to your mother," she said, blushing with pleasure and the implied compliment, remembering when he'd started growing and she'd thought of such things in the loneliness of her bed and then suffered the shame afterwards.

"Well, we got up there on the pile of crates. 'Perfectly safe,' they said. 'Supported from inside,' they said. The whole goddam thing came tumbling down. I mean, you should've seen it. All asses and elbows flying all over the goddam place." He was on his feet, flailing his arms like a windmill, acting it out, making her laugh so hard she began to sound angry. "Ass over teakettle onto the concrete, right on my wrist. I mean, I threw out my hand like you do, you know?"

"Instinct," she said.

"And whammo! There goes the wrist. I could hear it snap."

"Oh, baby, baby," she was moaning through her laughter, grabbing the arm with the cast and drawing it toward her breasts, kissing the exposed fingertips.

He jerked his arm away and went to sit down across from her again at the rickety kitchen table with the oilcloth on it.

"They give you the adjustment?"

"Sure. But the check won't be ready for ten days. You know how they do."

"You going on workman's comp?"

"Oh, sure. I'll go on comp, but I'll work some rides off the books. Hell, you got to take your opportunities. Get ahead of the game a little bit. Right?"

She could smell it coming, but knew there was nothing she could do about it. She felt this sinking feeling in her chest and she wondered for a fraction of a second if it was overwhelming love for her boy she was feeling or rage at the way he was going to work her again.

"Trouble is I got a lot of pain and won't be able to drive the cab two, maybe three, days," he said. "There's the rent."

"Haven't you got anything put away for a rainy day?"

"What rainy day?" he said, making a big show with his eyebrows, making a joke, keeping her spirits up. "This is L.A."

"You know what I mean. Don't get smart. Ain't you been saving your pennies like I've always told you? Or is that wife of yours still spending like you're a millionaire?"

"Don't get on Lisa's case, please, Ma. You don't want to advance me a little walking-around money, just say so."

"You already owe me..."

"If you're going to start again on what I owe you, I don't want to hear it," he said angrily, jumping up from the table.

Distress lines appeared between her eyebrows, making her look like an irritated cat. "For God's sake, Sonny..."

"Don't call me Sonny. It's bad enough everybody calls me Billy and me almost thirty-five."

"Almost forty-three."

"Jesus Christ! You just won't let up, will you? First you start hammering at Lisa and now you're going to start hammering at me."

"I'm not hammering. I just said—"

"I know what the hell you just said!" he shouted. A note in his voice got picked up by some piece of metal in the kitchen. It rang with sympathetic vibrations. Then it was very still, the silence stretching out like a rubber band, both of them waiting to see how long it'd take before it broke.

"How much do you need?" Maggie finally said.

"Three hundred dollars would just about do it."

"Three hundred dollars? I haven't got anything what even *looks* like three hundred dollars."

"Well, how much *do* you have?"

"Thirty, forty dollars maybe," she said, reaching quickly for her purse that was never far outside her reach, as though afraid he was going to snatch it up and spill its contents out on the oilcloth.

"If you don't want to give me the money, just say so, but please don't lie to me," he said.

She dumped the contents of the purse out on the table herself.

"So go ahead and look. Go ahead and count. I got expenses too, you know. I've got the rent to pay on this dump. I got the gas and electric."

He counted the money in her wallet.

"I make it a hundred and twenty bucks."

"You forgot this," she said, picking up her change purse and throwing it at him. She turned away, leaning on the back of the chair, hurt to the heart. All he wanted her for was to suck her dry of every dime she worked and slaved for at the laundromat.

He didn't even look inside the little purse. He just shoved it and the wadded bills closer to her. "Here, I don't want it. I don't want your money. You still got your own rent to pay, just like you say."

"Well, I already paid the rent for this month," she said. "I can spare a little."

"How much? I don't want you to short yourself."

She turned around to face him again, put her arms on the table and pushed the money around with her fingers, looking up at him from under her lashes like a flirtatious girl.

"Seventy-five?"

"Sure, if that's what you can spare."

He sat there with his forearms on the table, the one in the cast reminding her of his injury, the other with the hand palm up, like a beggar waiting for a crumb. She counted out seventy-five dollars, hesitated, then added another twenty-five.

"Make it an even hundred. For my Sonny," she said.

He didn't protest the name. He folded up the bills and put them in his pocket. "Well, I got to get home. Lisa doesn't know about this yet."

He started to rise. She reached out and held him down with her hand on the cast.

"Let me sign your cast, Sonny, the way I did before, a long time ago. Remember?"

"Sure. When I fell off George Wager's bike."

She drew two intertwined hearts on the plaster with a red ballpoint pen. Then she wrote, "Love, Mom."

The white Mercedes crawled along as close to the curb as it could get, prowling along after the woman in the light summer dress, the driver leaning over trying to make conversation.

Some women look more naked with clothes on than most women

do with them off. Even if they don't want to be an invitation, they're an invitation. It was no wonder the asshole took her for a whore the way the breeze was plastering her skirt to her thighs and belly.

The driver made a long kissing sound.

The woman left the sidewalk and stepped across the curb between two parked cars as though she was ready to get in the car. She stuck her head in the window when he stopped.

"You want to pop back into your hole, or would you like me to haul your ass in on soliciting an immoral act?"

"You trying to tell me you're a police officer?" he said, half believing.

"You want to see a badge? I show you a badge, then I've got to carry through. I've got to take you in. I'm almost off shift. I take you down it's another hour, two hours before I get a shower. You want to see a badge?"

He accelerated out of there, almost hitting two hookers and a pick-pocket on the corner.

The woman, Billy Ray's wife, Lisa, stepped back on the sidewalk and went on looking for Panama Heath, who'd been her boyfriend until six years before when she got the hots for Billy Ray.

She and Heath hadn't seen each other for two years and some months the week she went looking for him along the hookers' stroll, in the bars, coffee shops and restaurants, in the used-book stores and record shops, in the massage shops and sex parlors and all-day-all-night X-rated movie houses. Besides the man in the Mercedes and the usual suggestions from the loafers, she was offered work in three different "hot box" display parlors and in two pimps' stables before she finally ran him down sitting in the cool dark of the Old Time Movie House watching Charlie Chaplin eat his shoe.

When she slid into the chair next to him and tapped him on the knee, he started and said, "I got to tell you, lady, I'm a cop, so don't make me any offers."

"All I was going to do was say hello, Panama. Just say hello and ask you what a good-looking guy like you was doing hanging around a joint like this."

He sat straight up and turned his head to look at her, then turned it to the front again because, in that instant, he was afraid to see her outside his dreams.

"I could ask you the same," he said.

"I came looking for you."

There was an apple stuck in his throat and his pulse was beating so hard across his chest it was almost painful. He tried to cool himself down like he did when he had to go into someplace where bodies lay smashed and blood painted the floors and walls. Turn himself to ice so that witnesses later talked about the tall, sad-eyed, hard-eyed, cold-eyed cop who went around seeing things were cleaned up right and never shed a tear. But it was no good. He felt her sitting next to him like she was naked and he was naked and they were both one creature, melted altogether on a hot bed with a cool breeze blowing in all the way from Santa Monica through the window of his bedroom in his apartment above the garage.

He reached out a hand—it was like it wasn't even his own hand—and cupped her knee on the soft, tender place just above the shifting bone. She gave a little moan and shifted her legs to open them wider just a fraction, then put them both together and jerked them away from him. "No!"

"What is it you want, Lisa?" Heath managed to ask, through the sand and honey in his throat.

"I need a favor."

"What kind of favor?"

"Billy's into some shylock for more than we can pay."

"You need a loan?"

"I couldn't ask for money."

"Then what is it you could ask for?"

"Just a favor."

"How much is Billy into the shy for?"

"A thousand dollars."

"You know who is this shy?" he asked, thinking how she was asking him to go to a lot of trouble and put himself on the line for what amounted to chump change.

"A man named Pachoulo."

He grunted.

"You know him?" Lisa said.

"Oh, yes. Everybody in this part of town knows Pachoulo. He's Santa Claus. All he needs is a red suit and a bell. How long has Billy had this loan outstanding?"

"I don't know. He won't tell me."

"How come he told you he owed the money?"

"I caught him going through my pocketbook looking to make up the two hundred dollars interest he's got to pay this week."

"He took two hundred from your purse?"

"He took all I had. Thirty dollars. He had a hundred from his mother. He said not to worry, he'd get the rest."

"How is he going to get the rest?"

"Drive the cab off the flag. Pick it up five dollars at a time from all the people he knows and hangs around with. I don't know."

Up on the screen Charlie was being chased by two Keystone Kops. One of them looked like their chief of detectives, Bondo Hefferman. Charlie was acting scared but was getting the best of it.

She stirred. "I just thought I'd ask you for the favor. I don't know what else to do."

"You could let him pay the price."

"They punched him in the stomach and broke his wrist. They did that already. For being late with two hundred dollars."

A large man loomed up in the aisle. It was Wilber Monk. He knew exactly where to find Heath. He put his big head down next to Heath's.

"You in the middle of an investigation or some recreation, Panama?" he whispered.

"Take a look. Can't you see who's here?" Heath said.

Monk leaned halfway across Heath, peering into Lisa's face. "Hey, Lisa, what do you know? Long time no see."

"Hello, Wilbur. How's Jessie and the kids?"

"Doing good. Jessie's taking bookkeeping in night school. Henry's playing junior varsity basketball. He's a goddam ladder. Hilly's going to have the lead in the class play."

"Oh, that's good."

"Yeah."

"Why did you come looking for me?" Heath asked, as though impatient, as though *annoyed* with Monk for breaking up something he had going even though he didn't have anything going.

"We got to look into a little something over on Sweetzer."

"A little what?"

"Well," Monk said, getting his mouth closer to Heath's ear, half turning away from Lisa so that she couldn't accidentally hear a word, "it seems that some twangy boy was doing a pickup with a soda bottle and his lover walked in on them and rammed it home. Made a suction and . . . you know."

"They're sending a detective team over to bust a soda bottle out of a faggot's keister?" Heath said, hardly believing what he'd just been told. "That's what they call proper use of manpower?"

"The lover already broke the bottle, Panama. Broke it and twisted it. They tried to stop the bleeding with towels. It didn't do any good. We got a homicide. What the hell, Panama, I didn't know you had something on."

Heath got up, almost knocking Monk's cheekbone with his head.

"I haven't got anything on. Lisa was just asking me to do her a favor."

"Sure," Monk said. "See you, Lisa." He took a couple of steps away and up the aisle.

Heath looked down at Lisa, who was looking back up at him. He could see enough of her face through the gloom to know that she'd aged twice as much in the last two years as she should have. There were stains around her eyes and little puffs of flesh under them as though she didn't sleep enough or cried too much.

"I'll see what I can do," he said.

She smiled and was a girl again, the dimple at the corner of her mouth winking to life, playing hell with his adrenaline again.

"Thanks," she said.

"You want to see me again," he said, "don't come looking for me in places like this. Leave a message at the register over at the coffee shop across from the Chinese."

"All right, Panama," she said.

Heath turned and grabbed Monk by the elbow, turning him away from the screen. He practically pushed him up the aisle, like he was in a hurry to get to the scene of the ridiculous, pitiful, messy killing.

"God, they just don't make them like Charlie Chaplin anymore," Monk said.

"They wouldn't even be able to make Charlie like Charlie anymore," Heath replied, taking one more look at the screen, which really looked like a silver screen.

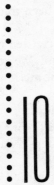

10

"Lisa asked me to do her a favor," Heath said again when they walked out of the popcorn-smelling lobby into the evil-smelling air. He said it like he expected Monk to call him a liar.

"What did I say?" Monk asked.

"I know what you're thinking."

"No, you don't know what I'm thinking."

"You telling me I don't know what you're thinking?"

"All right, so you know. It's none of my business. Lisa's marriage to Billy Ray's a disaster area, so why shouldn't she look up an old friend and talk about better times?"

"You were thinking she and me was meeting so we could make it in the back of a movie house."

"Well, no, I didn't get *that* far," Monk said.

"If you've got to know—"

"I don't have to know."

"—Billy Ray's in hock to a shy who just busted his wrist for being late."

"That Ray's got the disease."

"I know that."

"I got no patience with people who gamble till they're broke."

"I got no patience either."

"I got no patience with gamooshes who go drown their mistakes in some saloon with the last five they got left to their name, then go to some pizza parlor and float a loan with strangers."

"I got no patience either."

"So let him drown."

"I can't do that."

"Why? Because you're getting it on with his wife?"

Heath stopped flat-footed and turned, his hands coming up as though he were ready to fight.

Monk threw up his hands, palms out, and drifted away a step. "If you ain't got something on, you're sure as hell thinking about getting something on."

"You're calling me an asshole."

"No, I'm not calling you an asshole."

"That's an asshole's game, so you're calling me an asshole."

"I'm just telling you *not* to start getting round and puckered."

"I've got no intention."

"You were inside there, looking at Charlie Chaplin, with Lisa's leg leaning against your leg. You help out Billy Ray, Lisa feels grateful. She wants to pay you back. She's got nothing to pay you back with except herself. What the hell, you're not getting so much you can refuse an offer. Just the once you'll tell yourself. But it'll never end. It'll be very bad for everybody."

"I'll think about it," Heath said.

Heath thought about it as they went in past the uniform at the door. He thought about it while he stood around in the middle of the court apartment that had once been a home and now was the scene of a crime. He thought about it while he questioned the pale-faced bare-footed boy, in tight jeans and open shirt hanging loose on his skinny bones, and the middle-aged, balding, paunchy man who'd done the deed and who stood there staring at his young lover as though his heart would break. He decided that if you wanted to play it safe you'd be smart never to want or need another person.

So he'd be smart where Lisa was concerned.

But he also thought that he'd once loved her, maybe he still loved her. But, even if he didn't, men kept on helping old girlfriends even after it was over. That was a woman's edge.

Billy Ray came out of the coffee shop and put on his yellow cap, putting himself back in business. He felt rocky as hell, the pain of his broken wrist radiating up his arm to his neck, making him hold his head over to the side like Frankie the Gimp. Getting mad and yelling at Lisa hadn't done the pain any good, either.

It was a hell of a note when a man had to go out, tired as a dog, and work a double shift pushing a goddam hack all over the goddam filthy streets with whores doing things in doorways and gonnifs shoving knives in your neck to steal your book, just because a not-so-loving wife wouldn't cough up the scratch to save a man's life.

"Hey, hey, hey, Billy Ray," a voice said, and Ray nearly dumped in his drawers, thinking it was Sam's Man come back because his boss, Pachoulo, wasn't satisfied with a broken wrist, he wanted also a broken nose or a busted leg.

He turned around and saw Benny Checks, a small-time bookie, who wore suits that looked like he'd lifted them from the trunk of an old-time vaudeville second banana, standing there with a grin and a toothpick in his kisser. Sam's Man wasn't the only asshole who went through that "Hey, hey, hey, Billy Ray" bullshit.

Ray showed Checks his cast. "Don't tell me I owe you, too, fachrissake," he said.

"How can you owe me, you don't bet with me lately?"

Jesus Christ, Ray thought, he'd forgotten all about he didn't owe Benny Checks. But if he didn't owe him, he was the only one he didn't owe. He owed everybody else.

"Well, I been going out to the track in person, lately. I like to see them run."

"That's what the Queen of England always says when she goes to the track."

"But, as a matter of fact, I was just about to lay a little action on you."

"I don't think so."

"What's that?"

"I don't think you're going to lay a little action on me, because I ain't going to let you."

"Why the hell not?"

"Because you ain't good for it."

"Why don't you fuck off, then, stop wasting my time? I got to make my living."

"So drive me up to Mulholland," Checks said and walked over to Ray's cab.

"Since when you take a cab anywhere?" Ray asked, trailing after him.

"Since I totaled my Mustang down on Pacific Coast Highway. Not my fault. Some asshole ran the light down there by the shopping center. You know?"

"So you're scared to drive?"

"The gamoosh that hit me lives over to the Colony. Television writer. Director. Something like that. I'm going for a settlement."

"Those sort of people turn it over to their lawyers. You could grow old and die before you get a judgment. Well, if you're getting in, get in."

"Ain't you going to open the door for me?"

Ray made a noise like a train pulling into the station and went around to get behind the wheel. Checks got into the back.

"You try to throw a little business to a friend," he said.

"You want to do a little business, take my action at Hollywood for tomorrow."

"You don't get my meaning," Checks said. "Betting's *my* business. I don't want to give you a piece of that. Driving a hack's *your* business so here I am doing you a favor riding with you, I could be riding with a cabbie opens the door for his customers."

"You take my action, two, three races, I'll open the goddam door for you."

"Never mind. I'm already in the cab. Take me up to Mulholland."

"Where Mulholland?"

"Over by Woodrow Wilson Drive."

Ray pulled out into traffic very smoothly and caught the light so he could cross the boulevard. "What are you doing going up to Mulholland and Wilson?"

"Got a client up there."

"What kind of client?"

"Old retired whore. Got a ten-room pink stucco overlooks the city. Eats off silver and wipes her ass with ten-dollar bills. Likes to play the ponies a little every now and then."

"So how come she can't lay the bets on the phone?"

"Oh, she can lay the *bets,*" Checks said, catching Ray's eyes in the rearview and popping his eyebrows up and down like a clown.

"What are you saying here?" Ray asked. "You saying she's the customer or you saying you're the customer?"

"I ain't paying for it," Checks said defensively, wanting to make that clear right off the bat. "She pays her losses."

"Come on. Don't tell me you don't let her bet a maiden, maybe a little claimer, you take it out in trade."

"I don't pay a goddam cent."

Ray's eyes flicked from road to rearview to side mirror. Flick, flick, flick. He was a good driver. He saw Checks smile a smile that was sort of sweet and shy.

"She calls me her little prince," Checks said.

"Jesus Christ, Benny, she must be a very old whore indeed."

"You wouldn't know to look at her. She goes to the gym every day, the Golden Door every three months and Switzerland once a year. She looks forty, forty-five tops."

"Don't it give you the creeps not knowing maybe she's seventy, eighty? Who the hell knows how old?"

"You know what old Satchel Paige once said?"

"How's that?"

"How old would you be if you didn't know how old you was?"

They were climbing up into the hills along Nichols Canyon, Checks wondering how old his customer really was, Ray wondering what it would be like to have an old whore who wiped her ass with ten-dollar bills in love with you. Christ, it'd be like having a key to the bank.

All of a sudden Checks said, "I don't give a good goddam how old she is, she gives the best head, New Orleans style, I ever had in my life."

"Well, that comes from long experience, don't it?" Ray smirked, not letting Checks get off that easy.

"For Christ's sake, Billy Ray, you're the kind of sport what sits in the cake at the wedding. Just can't stand to see other people got it good, can you?"

"I never said that," Ray said, instantly contrite. "I was just having a little fun. You want to know the truth, the truth is maybe I'm a little jealous you got this lady in the pink stucco house, calls you her little prince. I mean that must be love she calls you that because whatever you are, you're not little."

"What are you talking about," Checks said, pleased as punch, "you've got Lisa. That's a winner you got there."

"Maybe it's a winner I got there, but mostly it's a woman I got there always needing this and that. I mean she spends as much on underwear as I do on a little wager now and then. Do I begrudge she should put pretty silk on her ass? Not likely. Does she grudge me a little recreation? You bet your sweet ass she does. Now, your lady, from what you tell me, she don't object to your profession, she don't whine and carry on you should go out and make something of yourself, get a regular job. She places her bets and gives you the greatest New Orleans head you ever got. How lucky can you get?"

"What ideas you got about Hollywood Park tomorrow?" Checks asked, suddenly feeling very good.

Ray's eyes went flick, flick, flick as they made the turn onto Woodrow Wilson Drive even though there was no traffic anywhere.

"Wapati in the third looks very good to me."

Checks nodded sagely, not saying yes or no.

"Also Boogaloo in the fourth. But if I had a place to make a wager, I'd bet the farm on Erin's Boy in the seventh."

"You bet the farm on Erin's Boy, Sam's Man and Machado'll be hanging you up on a butcher's hook."

"Don't talk like that! It gives me the chills. Those bastards are haunting my life."

"Why don't you pay Pachoulo off?"

"I shouldn't have to pay him off, the sonofabitch, all the trade I've sent his way. No more. The bastard squeezes me like he does, does me an injury, fuck him. I'll steer any inquiries elsewhere."

"So, you still don't tell me why you don't pay him off."

"It's all I can do to get the C-note every week. Where am I going to get the bone?"

Flick, flick, flick.

Checks took out a roll as big as a sausage in a bun, held together with a rubber band.

"You shouldn't be walking around with a stake like that," Ray said.

Checks caught Ray's eyes in the rearview, to make sure he was watching, and lifted his jacket away so Ray could see the butt of the gun nestled in his armpit. He grinned, thinking it was a shark's grin.

Oh-oh, Billy Ray thought, some thief catches you with that gun, he'll take it away, shove it up your ass and pull the trigger.

Checks flicked off one C-note after another.

Flick, flick, flick.

"Over there," Checks said, pointing to the pink stucco back up the hill with his chin.

"I see it," Ray said.

"Drop me at the bottom of the drive."

Ray pulled in to the curb. "You want me to wait?"

"You want to wait off the meter?" Checks asked, testing him.

"Would I have a reason to wait off the meter?"

Checks shoved a small tube of money through the grill.

"What's this?" Ray asked, hardly believing what was happening.

"That's fifteen hundred dollars," Checks said. "Go pay off Pachoulo."

"You spreading out, Benny?"

"There comes a time when a man's got to diversify his business."

"Aren't you worried Pachoulo takes exception?"

"What he don't know don't hurt him. If he finds out . . ." He patted his jacket.

He got out of the cab and stood there at the curb, bent over, his arm supporting him on the car door.

"You understand what's happening here? You pay off Pachoulo. So, now you owe me. That don't mean I'm going to be kind to you, you don't pay up on time."

Ray shoved the roll of bills back at Checks. "So what do I get for moving my loan from one bank to another?"

"You get room to breathe, you get three cees to bet Erin's Boy in the seventh—if you got shit for brains—and you get eight percent vigorish per week instead of ten. You can't do better than that, Billy Ray. Also, you steer any business my way, I give you a finder's fee."

"Well, okay," Ray said, pulling back the roll, which he'd never really intended to give up in the first place. He counted off a hundred bucks. "Do me twenty, twenty and twenty on Wapati in the third—"

Checks put his hand out, showing the palm. "I won't take your bet this evening, Billy Ray. I'd be working against my own interests. You take my advice. Don't be in such a hurry to spend that money. Make sure you pay Pachoulo. You don't pay Pachoulo, I just pissed away fifteen hundred on a corpse. You pay him. You maybe take a cee and buy Lisa some silkies. Then you call me tomorrow, the next day, maybe I'll take your action."

Ray didn't argue. He tucked the roll in his pocket.

"That's four-eighty on the meter," he said, after taking a glance.

"Don't fuck with my good nature," Checks said, and started to walk away.

"That's some house," Ray called after him.

Checks stared up at the pink stucco, which looked sickly in the failing light of day, big patches of plaster falling off here and there. An old dinosaur of a house ready to roll over and die.

"Looks like one of them haunted houses in a horror movie, don't it?" Ray said, conversationally. "Watch yourself."

"What do you mean?"

"Maybe that old whore stays looking like she looks sucking the blood of people younger than herself. It's just a thought."

He drove away, leaving Benny Checks standing there thinking about *that*.

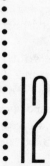

12

Billy Ray strolled into Benito's and ambled through the early diners to the table in the back where Pachoulo could almost always be found. He was sitting there alone except for Iggie Deetch. No sign of Sam's Man or Machado, which filled Ray with a sense of relief on the one hand, and regret on the other. After the humiliation of being on his knees and taking Machado's punches, without being able to defend himself, it would have done his heart good to look Machado in the eye, telling him silently what a fuck he was, as he paid Pachoulo off, knowing that Pachoulo would never allow Machado to take personal action even if Machado became offended. Pachoulo was a great conserver of energy, his own and anybody's who worked for him.

"Look who's here. Did anybody call a cab?" Pachoulo asked, looking up from his spaghetti carbonara.

"I come to pay the interest," Ray said.

"Sit down, sit down," Pachoulo said amiably. "You didn't have to make a special trip."

"I wanted to make a special trip."

Pachoulo looked at Deetch. "You know the secret of a successful business? You got to have steady, reliable customers. Well, you know that, don't you? Working with felons the way you do. Got to have regular customers with strong appetites." He looked back at Ray as though his own remark reminded him of his family's long tradition of hospitality. "You want a plate?"

Ray nipped two fingers into his cast and came out with two folded hundred-dollar bills. He unfolded them and spread them out on the table one-handed, deliberately awkward, making a production of it.

Pachoulo didn't touch the money. "You know, by rights, I should charge you interest on the interest for being late. The way the banks do."

"You'd squeeze blood out of a stone," Ray said.

Pachoulo, perversely, took it as a compliment and smiled. "You want a glass of wine?"

"That sounds good," Ray said.

"Would you pour my good friend a glass of wine?" Pachoulo said.

Deetch poured a glass of red, smiling under his breath at the sight of Pachoulo playing cat and mouse.

Ray took a swallow.

"Hey," Pachoulo said.

"What's the matter?" Ray asked.

"Ain't you going to drink my health? Where I come from, you ask a guest to sit down have a meal, have a glass of wine, the guest always shows respect with a toast. You know what I mean? It's the custom of my country."

"I thought you were born in Wilmington, down by the docks."

"How would you know where I was born?"

"I thought I heard it somewhere. So, where were you born?"

"That's none of your business."

It was quiet for a little, then Ray lifted his glass and said, "Here's to your health, Puffy."

"Well, thank you. Now, you better go do some business. You shouldn't be late with next week's payment."

Ray fingered the larger wad of bills out of the cast. "I want to pay off the bone, Puffy. There it is," he said, spreading out the ten C-notes, enjoying the moment.

"Somebody die and leave you?" Pachoulo said. "Where'd you get it?"

"That's none of your business."

"Don't get smart."

"That's what you said to me, that's what I say to you," Ray said, looking to Deetch for confirmation that fair was fair.

Pachoulo dropped his fork and leaned back in his chair. "I ask a friendly question and I get one of my best customers mad at me. How does that figure?" He was all butter and olive oil all of a sudden, working the napkin over each of his fingers like he was making very sure his hands were clean before shaking hands with Ray and complimenting him on his good fortune. "It was just what you could call an idle question. You know what I mean?"

"Well, okay, Puffy, I know what you mean and I don't take any offense." Ray stood up. "But I'm not going to tell you."

"This mean we don't do no more business?" Pachoulo asked, picking up the thousand dollars and adding it to his roll.

"This means we're quits except maybe you call for a cab some night and I catch the call."

"You find another bank?"

"Give it a rest, Puffy, I'm not telling you," Ray said, smiling, pleased to see Pachoulo squirming around trying to get it out of him, trying to find out just who it was gave Billy Ray, the cabbie, the chance to flick him the finger.

"I'm jealous," Deetch suddenly piped up. "I'm jealous all this money flying around the table and I don't get any. You haven't got a bone or two for me tucked up there?"

"You tapped out, Billy Ray?" Pachoulo chimed in.

"I got what I need," Ray said.

"You got enough for your appetite?" Pachoulo asked.

"I got enough to place a bet, I want to place a bet."

"Who do you like at Hollywood tomorrow?" Deetch asked.

"I'm not in the mood."

A horse player saying he doesn't want to talk horses is like a head saying he doesn't want to snort coke.

"There's a horse in the seventh . . ." Deetch said.

"Erin's Boy?" Ray said.

"What makes you say Erin's Boy? Who told you about Erin's Boy?"

"Who told me about Erin's Boy told me to save my money."

"Your mother tells you to save your money. Your wife tells you to save your money. Anybody knows anything about horses doesn't tell you to save your money."

"Benny Checks told me to save my money."

"You try to lay a bet with Benny Checks?"

"I had the notion."

"A bookie tells you not to bet a horse with him, do you stop to wonder why he don't want you to bet the horse with him?"

Everybody said that Billy Ray was good-looking, not many said he was smart. He stood there working the equation through his head. Why wouldn't Checks take his bet on Erin's Boy? Because with the three hundred extra he'd borrowed from Checks he could've won all he needed to get off the hook with Checks just like the bone the bookie advanced him just got him off the hook with Pachoulo.

Deetch and Pachoulo were looking at Ray as though they were waiting to see if some woman they just propositioned was going to lay down and do a triple.

"It's not my business, but Checks won't take your bet, I'll place your bet with my bookie," Deetch said temptingly.

Ray's good fingers snaked into the cast again as though of their own volition and drew out the three smalls. He laid them out on the table as though he were under a hypnotic trance.

"Erin's Boy on the nose?" Deetch asked.

Ray reached out, snatched up one of the bills and shoved it in his pocket. "I want to buy a present for the wife."

"So, on the nose?" Deetch asked again.

"One to place and one to show."

Deetch scribbled out the bet on a slip of paper and handed it over to Ray. Ray stared at it for a few seconds. "So, I got to go."

"Good luck," Pachoulo said, the words bubbling up and bursting gaseously, like the eruptions of tar down at the La Brea pits.

Ray made his way through the tables toward the door. He was suffering a terrible crisis of confidence. If he was known for anything around town, he thought, he was known for risking everything, going for broke and never holding back. Nothing cheap and chintzy about Billy Ray. He spun around and strode back to the table where Deetch awaited him.

"Hey, hey, hey, it's Billy Ray," Pachoulo mumbled, under his breath.

"On the nose," Ray said, throwing down the slip to be amended. "Two hundred on the nose."

After he'd left the second time, Pachoulo looked at Deetch. "Looks like that Benny Checks stole one of my stones. I got to have a talk with him he shouldn't get the idea he can make it a habit."

13

It wasn't half an hour after Ray had left that Eddie "Panama" Heath came out of the sun and into the restaurant. The air conditioner sent waves of cold air over his back and shoulders. His sweat turned to ice water. He shivered like he was shrugging off the heat.

He went up to Pachoulo's table, grabbed a chair, turned it around and straddled it. Took off his panama and wiped the sweatband with a blue-and-white bandanna plucked from the back pocket of his jeans.

"Why don't you buy yourself a new hat," Pachoulo said, pushing over a C-note.

"I'm not on your pad, Pachoulo."

"So, get smart. Your boss is on my pad."

"That's your say-so. I don't take the word of gonnifs, pimps and juicemen."

"So, you don't stop in for a new hat, maybe you stop in for a meal."

"Guinea food makes you sweat olive oil. Who needs to sweat olive oil on a day like this?"

"You don't sweat anything if you don't got to be out on them hot streets." Pachoulo smiled. "Gimme your size, I'll send somebody out to get you a new hat. You wait in here where it's cool. Have a little spaghetti, a little fettuccine, a little lasagna."

"I like this hat. This is my made hat. You know what I mean when I say this is my made hat?"

"You mean like the mafioso are supposed to talk about made men? Men what have done a killing?" Deetch said.

"Men you'd be smart to be afraid of, that's right."

"So, I'm supposed to be afraid of that hat?" Pachoulo asked.

"Anybody on the street who's got any brains knows enough to straighten up, get their act together, when they see this hat coming."

"You'd better stop talking like that. You're going to scare the kiddies."

Heath put the hat back on his head, making sure the brim was turned down all the way around, making sure it was tipped at just a certain angle. Just a little, not too much. He straightened up a bit and turned his whole upper body toward Pachoulo as though asking the shylock to comment on the proper setting of his hat. He was smiling in the friendliest way, and his tone of voice, when he spoke, was cordial and unthreatening.

"You better listen to what I'm going to tell you, or I'll step on your wop face."

"You got no right to come in here, I'm having a quiet meal with a friend, and abuse me," Pachoulo said, mightily offended.

"Listen to me. I want you to give a certain person some air."

"What certain person?"

Heath was reluctant to say, because he knew that when he named the name smirks would appear on the faces of the two gonnifs facing him. Was there a soul along the stroll that didn't know that a half-assed actor who pushed a cab had stolen Eddie "Panama" Heath's love right out of his bed?

"Billy Ray."

The smirks appeared just as expected. Heath sat there and held his temper.

"I want you to give him a chance to work it out—"

"Wait a second," Pachoulo interrupted. "I ain't even going to point out you got no business sticking your nose into my living. I ain't even going to ask me do you expect me to scratch what the cabbie owes me off my books. I ain't even going to ask you if you got the nerve to set my a . . ." He looked at Deetch.

"Agenda?"

"No. What to do with paying off a debt."

"Amortization?"

". . . amortization schedules for me. Because the whole situation is . . ." He looked at Deetch again.

"Moot."

". . . a mutt. This Ray just paid me what he owes me. Interest and principal. I just closed his account."

Heath got up, feeling foolish. If what Pachoulo told him was true, he'd just made a damned fool of himself for nothing. Asked a favor of a shy, putting himself in his debt according to the bookkeeping of the street by which both cop and criminal abided. Revealed himself still at the beck and call of another man's woman. Opened himself up to speculation.

"She sent you out on a wild goose chase, Panama," Pachoulo said.

"Watch your mouth," Heath said, but there wasn't much fire in it.

There was nothing more to say, so he walked away, wondering where in the hell Billy Ray had glommed on to enough money to pay off Pachoulo a bone and two dimes.

Outside the restaurant, Monk was waiting for him. "How'd it go?" he asked.

"Lisa made me a fool. I don't think she knew she was doing it, I don't think she knew the situation had changed, but she asked me to go in there and made me a fool."

"You'll get over it."

"Who said I wasn't over her?" Heath snapped.

"I didn't say 'her,' I said 'it.' I said you'd get over looking like a fool in front of that guinea."

"Oh," Heath said awkwardly. "I didn't hear you right. I'm sorry."

"That's okay. We got a call. They want us over to the Rampart Street jail."

"What for?"

"They named a special prosecutor to look into vice and racketeering. I think we've been volunteered for the task force."

14

The word raced down the boulevard like a tongue of flame. Puffy Pachoulo's henchmen were out on the streets looking for Benny Checks. Even Pachoulo himself was in the back of his car with his driver, a big black gamoosh named Howard, threading the side streets, looking for a sign.

When they found him, the word said, they were going to stop his clock and stuff his mouth with a dead herring. Checks had dared to move off his own turf and stick a finger into Puffy Pachoulo's pie.

Notice of the danger even reached the ears of Benny's wife when she overheard the butcher talking about it to a couple of customers before they knew she was in the shop.

She was a pretty woman whose good looks were spoiled a little by the sorrowful expression she always had on her face, like a cat that could never settle down for a good rest for fear of the dog next door. She'd come out of Poland or Czechoslovakia somehow and had been working as a domestic in a Beverly Hills household when Benny Checks struck up a conversation with her over the bagels and challah bread while waiting for service in the delicatessen on Rodeo.

She hardly ever talked when he took her out, though she spoke a perfect, precise and nearly unaccented English that made Benny Checks sound like the one who came from the old country. She had a solemn face with a complexion like milk, and eyes like pieces of coal. She had a body that looked chunky and ungainly in her maid's uniform and low-heeled shoes. Even when she was dressed up Checks didn't think she looked like much. When he finally talked her out of her clothes he couldn't believe what he saw. She was so beautiful it could stop your heart. This perfect white shape, with tits like mounds of frozen snow, except for pink peppermint nipples. Between her legs she had a bush like spun-gold floss. She'd made love that first time like someone who hadn't had a decent meal in years. When they were done, she went to bathe and came back all dressed again. Checks learned that Ana wasn't one to linger. What was done was done. What was to come was to come. She wanted to be ready for anything, good or bad, but mostly bad.

Ever since that night, he walked around with this woman, who looked dowdy and clumsy to the average person, knowing the mystery she hid beneath her dress.

Six months later they were married because, Checks declared, it was the only way he could think of to get her to smile. He'd tried and tried without success and he figured he needed time. But, according to him, she'd only smiled once or twice in the four years since they'd tied the knot and now he accepted the fact that whenever she looked less troubled than usual, she was probably hysterically happy. He hadn't learned much more about her than that, and she hadn't responded with such passion in his bed ever again. Once she'd said, by way of explanation, that it wasn't becoming to a married woman.

She kept a perfect house, not a picture or magazine out of place. Any spaces left on the walls between the dark paintings of lakes and mountains, peasant festivals and religious icons were filled with Bohemian chinaware, held in place with brass hangers. Every piece of furniture had its company of porcelain animals, ducks, mice and rabbits. Little dishes of hard candies were scattered around here and there, sitting on little doilies. There were always cakes and oily cookies in the breadbox. Always ice cream and frozen desserts in the freezer. She never ate them herself—she had to watch her weight—and Checks wasn't much for sweets, but they were always around, signs of plenty, hospitality for any guests they might have, even though there were very few. It didn't take a shrink to know that Ana had been a deprived child and that nothing could ever make up for it. Not even if Benny Checks made a million. Not even if Benny Checks became an aristocrat.

"There is a hoodlum by the name of Pachoulo who is sending us threats on your health, even your life," Ana said, when Checks came through the door of their West Hollywood apartment around suppertime.

Checks coughed, laughed and cleared his throat, one thing right after the other, as if he couldn't make up his mind how to take the news.

"I think you have reason to be afraid," she said.

"What are you talking about? This is just a little commercial dispute. I do a little charity work with some of his customers and it sticks a wild hair up Pachoulo's ass. He's just making noises."

"When violent men make noises, that is reason to be afraid."

"What do you want me to do? You want me to go down on my knees to that greaser over in that wop hangout where he hangs out, stuffing his face and listening to that asshole Iggie Deetch telling him what a fine, upstanding citizen he is?"

"Is this the first time you stole a client away?"

"I nibbled him a couple times, but he never knew it. I should have known this Billy Ray would have a big mouth."

"Pachoulo has done violence before, is that right?"

"Well, he's done some violence to customers who didn't pay up."

"Why did he do this?"

"Because they was taking money out of his pocket, I guess. By way of doing business."

"What is this business?"

"Lending money."

"This is the business you want to make for yourself?"

"It pays better than writing bets."

"And, if your new customers don't pay on time, will you do them violence?"

"If I have to."

She sat there in their clean but cluttered living room and shook her head as though she were bringing down a judgment against him. All of a sudden Checks felt his anger boiling up. Great tits or no great tits, was it worth it living with a woman who never smiled and rarely spoke? Who didn't want to know about her husband's business but now, all of a sudden, decided to stick her nose in his business?

The anger burned in him with a fine, blue flame. His whole body was alive with anger. Anger that made him feel, in that moment, capable of fighting it out with Pachoulo and his muscle toe to toe. He could smell the candy in the dish on the coffee table. He could smell the talcum powder she sprinkled on her breasts. He could hear the sea all the way from Malibu and could feel the rug through the soles of his shoes.

"I could do it if I have to," he practically shouted.

"No. It's not in you to hurt another person. If I had thought it was in you to hurt another person I never would have agreed to be your wife. You are not a strong man, Benny, and that gun you carry under your arm won't make you something you are not."

Checks stood there as though she'd poleaxed him.

"That's a hell of a thing to say."

She frowned, as though the fact that she was there, keeping his house, cooking his meals, lying next to him in their bed and allowing him to use her body now and then, was all he could expect. For her to think him brave was more than he should expect.

He felt his balls retreat up into his belly. He felt his scrotum shrink. The fine anger was replaced by fear.

"What should I do?" he asked.

"Go away for a little while."

"Go where?"

"Go to San Diego and visit your relatives."

"I don't even like my relatives in San Diego. I wouldn't even be welcome in their house."

"Stay in a hotel. Stay anywhere you please."

"You want me to run because this guinea is making threats?"

"You do not have to prove yourself to me. You are what you are. I know it. It is time for you to know it. Go to San Diego or anywhere. But first call your lawyer friend."

"Allan Nadeau?"

"Call Mr. Nadeau and ask him to act as your intermediary with Pachoulo. Have him tell Pachoulo that you have no plans to be his competitor."

"I can tell the guinea myself."

She shook her head and shifted herself in the chair. The warm smell of her came at Checks in waves. "He has made a threat and a boast. If you go to speak to him yourself, you may not have the chance to say what you have to say before he does you violence. If he picks you up off the street or comes here to our home you may not have any chance at all."

"You're asking me to show the flag."

"What flag?"

"The white flag. You're asking me to stand back and have somebody else plead my case."

"Sometimes it is better to be smart than brave."

"You want me to assume the position," Checks complained, still trying to hold on to something.

"What position?"

"Bent over, with my ass in the air, so he can kick me anytime he wants."

"It is no shame. It is what even the monkeys do in order to survive. Will you call Mr. Nadeau?"

"If it'll make you happy."

15

Every once in a while, maybe it's election time coming up, maybe there's big trouble with the garbage collection or the firemen are threatening to strike, maybe it's some television preacher gets on about Sodom and Gomorrah one more time, somebody, the mayor, a councilman, a citizens' committee, calls for a special commission to look into vice and corruption. The theory being that even if you can't change human nature by sweeping the bookies, the skag dealers, the hookers, pimps and twangy boys off the streets, hassling the dirty-book shops and the porno movie houses until they're forced to shut their doors, doing whatever it takes to condemn certain activities that have been going on for ten thousand years, you can give the good people of the city the *idea* that something's being done about it.

The trick is in finding somebody to head up such a task force, the local district attorneys or public prosecutors being, as a rule, street fighters who have themselves been known to snort a line or two or avail themselves of the high-tech party girls in the hours immediately following public functions. Being, also, tangled up in the power structure in which there are no white hats and no black hats; in which, as the lady who entertained a president and a gang lord on alternating nights once said, "Everybody does business."

When even ministers of Christ are going around despoiling virgins, while their wives pop pills and their associates threaten to hold their breaths, turn blue and die if the faithful don't put themselves in hock for the million-dollar houses and the ten-million-dollar glass edifices, you can see how hard it is to find a person at least *perceived* as being above suspicion or reproach.

It's usually a good idea to go outside the local power structure and pluck, from elsewhere, somebody with plenty of ambition but no name. Onetime seminary students with leanings toward Zen philosophy are good. New England scions of the very rich, with loose hair flopping over their eyebrows and an easy way of walking around with one hand in their pockets, are very good. Anal retentives with young faces and white hair are maybe the best.

Francis Michael Fitzsimmons had it all, plus skin that looked like it had been just freshly scrubbed and waxed, a black plume in his snowy hair, and killer blue eyes.

"Where's this alien come from?" Heath asked Monk as they slouched through the door and into the main reception room of Rampart Area Jail, a decaying facility long out of service that was aired out every now and then when a neutral jurisdiction was needed.

The white-haired stranger from the East was standing up on the charge desk platform with Buck Choola, the commission services coordinator; Howard Bradford, from the office of the administrative commander; Gunnar Norenson, the first deputy and assistant chief of police, and a few others unknown to Heath and Monk even by sight.

"He's some rich kid used to be a congressman from Rhode Island, I think," Monk said.

"What's the matter, we haven't got enough assholes right here in California, we got to bring them in from the other side of the country?"

"Don't ask me. Maybe they want somebody with clear eyes and clean lungs."

"Jesus Christ, look what we got here," Heath said, casing the hall, which was crowded with maybe fifty men and women, and more coming in every minute. "Will you look at the members of the congregation."

"There's Jacoby and Matz from Organized Crime," Monk said.

"There's Chuka from Newton Street and Mandingo from Hollenbeck."

"The animals out on the streets must think it's Christmas with all the keepers in here having coffee."

"You want a coffee?" Heath asked. "There's a crowd over in the corner. I think that's where they got the coffee."

"All they got is them Styrofoam cups," Monk complained.

"What's the matter, you drink coffee out of them cups all the time."

"No, mostly I drink cold drinks out of Styrofoam. I always try to get cardboard when I get coffee to go."

"Paper makes the coffee taste like wax. So you don't want any?"

"I see some people are chewing on sweet rolls. You think they brought their own sweet rolls?" Monk asked.

"Who'd bring their own sweet rolls?"

"So you think the administration sprung for the sweet rolls?"

"How the hell would I know? Who gives a rat's ass?"

"I was just thinking, they sprung for the sweet rolls, maybe this operation is going to be funded pretty good for a change."

"So you want a coffee with your sweet roll?"

They made their way through the crowd to the coffee urns, three of them, fifty cups apiece, lined up in a row. With cardboard boxes still half full of sweet rolls, all kinds, lying beside them.

Every time they bumped a shoulder or laid a hand on an arm with an "excuse me," they said hello to a cop they knew or had worked with, or looked into the eyes of a stranger, sizing each other up in case they found themselves together in a team.

"You in on this, too, Missy?" Heath asked a little Chicana woman with a cloud of black hair flying around her face.

"Whatta you think, I shou'n' be in on this? Is this one jus' for the boys?" she said, ready to fight, her words like little firecrackers going off.

"For God's sake, Missy, I was just wondering what Juvenile was doing here. Why do you jump on me every time I say hello?"

"Is tha' wha' tha' was? Hello? You wan' to say hello, say hello. You wan' to know wha' Juvie's doing here, it's because tha's where it's all fallin' apart, ain' you heard?"

"Well *excuse* me."

"I ain' mad at you, Panama," Missy Guevera said, smiling a brilliant smile. "How come they don' have maybe some burritos at these briefing sessions?"

"You already got too many beans in you," Heath said, grinning.

She patted him on his ass. "You come aroun' sometime, maybe I show you."

The noise level had been climbing and climbing. There were maybe seventy people in the echoing cavern of the main reception room by now and some of them were shouting to be heard.

Then this thin, sharp voice said, "People!" and kept on saying it. The words were pieces of polished brass hammered flat, ringing in the air.

"People," Chief Norenson said, and the noise level dropped like the sound of surf falling behind as you drove away from the sea. "We're going to keep this short and sweet. That's why we didn't lay out a bunch of chairs so you could rest your feet. I don't have to tell you the tide is rising out there. You're the ones swimming in it. Now we're going to start pulling some plugs. Captain Choola's got something to say to you about Miranda and Escobedo."

Choola wasn't in uniform. He looked like every banker that ever turned you down for a loan, mouth like butter and little eyes magnified by his eyeglasses until they were too large for his face.

"The authority and singular powers of a task force assigned to carry out the wishes and commands of a special antivice and antiracketeering commission do not alter the legal necessity of Mirandizing everyone brought in for questioning or placed under arrest. In fact, you have to be twice as careful as you ordinarily might be about this point, since the entire operation is going to be under constant and considerable media scrutiny. Note that this is not intended to be a sweep of the streets and parks. There are to be no random or wholesale pickups. We are looking for the structure of vice and racketeering throughout the city. That means we are willing to pay off the little ones so we can climb on their backs to the big ones."

"So, what else is new?" Heath murmured.

"What does he know?" Monk murmured back. "The man lives in an office."

Choola kept going. "When the time comes to gather up the sharks and barracudas in the nets . . ."

"He's a fisherman," Heath murmured.

"... there will be some door kicking..."

"Also a carpenter," Monk replied.

"... and that is another matter we should talk about. More and more the courts are taking the position that society should not be punished for the procedural mistakes or even misconduct of the arresting officers."

A murmur passed through the crowd.

"Evidence acquired through honest error or misunderstanding will no longer be considered illegal and inadmissible. It will *not* poison the well. In other words, if you happen to have the wrong date on a court order to search a premises, the defense won't be able to cry foul and get the evidence thrown out."

"What's he telling us? What's he telling us?" Heath asked.

"He tellin' us, we kick somebody's ass with a pointy shoe, all we got to say is we forgot we was wearin' our hooker's heels," Missy said at his elbow.

"Suppose we conduct a search and seizure at a wrong location and find guns or illegal substances?" a cop with a young, freckled face piped up.

"What's the matter with that gamoosh? Ain't he listening?" Monk said. "Choola just told us we'll all be walking around with blank warrants. Fill them in afterwards. What kind of schmuck we got on this task force?"

"Tha's Jimmy Kelly from over to Venice Detective," Missy said. "He ain' dumb. He jus' wan' to see can he make Choola say it."

"Say what?"

"Say we supposed to go out there an' scare the shit outta ever'body on the street. Knock the statistics flat for a month, two months. You don' really think they mean it wit' all this bullshit? They jus' blowin' smoke. That white-haired asshole is prob'ly goin' to run for president. We make his reputation, ever'thin' goes back the way it was."

Heath and Monk didn't want to think about it, so they just shushed her and tried to hear what Choola was saying.

"What did he say? What did he say?" Heath asked.

"He didn' say nothin'. What you don' say out loud, you don' get shoved down your throat or up your ass."

Choola turned to the white-haired stranger and took a step back, inviting Fitzsimmons to belly up to the podium.

Fitzsimmons ran a hand through his white hair and ducked his head as if he were about to ask a girl to dance. The black streak settled right back into place and every woman in the station house felt a twitch below her belly button, even old Aggie Felton, who didn't even like men.

"Oooo, oooo, oooo," Missy moaned.

"Jesus Christ, you disgust me," Heath said.

"You jus' jealous, Panama."

"You'll notice there aren't any newspapermen or television crews here for this little get-together," Fitzsimmons said. "Only family. That's so we can speak up if we have any questions and expect to get straight answers. I don't think Captain Choola caught your inquiry, officer."

"Well, no, I didn't quite understand what was said," Choola said, very seriously.

"We're all nervous today. We're about to embark on matters of great moment for this city. We're about to give the criminal element the word that we're mad and we're not going to take it anymore," Fitzsimmons went on.

"I saw that picture," Heath murmured.

"So to answer your question, Officer . . . ?"

"Kelly. James Kelly."

"Okay, Jimmy. It means you're to go where you have to go and do what you have to do in order to gather the evidence and build the cases that'll result in arrests, prosecutions and convictions. No place is sacred. No place can be defended by a tangle of legal paper. That doesn't mean you can grossly abuse anyone's rights, or settle any personal vendettas. But you show me that your actions were well meant and you won't have to worry about Internal Affairs putting you on the griddle or the state's attorney hanging you out to dry. I, personally, will be your shield against any accusation of improper or illegal conduct, within the guidelines I've just given you."

"I didn't hear any guidelines," Monk said, under his breath.

"You attend to the spirit of the law and I'll take care of the letter," Fitzsimmons went on, with a lift to his voice as though he were ready to accept applause. When none came he asked if there were any questions.

After two or three, worrying the same issues of search and seizure, arrest and interrogation, trying to pin down just exactly what would be considered suitable and what would not, Fitzsimmons cut off any more questions and referred them to the leaders of the newly formed teams as noted on the rosters by the door.

Then he waved a hand like he was already a candidate for public office and disappeared through the door behind the charge desk with a little man named Charlie Swale who had a permanent smile stuck on his kisser and who was the Democratic Party guide through the politics of the city and the state.

"Look at Charlie Swale," Monk said.

"In case there was any doubt about Fitzsimmons running for higher office," Heath replied.

16

The newly formed fifth squad walked together down the street until they found a coffee shop with booths where they could all crowd in, have a cup of coffee and introduce themselves to one another. Missy knew Kelly, and Heath had bumped into Mandingo once or twice. Some of the others had nodding acquaintances but none of them had ever worked with any of the others before. It was like going to summer camp and sizing up the strangers you were going to have to live ass to ass with for two whole months, eating the same food, doing the same things, sharing sleeping breaths and farts in common.

Poke Kopcha was the only one who ordered any food.

They sat there, wondering how to start.

"So, how's this supposed to work?" Jimmy Kelly asked. "We all go running around holding hands and catching perpetrators?"

"We go out there kicking doors and busting heads?" Mandingo asked in his bass rumble. Mandingo's real name was Ainsley Washington, but it had been so long since he'd been called by either of his given names he'd almost forgotten that he had them. Some people called him Mandingo but most, too lazy to go the distance, called him Man. Since "man" is commonly used as a neutral designation like Mac or Jack and since "man" is also used generically when referring to persons in authority, Ainsley Washington was made to feel like everyman on the one hand and the living symbol of the police on the other. Assaulted with what had become his proper name a thousand times and more a day he had, unbeknownst to himself, taken on the attitude of a living totem or a tribal shaman.

Sergeant Harvey Becker sat back in the vinyl-upholstered booth and looked worried. Becker rarely looked anything else but worried. With his thinning hair, pinched nose, receding chin and steel-rimmed eyeglasses, he looked like everybody's uncle, the one the family called upon to sort out arguments, decide disputes, check insurance rates and arrange for the burial of the dead. The uncle you could depend on to think things through and get things done, but could never depend on in a bar brawl. What hardly anybody knew, because he certainly would never tell them, was that Becker had half a dozen citations for bravery and had once walked into a gang hangout down in Chinatown and dragged out their warlord by the scruff of the neck while the gang looked on with their mouths open. In dangerous situations, he acted like he wasn't afraid of anything but he always *looked* like he was about to fall down in a faint if anybody said boo.

He kept looking at the door and then at the faces of each of the cops stuffed three to a side in the coffee-shop booth as though he were counting noses. There were supposed to be seven to a squad, including the leader, but he had only six.

Missy wiggled around. She was sandwiched between Mandingo and Poke Kopcha, two hundred eighty pounds and sweating. It was a wonder he was still on the force, the condition he was in, but there he was, still working the streets and alleys in the Harbor area, scaring the hell out of everybody, avoiding the yearly physical, ducking reprimands and warnings, hanging in until his retirement came through eight months down the line.

"You got ants in your pants, little girl?" he asked.

"I don' know you, whattaya t'ink, talkin' about my pants. I'm sittin' between two lard barrels an' my feet don' reach the floor."

"You want, you can sit on my lap."

"You ain' got no lap. You probably ain' seen your pecker in twenny years."

"So maybe you'll take a feel, tell me is it still there."

"I take a feel, you'd keel over with a hard attack. I ain' no murderer."

Monk came through the door and strolled over to the booth, picking up a loose chair on the way. "I think this whole operation is a lot of bullshit," he said.

"What are you doing here, Monk?" Heath asked. "They didn't assign any teams intact."

"Monk? That your name?" Becker asked. "I haven't got you on my roster."

"I traded off with Heinie Weiss."

"Why did you do that?"

"Because Panama and me are married."

"I don't know about this...." Becker didn't have to say what he didn't know about because everybody knew these special commissions set great store by tables of organization, personnel charts and other symbols of efficiency. It was as though, by setting up these neat little trees of command, they believed they'd done more than half the job. All the names in the boxes had to do was go out there and bring back the news, which would be sorted, collated, shuffled, alphabetized and taken to the courts, where a thousand villains would be arraigned, charged, some tried, a few convicted, many appealed and one or two tossed into the slam.

"Whattaya t'ink, the rest of us ain' got no partners? Hey, how come they break up the teams? Tha's no way to do."

"What we're looking at here is a crusade against chicanery and corruption," Kopcha said. "The assumption is that every working team of cops has got a pad to which this bookie and that pimp contributes a little something. You decide to sweep the garbage off the streets you want to be sure—one—the gonnifs don't get any protection and—two—none of the cops accidentally get swept up, too."

"I don't know if that's all of it," Becker said.

Everybody looked at him, their uncle, ready to listen to what the old worrywart had to say.

"There's another angle to it when you break up partners. Two people work the same streets day in day out, they start seeing the same things and not seeing the same things. They spend a lot of time talking about their gallstones and athlete's foot. You bust them up and toss them out on streets they never saw much of before, all of a sudden their eyes get sharper and their noses smell better. Not only that. They miss each other or maybe they already share a social life. So they get together and they compare notes. All of a sudden they're seeing things they never saw before. They're covering twice the ground and they don't even know it."

"I still say it's bullshit," Monk said. "It won't do no good. We'll clean up some of it, the politicians'll get their headlines, and the crap will all be back on the street the next day."

"So wha'?" Missy said. "It's like you got a garden. So you let it go ever' now and then. The weeds get so high you can' see over them. So you go out an' cut the grass an' pull the weeds and the flowers got a chance for a while. It's better than lettin' it go to hell altogether."

"Jesus Christ," Kopcha said, "now we're talking about fucking flowers."

Missy fixed him with her black eyes. "Be grateful. For a man in your condition, fuckin' flowers is better than nothin'."

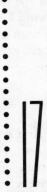

Allan Nadeau agreed to squeeze Benny Checks in while he was having his lunch over at Musso Frank's on Hollywood Boulevard. Checks himself ate there a lot, preferring the counter, where you could talk to this guy and that guy, either side of you, out of the corner of your mouth, do business with one or the other, the other guy doesn't know, looking straight down at your plate if you didn't want anyone to read your expression.

But Nadeau liked the wood-paneled grill room in the back where the high rollers put on the feedbag.

They were sitting across from one another, Checks wondering where he should look because he hated it that Nadeau would see the fear in his eyes as he told his story.

"I can't understand why you'd do anything so dumb, Benny," Nadeau said.

"Well, four, five months ago I got to thinking a man can't just keep stepping along in one place. A man's got to diversify his investment portfolio a little bit."

"You're been shying for five months?" Nadeau exclaimed.

"Just a little. A bone here and a bone there."

"How did you keep it quiet so long?"

"I told the people it was between them and me. They don't talk because they don't want I should cut off their water."

"How come it didn't work this time?"

"How can I figure Billy Ray—he knows the streets like I know the streets—gets a case of the stupids and brags to Pachoulo that he's got a new banker?"

Nadeau felt like telling him that with the kind of people he dealt with Checks could *always* expect his friends and acquaintances to do the stupid thing just like anyone could depend on Checks to do the stupid thing. It was why they were making their livings on the edge, they couldn't cut it otherwise. He didn't give in to the urge because he expected he'd told Checks what was what more than once before, and besides, it was the stupidity of people that put some of the steak and potatoes on his plate.

"What are you having?" he asked, as he saw the waiter approaching.

"I usually eat at the counter."

"The food's the same."

"Oh, I guess that's right. I suppose I'll have a hamburger with fries."

"That's what you'll have? You're in the best grill in Hollywood and you're going to have a hamburger and fries?"

"What are you having?"

"Kidneys Torbego," Nadeau said to the waiter.

"What's that?" Checks asked.

"Kidneys, chipolata sausages and mushrooms prepared with a light red-wine sauce." He ticked the menu with a well-manicured finger. "Corn. Sliced off the cob. Potato puffs." He looked at Checks.

"I'll have a *cheese*burger and fries," Checks said.

When the waiter left, Checks looked at Nadeau and said, "I didn't come here to eat, Al, I came here for a little advice."

"You tell Ana about this?"

"Sure."

"What did she say?"

"She said I should leave town for a little while."

"That's good."

"She said I should ask you to speak to Pachoulo for me."

"That's good."

"You telling me I should let that fat greaser run me out of town?"

"You'd rather stay and have it out?"

"Well, no, I didn't say that."

"Spell it out for me."

"What do you mean?"

"I mean tell me what else you can do except stay here and maybe get your arms and legs broken—maybe worse—or you take yourself a little vacation and I make it right with Pachoulo."

"How do you make it right with him?"

"Don't worry. I'll put it to Pachoulo, one businessman to another businessman. I'll call it a territorial dispute. I'll redefine spheres of influence. I'll tell him you're ready to agree to certain restrictions and covenants."

"Yeah?" Checks said, brightening at the news.

"In other words we'll agree not to shit in his yard and he'll agree not to shit on you."

"Oh."

"You're worried about losing face. Don't. Pachoulo and his friends may think you've lost some face. That's what we want them to think, isn't it? Maybe even a couple of people you know will have a laugh behind your back. But your friends won't think you lost face. I won't think you lost face."

"Will Ana think I lost it?"

"She advised you to take a trip, didn't she?"

"Like I was her kid she wanted to keep out of trouble."

"Hey," Nadeau said softly, "is that such a bad thing, a wife wants to treat her husband like her kid?"

The waiter came up with the trolley and started laying out the plates of food.

"So, now you tell me where you'll be going and where you'll be staying so I can give you a call in a day or two and tell you everything's hunky-dory," Nadeau said, biting down on a piece of sausage. A drop of juice escaped from the corner of his mouth and ran down his chin as he grinned with great satisfaction.

"Maybe I should have had the kidneys and sausage," Checks said.

Millie Polachevsky, Nadeau's receptionist, often met with Judy Elkins, the receptionist from another legal firm on the floor above in the Century City East tower where agents, business managers, certified public accountants and attorneys all did business in a thick stew of deals and counterdeals. Whereas their bosses talked mergers, contracts, points, buy-backs and bottom lines, the receptionists and secretaries, truer to the only bottom line of any real consequence, talked about people. They played a game of comparing clients to animals, birds and other creatures. One was a hawk, another a cockroach, and maybe another a sharp-nosed fox.

"This Pachoulo is a frog," Millie said. "He's got this flat face and practically no nose and this smile that runs from ear to ear. You know what I mean?"

"Ugh!" Judy said, and shivered.

"You ever see a frog sitting on a riverbank? It squats there with its fingers all spread out in front of itself and this smile on its face which is very evil."

"Oh, my God. What does he do for a living?"

"I don't know and I never asked. He's up in Allan's office right now with these two men he always travels around with. One of them looks like a mean pig and the other one looks like a wolf. His hairline's practically down to his eyebrows."

"Oh, God, what would you give to be a fly on the wall?"

"What I mean is," Pachoulo said, dragging the words up out of his belly, "you got a legitimate obligation here—"

"Which I have every intention of honoring."

"Well, honoring's one thing and paying up is another."

Nadeau was leaning his elbow on the arm of his leather executive chair with his shirt sleeves rolled back, hand upraised, displaying a Rolex on a loose heavy gold link chain looping his wrist. "You'll be paid. I would have had the money ready for you yesterday, but there was a little eddy in the cash flow."

"I don't know who is this Eddie. What I know is how I got to run my business if I'm gonna—"

"I'm trying to reassure you, Puffy, that I'll have the money for you in a day or two. Three at the most."

Pachoulo sighed as if his patience was wearing very thin. He looked at the floor-to-ceiling windows.

"What floor is this?" he asked.

"The eighth."

"You think that glass could break?"

"I suppose it would if you really wanted to break it."

"Like throwing a chair through it?"

"Well, yes, like that." Nadeau dropped the languid pose, straightened up, planted both feet on the floor, as though pinning himself safely to the rug, and folded his hands on the desk. "But if you stumbled against it by accident, it wouldn't break. You don't have to worry about anything like that."

"Oh, good. How about if you tossed a body through it? You think if it wasn't like a stumble but like a real hard push the glass would break?"

"It might."

"Now, you mind if I tell you something about how I got to run my business without you butting in?"

"Go ahead. I'd be happy to be informed."

"That's good, because my business is very tricky. It's like there ain't no rules anybody thinks they got to follow. People come to me for loans when they run out of credit everywhere else. With me they don't put up their cars or houses for collateral, you understand what I'm saying? They don't even sign a paper. What am I gonna do with a paper, take it to the sheriff? Take it to the court? Maybe take it to some lawyer like yourself and say go sue this sucker, I should get my money back?"

Nadeau opened his mouth as if he wanted to say he understood and that there was no need for this long harangue, but Pachoulo simply raised his voice a trifle and anything Nadeau had to say was left unsaid.

"I try to do anything like that, what do you think happens? They come after me for what they call usury. For charging more than the legal rate. You see how it works, they got a legal rate and you can't charge more than that, until somebody high up fucks up, like somebody did nine, ten years ago, and all of a sudden what the banks are paying on passbooks is less than the rate of inflation and what the credit card companies can charge their customers gives them a loss instead of a profit on every transaction. So then, you understand, they change the rules. The rates on the credit cards shoot up to eighteen, twenty, maybe twenty-two percent and everybody says, okay, that's all right, that's legal. You see what I'm getting at here?"

Pachoulo was enjoying himself. He was making a man who ordinarily wouldn't give the likes of him the time of day sit there and listen to his bullshit go on and on and on.

"You understand what I'm saying here?" he asked again.

"Yes," Nadeau responded. His voice came out through clots of cotton. He cleared his throat.

"You think because I don't talk too good, I'm an asshole? I'm not an asshole. I'm a small businessman," Pachoulo said. "I fuck up, I can't change the rules. So the rules I make, I have to see everybody keeps. Otherwise people take my money and I never see it again. They spread the word that Puffy Pachoulo can be sweet-talked out of his rights. Puffy Pachoulo's a patsy. Everybody breaks my balls. I can't let that happen. So I got to break *their* balls. You get my drift?"

"I'll have the money for you tomorrow."

"That's still three days late. It's not like this is the first time it happens. It happens practically every week. You always got this cash-flow problem. I sympathize. But I got fifty of the same kind of problem. I got to work my ass off trying to keep up with all these goddam cash-flow problems. You sit there dangling your fucking wrist in the air wearing maybe three, four thousand dollars' worth of watch. Look what I wear. A Casio. Seventeen, eighteen dollars. Tells the time. It's also a stopwatch. I can even put ten telephone numbers in it. I got your number in it. I got your number. So, how come you owe me twenty large and you're flashing that gold in my face? You trying to make me look like a fucking fool?"

Nadeau started unclasping the watchband. "How about I give you the watch for this week's interest?"

"What do I look like, a hock shop? I ain't a hock shop. I give you hard cash, I want hard cash back."

"Well, I don't know what else to do, then."

"You got to get up the money. You got to scrape it up. You owe me twenty bones and you sit there without a mark on you. Another client of mine, this cabdriver, this Billy Ray, he owes me a bone, he don't pay the interest and Manny and Carmine here bust his wrist."

"We done him a favor," Sam's Man explained, speaking up for the first time.

"A favor?" Nadeau murmured.

"I tell my boys not to bust his face," Pachoulo said. "The man wants to be an actor. You think I'd take a man's future away for two cees?"

"No, of course not," Nadeau said.

"But for one bone against twenty, what do you think is fair? I mean compared to what happened to Billy Ray?"

"I don't know," Nadeau said after a while. "Maybe I can do you a service."

"What kind of service?"

"Maybe I can arrange for some of your competition to leave the streets."

"You know somebody who's lending money on the street?"

"Benny Checks."

"How come you know this Benny Checks?"

"He's a client of mine."

"What do you do for him?"

"I handle some of his personal affairs. I wrote up his will. I drew up the papers for some real estate ventures his wife, Ana, got into."

"You wrote up his will?"

"Yes."

"That's good. Benny Checks is gonna need a will very soon."

"How's that?"

"He tried to move in on my business."

"That's just what I'm telling you I can do for you. Benny listens to me. I'll advise him to stop his lending activities and turn over any of his current accounts to you. For, let's say, twenty cents on the dollar?"

"You cutting a deal with me?"

"I'm saying I could meet with Benny and make the offer."

"How about ten cents on the dollar?"

"I'll make that offer."

"How about nothing?"

Nadeau hesitated, stammered, tried to grab back the initiative by frowning as though he didn't understand what Pachoulo was getting at.

Pachoulo smiled. "Where you going to have this meeting with Checks?"

"I don't know. Musso Frank's. Whenever we've conducted any business we've met at Musso Frank's."

"How's he going to meet you in Musso Frank's if he's out of town?"

Nadeau lifted his eyebrows. "Oh? Is Benny out of town?"

"Oh, yes. You know why he's out of town? He's out of town because I put out the word I was going to clean his clock."

"Clean his clock?"

"Oh, you know what is this clean his clock. But I got an idea you still don't understand how I got to run my business. Some gamoosh like Benny Checks steps on my shoeshine I got to make an example of him."

"An example?"

Pachoulo looked at Sam's Man, having to turn his whole body to do it because there was so little play to his neck. "Whatta you think of this here lawyer?"

"He sounds like a parrot."

"That's because he's trying to learn." Froglike, he turned his body straight again and stared at Nadeau.

"So, see, there's nothing you can do for me with Checks out of town."

"I can call him," Nadeau blurted out.

"You know where he is?"

Nadeau felt the blood leave his face. His hands were suddenly cold.

Pachoulo shifted in his chair and tilted forward, staring at Nadeau with his slightly bulging eyes. "So you tell us where he is, you buy yourself the three days of grace, no charge."

The room wasn't breathing. A clock that couldn't be heard before was suddenly making a racket, and the traffic from way down below came through the double glazing like the rumble of tanks along an iron road.

"San Diego," Nadeau heard somebody say. Had he said it? He thought all he'd done was take a breath.

"You got a shovel handy?" Pachoulo asked.

"What's that?"

"Never mind. We pick one up at a hardware store on the way out of town."

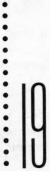

Heath and Missy were having some Mexican at a taco stand on Magnolia Boulevard in North Hollywood.

"This is good, huh?" Missy said, having convinced her new partner that he should change his diet from black coffee and greasy hamburgers to something better for his health.

Heath watched her eat her tostada, biting into it with her little white teeth, leaving the scarlet marks of her lipstick on it.

"I don't know what the hell I'm doing out here," he said.

"So, you don' like the food, you don' got to eat with me. You eat where you wanna an' I'll eat where I wanna," she snapped.

"I don't mean what am I doing eating at a taco stand. I mean what am I doing out here in North Hollywood? I don't know a goddam thing about this area. I hardly ever come over the hills."

"Me neither."

"So what we got is a unit leader who's been working Foothill for nine, ten years, Mandingo out of Hollenbeck and Kelly out of Venice. We got Kopcha from Harbor and you from Wilshire. Me an Monk've been working Hollywood for years. Not only do they pull everybody off the streets they know but Becker don't even let me and Monk work together, we been partners for six years."

"You don' like me?"

"Dammit, if you're going to get a wild hair up your Mexican patootie every time I make a comment about something that's going on, I'm not even going to talk to you."

"How come you always talkin' about my patootie? You got my patootie on your min'?" She grinned.

He grinned back. "Well, that wouldn't be such a bad thing to think about."

"You jus' keep thinkin' about it, Buster, one of these days maybe I let you have a little feel."

"You don't have to talk like one of the boys with me. I'm not like that."

"Like wha'?"

"I don't go around putting lady cops down."

"Ain' you sweet? You don' have to come on liberal aroun' me. It's no skin off my patootie..."

"I'm just saying."

"...you like women cops, you don' like women cops."

"Oh, for God's sake."

"Hey, don' you understan' why this crusader breaks up the teams, drags us in from here an' there, then puts us down here an' there?"

"Because he's an asshole."

"Oh, sure, there's that. It's because he t'inks all cops are crooked.

Maybe not a lot crooked but a little crooked. He t'inks we're all sippin' from the bottle."

"That's a lousy thing to think."

"I don' know. I come into a town like this from somewhere else, I think I'd do the same thing. Why take chances?"

"How the hell are we supposed to do a job? It takes years to get to know the nooks and crannies. Years to get a pocketful of snitches. Informers don't just grow on trees. You got to cultivate them."

"So we got to plant a new crop, tha's all."

"You make it sound easy."

"It ain' easy, but it ain' too hard, either." She glanced over at the young Latino working the grill, knowing that he'd been admiring her all the time they'd been sitting on the stools. She spoke to him in Spanish and called him friend.

Heath didn't know a lot of Spanish but he understood a little. Enough to get the meaning of what they were saying.

"Are you doing a good business?" she asked.

"Sufficient."

"Is this your stand?"

"No, I work for my uncle."

"Your uncle American?"

"I don't understand?"

"He born and raised here?"

"He came from Mexico twenty-five years ago."

"How long has it been since you came to America?"

"Two years."

"But not from Mexico?"

"Yes, from Mexico." His eyes shifted away from her face.

"No, not from Mexico. I think from Colombia."

He stared at her, his eyes going flat.

Missy sighed, opened her purse and took out her badge and gun.

"Hey, for chrissake," Heath said.

"I don' wan' the fool to run," she said in English. Then she went back to Spanish. "They make a lot of cocaine in Colombia?"

His face practically fell apart. He stared at the gun. His arms and legs started to tremble.

"I don't know anything about any cocaine, excellency."

"Why the hell's he calling you excellency?" Heath asked.

"He knows authority when he sees it," she said in English, without cracking a smile.

"Your gun's scaring him spitless. What the hell, you crazy flashing your piece out in public like that?"

"I'm plantin' a seed."

"Next thing you know he'll be hollering intimidation and police harassment."

"He wouldn't be hollerin' that even if he knew the words. He's an illegal. He sees a badge his *cojones* turn to marshmallows."

"Are you enjoying scaring the poor bastard?"

She fixed him with her black eyes. "You gonna tell me you don' enjoy it?"

He dropped his eyes first. She went back to working the illegal, who, with promises of protection, would, for a while at least, be a dependable informer.

If he hadn't known better, there were moments when Nadeau would have thought he was with a bunch of friends on a fishing trip or an excursion to the beach. Except what talk there was wasn't about the expectation of seeing beautiful broads in string bikinis or the big fishes that once got away. It was about kinky sexual adventures with hookers and how a welsher looked hanging on a hook when Machado and Sam's Man were done with him. Machado, behind the wheel, even started looking in his pockets for pictures of a recently mutilated dead man which he kept as souvenirs.

Now they were silent, Pachoulo sitting next to Machado up front, half dozing, eyes closed and face lifted sideways to catch the sea breeze blowing into the car through the half-opened window as they hurried down the Pacific Coast Highway toward San Diego. He had a hand-kerchief, knotted in the four corners to make a hat, protecting his balding head.

Nadeau was in the back with Sam's Man, scrunched over into the corner, a Styrofoam cooler full of ice and canned beer on the seat between them and the dog's heavy head lying on his foot, turning it numb.

Machado tilted his head back and drained a can of beer. The car drifted over into the next lane. A trucker leaned on his brakes and sounded his horn, swinging around them, the huge weight of the load tilting the trailer away and then toward them as he dropped the hammer and fought to regain control.

"Whatsamatter with you, Manny?" Pachoulo complained, starting up out of his doze. "You see how close that truck come to falling over and squashing us flat?"

"Shouldn't allow them suckers to run over the limit the way they do," Machado said. "Gimme another beer, somebody."

Nadeau, white-faced and sick to his stomach, started to fill his request.

"Don't give him another beer," Pachoulo said.

"Hey!" Machado protested.

"You don't know how to drink a can of beer like a human being, you can't have any more."

"It's hot. My mouth's as dry as a goddam sock."

"What if a cop sees you sucking on a can of beer while you're driving?"

"So it's okay a cop sees them two in back sucking on beers, it ain't all right for me to suck on one?"

"They ain't driving a car. You see them driving a car?"

"I ain't even sucking on a beer," Sam's Man said.

"I don't think there's any left," Nadeau said.

"You telling me somebody already drank up three six-packs?" Pachoulo said, shifting his body around so he could look in back at the offending cooler.

"I only got two six-packs of beer," Sam's Man said. "Also some sodas."

"Sodas? Who the fuck drinks sodas?" Machado demanded.

"You drink sodas. I see you drink Pepsi when you eat."

"With pizzas I drink Pepsi, fachrissake."

"So you want a soda?"

"No, goddammit, I want a beer. Next turnoff I'll stop and we'll get a six-pack."

"Never mind the beer," Pachoulo said.

"I got to take a leak," Machado said.

"Piss in your sock."

"I ain't going to piss in my sock, for God's sake. It ain't natural. How come we can't make a pit stop? Benny Checks'll be there when we get there."

"We don't make a pit stop because I don't have to take a leak."

"Well, you could show the rest of us a little consideration."

"You got to take a leak, Al?" Pachoulo asked.

"I'm okay. I haven't had any beer."

"I could shake it out a little," Sam's Man said, before Pachoulo could ask.

"Like a couple of goddam kids," Pachoulo said. "All right, do what you got to do."

At San Clemente Machado pulled off the highway and found a gas station with rest rooms and a small convenience store attached. He hopped out and made a run for the toilets while Sam's Man labored to get out of the backseat, dragging Sam behind him. The dog promptly squatted and crapped on the hot pavement. The attendant started to come over, ready to complain, but there was something about the way the fat man on the other end of the leash looked at him that made him shut his mouth except to say, "That's some dog you got there."

"He can shit like a mule, can't he?" Sam's Man said, then lumbered off to the facilities when the dog was through.

"Carmine shouldn't scare people like that," Pachoulo said, pleased at the effect his best boy had on people. "It ain't polite."

"What am I doing on this trip, Puffy?" Nadeau said, hunching forward on the car seat.

"You're keeping me company. I get tired listening to them two all the time. A man needs a little intelligent conversation every now and then."

"Well, it looks like you're having a nice little snooze. I've got a desk full of work back at the office. I've got a living to make. How do you expect me to pay you what I owe you if I can't earn my pay?"

"So you're earning some money keeping me company."

"How's that?"

"I'm not going to charge you a penalty because you're late again this week."

"I appreciate that. But I haven't really got any reason for traveling all the way to San Diego. I could catch a Greyhound back to L.A."

"They don't make this run every hour on the hour."

"Well, that's true. I could grab a taxi."

"All the way back to L.A.? Fachrissake, that'd cost you a fortune. You got to save your pennies."

"Look, Puffy, I don't really want to be there when you talk to Benny Checks. I don't want him to know I gave him away."

"What's the difference?"

"Well, the difference is Benny will never trust me again."

"What do you care a dead man don't trust you?"

"Now, wait a minute. You don't really mean to kill Benny for one little mistake?"

"Whattaya think I got that shovel in the trunk for? You know how to use a shovel?"

Nadeau felt his bowels go loose. For a second he had the urge to let go right where he sat, to make himself so pitiable or offensive that Pachoulo, in disgust, would kick him out of the car.

Machado was coming back, a paper sack under his arm.

Nadeau scrambled out of the backseat and hurried toward the toilets.

"What's up?" Machado said.

"I've got to go," Nadeau replied, and duck-footed it into the rest room.

Machado got in behind the wheel.

"Don't got to go, got to go. That asshole can't make up his mind."

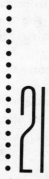

21

A married cop is an eighty percent cop. He's got a home to go to after shift, a wife and maybe some kids who see him as a husband and father first and a police officer second. Sometimes the balance gets out of whack and all they see is cop and then the marriage falls apart.

An unmarried cop is ninety-nine percent cop. He's got nothing but an empty apartment to go home to. Maybe a cat or a bird in a cage, but no people to see him as one thing before the other. Everything he does revolves around the job. The restaurants and coffee shops where he eats, the movies he goes to, the places he hangs around in all night and into the small hours of the early morning. He kids himself, while he's hanging around, that he's got nothing else to do so he might as well be on the eary and keep the feel of the street alive in his fingertips.

He knows as many hookers, pimps, gonnifs and twangy boys as he does cops, and more of them altogether than people in the straight world. If you could get the God's truth out of him, he'd admit that he doesn't understand or like the ordinary citizens very much, feels more than a little contempt for them the way combat soldiers feel about men who've never gone to war.

This goes for women cops, too, though they try to handle it a little differently, staying home nights more often, trying to live normally, growing little pots of chives in the kitchen window. It still doesn't look too good for a woman to hang around like she's got nowhere to go, nothing to do and nobody to do it with.

Missy had a good reason to hang out now that she was assigned to the task force and was working with a new partner. So when Heath said he was going to have his lunch in the coffee shop across from the Chinese Theater where he and Monk often took their break, she said she'd do the same and hung on to his shirttails all the way back to Hollywood.

Monk was already there, and the look on his face told the world that he didn't like to see his partner hanging out with a lady cop.

"You do any good?" he asked Heath, ignoring Missy altogether.

"We do some good," Missy said. "I make a connection with a Latino male workin' at a taco stand. I scare the hell out of him."

"So what's he going to do, turn in his people they deal a little crack, push a little skag, whatever?"

"He turn in his sister, she sellin' her patootie, if I ask him."

"You do any good?" Monk asked Heath again, as though the conversation he'd just had never happened.

"We walked the streets. We got a feel."

"I t'ink maybe it ain' such a bad idea we have our talks after shift in some place over in Nort' Hollywood," Missy said.

"What for?" Monk asked.

"Compare notes."

"We compare notes with Becker twice a week like he says. You know what would maybe be a good idea? Maybe it would be a good idea if you paired up with Kelly and me and Heath teamed up again."

"I don't think we can go on pulling Becker's chain," Heath said, trying to sound reasonable. "You put yourself in his unit without asking him shit about it. Now, you start rearranging his pairs, he's going to dump on you."

"I don' wanna," Missy said, flat out, no arguments.

Monk stared at her for a second. "You got to take a pee?"

"No, I don't got to take a pee."

"You got to take a pee, Panama? I got to take a pee."

Monk got up and went back to the men's room. Heath shrugged his shoulders and raised his eyebrows at Missy as if to say, what the hell you going to do when your partner gets a wild hair up his ass.

Monk was unzipped and pissing in the urinal when Heath walked in. Heath stooped a little and glanced under all the doors to the toilet compartments. Second nature. He went up to the mirror and carefully adjusted the tilt of the scrungy panama.

"That enchilada going to be pinned to your ass from now on?" Monk asked.

"What do you want me to do, slap her in the mouth and send her home?"

"How are we going to talk things over, she's hanging in there chattering away like a fucking parrot?"

"Don't look down your nose. She's no damn fool. She's maybe got more moves than you or me got."

"That's because she's got a pair of tits and a muff."

"That could be. I'm just saying she's got more moves. Speaking of moves, you shake it more than three times you're playing with it." He wanted to lighten Monk up, get a smile on his hound-dog kisser.

It didn't take. Monk pushed himself back in and zipped up, his mouth and jaw set in an unhappy expression.

"So how are we going to work it?" he said.

"Work what?"

"Chew over what we got at the end of the day?"

"Look, why the hell do you want to make a longer day? You got troubles with Jessie already. Make her happy. Go home for supper at a decent hour. You want to chew something over, chew it over with Kelly as you go along."

"All I get out of Kelly is Irish jokes. He's ambitious. He thinks this is an opportunity to make a reputation."

"He's not going to keep anything from his partner."

"Like hell he ain't. I'm nothing to him. He'd step on my face if he thought it'd give him an edge on a promotion."

"You're just feeling lonesome. There aren't a lot of partners as nice as me," Heath kidded.

Monk looked him in the eye. "You're not feeling lonesome?"

"For chrissake, what are you going on about? I'm not Jessie. I'm not your wife. I'm not leaving you."

"What made you say that?"

"That I'm not Jessie?"

"About leaving me."

"Oh, Christ, is Jessie threatening that again? She says she's going to leave you every Fourth of July and New Year."

Monk started walking to the door. "This time she says she means it."

"Hey, aren't you going to wash your hands? Where I come from we always wash our hands after we take a leak."

"Where I come from we don't piss on our fingers."

The place where Benny Checks was staying was a cheap travelers' motel on the fringe of the industrial part of town near the port facilities, a peeling collection of pink stucco blocks piled up two floors around a swimming pool which could be seen from the parking lot, lying still in the hot air just beyond a grilled gate.

"What a dump," Pachoulo said as Machado pulled in and started to park the car near the office. "Not here. Over there, in the back."

Machado shifted into drive and drove the car around back where a chain-link fence separated the parking area from some big dumpsters.

"I don't think Benny Checks is very successful," Nadeau said, trying to figure out a way to build a case that would save the bookie's life and keep *him* from being an accessory to murder. "Nobody but a loser would stay in a garbage can like this. Hardly seems worth the trouble."

"We already went to the trouble. Driving all the way down here in the heat was the trouble. What we're going to do now ain't any trouble. Hey, Manny, where you going?"

"I'm going to ask in the office which room Benny Checks is in."

"You going to leave your calling card? You going to stand there while the manager takes your picture?"

Machado stood there with his mouth open while he worked through the equation. Finally it filtered through to him that Pachoulo was telling him it would be better if they could work it so they weren't seen.

This was strange turf, and who could tell if the local citizens were the type that looked the other way or went running to the cops? They'd probably do the first instead of the second, like everybody else no matter where, but who could tell?

"So what should I do, Puffy?" Machado asked.

"You take a stroll around this dump. You take a little look, then you come back."

"If I see Benny Checks?"

"If you see him, you don't see him. And he don't see you."

"Manny ain't very smart," Sam's Man said, as though apologizing for him.

"He's all right," Pachoulo said.

"Suppose Manny doesn't see any sign of Benny?" Nadeau asked. "We can't hang around here without being seen by somebody sooner or later."

"Manny don't stumble on Checks, then we send you into the manager's office to find out what room he's in. You got a face harder to remember than the faces we got."

"Unless the manager's a nigger," Sam's Man said, making a joke, "then we all look alike to him."

Pachoulo started to laugh and was still laughing when Machado came hurrying back. He leaned on the edge of the open window on Pachoulo's side.

"He's laying right out there by the pool in a bathing suit."

"Anybody else by the pool?"

"A couple of broads, one fat, one not so bad. The fat one's old, the other one ain't."

"What the hell you wasting my time telling me about these broads?"

"They're wearing these little bathing suits which ain't any bigger than a couple of Band-Aids. Even the fat one."

"Oh, that's different," Pachoulo said, with heavy sarcasm. "Now I got all the time in the world to listen to your bullshit. That's all the people around the pool? How about any of the doors open on the first floor?"

"I didn't notice."

"You didn't notice was anybody sitting inside one of the apartments looking out at the broads around the swimming pool? You're a pip, you are." He sat there thinking about his next move, his lips popping in and out with the effort.

"Al, I want you to do me a favor. Take a walk in there and get Checks out here."

"What'll I say to him?"

"You're a goddam lawyer, you don't know what to say to a person like Benny Checks? You tell me you handle a little business for him every once in a while? A little real estate for his wife? So you tell him you were looking for him, you got a paper he's got to sign."

"He won't believe I'd drive all the way down to San Diego for him to sign a paper."

"You tell him you got the paper in your briefcase in your car."

"He'll know I'm setting him up. He'll never believe it."

"You make him believe it. You make him believe whatever it takes to get him to come out here without making a fuss or trying to make a run for it. I don't want to have to blow his head off by the pool, make a mess, scare the shit out of them two broads, maybe hit one of them with a stray bullet."

"Look, Puffy, I'm really going to have to refuse the favor. In fact, I'm going to get out now and go find a taxi or rent a car or something and go back home."

"There could be two bodies floating facedown in that pool."

"I don't think you'll do that. I think you're too smart to murder two people in front of witnesses. Even if you kill the women at the pool, you don't know how many people will come out to have a look. You can't shoot everybody in the motel. I don't think you'll do that."

"So what I'll do is have Manny and Carmine dig the hole for Benny Checks a little deeper. They could use the exercise."

"Well, maybe you could do that, if I just sat here. But I'm getting out now."

"Hey, Sam!" Sam's Man said in a certain tone of voice. The mastiff lifted up its huge head and stared at its master. "Look," Sam's Man said, and laid a hand on Nadeau's arm. The dog scrambled to his feet and took a position, watching Nadeau, his yellow eyes on the lawyer's throat.

"What's the argument we got here?" Pachoulo said. "You're not going anywhere."

"I won't do it, Puffy. I won't give Checks the Judas kiss."

"You know I got your wife on my books?"

"What?"

"That beautiful twat you're married to put herself in my hands. She's into me for two bones. I give her a price on the vigorish because her dealer, who's a friend of mine, asks me to. Five percent a week. I'm generous because she's so good-looking, you know what I mean?"

"Jesus Christ," Nadeau breathed.

"That's right, you should pray. So far, when she's late, I just tack it on the principal. I don't break her face. I don't put an icepick in her eye. I don't even threaten her."

"She's cute," Sam's Man said. "When I go to collect and she ain't got it, she laughs about it and pats me on the cheek. She thinks having an account with Puffy is like having one at MayCo. She's very cute."

"Go take a walk inside, counselor, but don't take a swim. We ain't got the time."

"Down, Sam," Sam's Man said, and the mastiff relaxed, lying down and putting his head on Nadeau's foot again. When Nadeau moved it to get out of the car the dog didn't object, he just sighed, worn out by the long ride and the heat.

Nadeau felt the sun hit him like a hammer right between the eyes. What the hell was happening here? he thought. He knew Helena snorted a line now and then, a little recreational drugs on a slow day. But what kind of a habit did she have that she was into a shy for two thousand dollars what with all the money he gave her? Then he asked himself why he was kidding himself. He'd known Helena was using heavy but had just talked himself out of it. What you didn't know didn't hurt you. Like a criminal lawyer trying not to face the fact that the scumbag he was defending had really raped, mutilated and murdered a six-year-old and didn't deserve a defense, didn't deserve any human consideration at all no matter all that bullshit about how everybody deserved counsel and how he was only doing his job the best way he knew how as provided by the law.

There were times when a monster like that should be judged out in the market square, knocked to the ground with a blow between the eyes like he was a goddam ox, and his balls cut off. Instead of giving him a defense and . . .

What the hell was he doing thinking about a hypothetical when Pachoulo had just told him his wife was into him for two bones and, if he wanted to put on the screws, there was nothing Nadeau could do about it? She'd put herself willingly into Pachoulo's hands just like he'd put himself willingly into Pachoulo's hands.

There was a little shade cast by some arching palms just where he passed from the parking lot into the courtyard where the pool lay like a patch of oil stinking of all kinds of chemicals, like a stale bathtub. The momentary coolness shocked him. He saw Benny Checks lying on a plastic chaise longue by the pool. He was wearing a pair of swim trunks, his belly slopping over the waistband, his legs coming out of the wide leg holes like white lamb legs covered with suet. He had a towel spread out on his chest and was resting a beer can on it, holding it in his two hands like a baby with a bottle.

For a minute Nadeau thought Checks was asleep behind the sunglasses, but when his shadow fell on Checks's face the bookie whipped the shades off as though dumbfounded to see him there.

"Well, will you look who's here?" Checks said. "What brings you all this way?"

"I wasn't sure you'd be here," Nadeau said.

"Where would I be? I always stay here when I come to San Diego, which ain't often, but anyways it's where I always stay. You want a beer? They got cold sodas in a machine over there. I can get you one. How about a cold soda?"

Checks was sitting up, draping the towel around his shoulders, talking fast as thought afraid to think about why Nadeau was there.

"So how come you don't tell me what brings you down here? Nothing's happened to Ana?"

"What? Oh, no. But it's about Ana I had to come down. One of the real estate deals she's got herself into needs your signature."

"How come? I never cosigned for anything before. What bank takes a bookie's signature for a cosigner?"

He stood up, getting his feet into his shoes.

"You hot? You must be hot. You want to go into the room? It's got air conditioning. It's a little noisy but it cools things down. I never signed nothing on one of Ana's deals before."

"This is a technical situation where your signature's needed to prove she's married to you."

"They got more goddam rules. Couldn't signing this piece of paper wait?"

"I thought it was better to get it over with. You never know on a real estate deal. The seller gets cold feet. You know what I mean?"

"Oh, sure. Where do I sign?"

"I left my briefcase out in the car. I didn't know you'd be sitting out here. I wanted to check if you were in before I lugged it around with me."

"So, okay, I'll go to my room—"

"Why don't you just walk out to my car with me? It'll only take a minute."

"What do you mean? You in some kind of hurry? My room's two twenty-two, right off the balcony up there. I'll sign the paper. You'll wait for me while I take a shower, get dressed. We'll have a little something to eat."

"Well, I was thinking about getting back."

"How come you drive all the way down here—"

"Well, it was a nice day and my friend wanted to take a little drive along the ocean."

"Your friend?"

"An acquaintance."

"Oh, I get you."

Nadeau could see Checks thinking what was he doing bringing some bimbo all the way down to San Diego when he had a stunner like Helena at home. Could see him saying something smart to himself like, I guess you can even get sick of lobster and filet mignon.

The opportunity to get a look at the kind of woman a highroller like Nadeau would consider reason to cheat on a wife like Helena removed Checks's last sneaking suspicion. He trotted out after his attorney like an eager pup, the towel, which he'd tied loosely around his waist, flapping behind him like a tail.

When they got close enough, and he got an angle on Pachoulo, he looked at Nadeau, as Christ must have looked at Judas, Nadeau thought, then started to turn, looking for a place to run.

"Fachrissake, it's too hot to chase you," Pachoulo said.

23

"I don't wanna break up no love affairs," Missy said.

"Don't mind Monk. He's having trouble with the wife. It makes him feel like everybody's against him."

"So Becker's doin' you a favor then. He's savin' you on laundry bills."

"How's that?"

"Monk can't cry on your shoulder an' wet your sleeve ten times a day."

"He doesn't do that. He just mentions it now and then."

"You must have a pretty back," Missy said.

"What?"

"There's some beauty staring a hole in it," she said, looking over his shoulder.

Heath turned around and saw Lisa standing by the cash register, a pencil in her hand. He started to slide out of the booth just as she looked away, put the pencil in the cup, crumpled up the piece of paper and started toward him, all in one quick move. He was halfway to his feet, still trapped by the table, when she stopped three strides away, and found himself in the middle of one of those awkward moments when the clock seems to stop and you've got egg all over your face, looking like a fool.

But nobody seemed to notice, least of all Lisa or Missy. They were too busy sizing one another up the way women do, these little cool smiles on their faces, claws neatly sheathed.

He mumbled an introduction, losing last names, hearing himself sounding guilty and wondering why he should be sounding guilty just because he was caught between these two women who had no holds on him at the moment.

"Missy, Lisa," Missy said. "Soun' like a sister act."

Lisa's cool smile turned a little brittle.

"You want to sit down?" Heath asked, hovering there like a bug on a pin.

"Sure, I'll sit down."

Missy leaned back and took a breath, showing that she might be short but she wasn't exactly small. "I got to go. My cat's goin' to be worried abou' me. See you at the taco stand, okay?"

"Okay," Heath said.

Lisa watched her go. Then she sat down where Missy had been sitting and Heath sat down facing her.

They both started talking at once. Then he leaned back and let her have first say.

"I came to tell you you don't have to bother about talking to that skylock."

"I already did."

"Oh. Then I'm sorry for sending you off on a wild goose chase. I suppose that Pachoulo told you that Billy paid him off in full?"

"It doesn't hurt to shake the cage every now and then."

"Billy bet the money he took from me and hit three long shots for the day."

"He did, did he? Lucky."

"I just want to say thank you, anyway."

"You didn't have to make a special trip."

"Are you still mad at me?"

"I just said it was okay."

"I don't mean about the favor."

"I know what you mean. That's okay, too."

"Is it?"

She ducked her head a little so she had to look up into his face, as though he was deliberately trying to avoid her eyes, which he wasn't. It was a trick she had. She used to use it on him when they were going together and they'd have a quarrel over something small. It was one of the things that irritated him a little about her.

"Don't do that," he said.

"Do what?"

"Look at me like that, like I'm trying not to look at you."

"Are you trying not to look at me?"

"I'm looking at you. Can't you see I'm looking at you straight in the face? There's no reason for you to go dipping your head and peeking at me like I'm hiding my head under the covers."

"You used to do that."

"Do what?"

"Hide your face under the covers."

"When I goddam didn't feel like talking."

She straightened up, a little frown appearing between her eyebrows. "Oh, dear, now I've really made you angry."

"I'm not angry, for chrissake."

She compressed her lips and folded her hands in front of her on the table.

"You want something?" he asked. "You want a coffee? You want a sweet roll?"

She shook her head. "You'd hide your head under the covers and then you'd bite my . . ." She left it lying there. She was trolling, throwing out bait, waiting for him to strike at it.

"Lisa, you don't have to thank me for a favor that turns out it wasn't even a favor."

"I want you to know it wasn't my intention to put you in an embarrassing position. You taught me pretty good about how a cop has to have face when he deals with criminals."

"I didn't lose any face with Pachoulo. It wasn't that big a deal. You don't have to thank me . . ."

"I want to thank you."

". . . but you've already thanked me. You better be getting back home. Don't you have to make supper for Billy?"

"He's working a shift. If he's hungry he'll probably stop over to his mother's."

"Well, so it wouldn't look too good if he cruises by and sees us sitting here like this."

"We're not doing anything. I'm just thanking an old friend for doing me a favor."

"I know we're not doing anything."

She stared at him with her eyes full of a hidden agenda.

Heath felt all kinds of turmoil in his stomach, chest and scrotum.

The old wry male wisdom about a stiff dick having no conscience popped into his head.

"I could use a favor every now and then," she said softly.

"Anytime," he said, as if he didn't get her double meaning. "Now, maybe you should be getting home. I've had a pretty hard day..."

She lifted one eyebrow at him, smiling her little smile, which you wouldn't know was a smile except this dimple appeared at the corner of her mouth.

"Get your mind out of the gutter," he said, laughing. "She's just my temporary partner."

"Like I was sort of your temporary partner?"

He slid out of the booth and stood up, the excitement turning a little sour on him because she just wouldn't let it go. Wouldn't let him get out of it smooth and easy so he could walk away feeling that he'd done the right thing, feeling good about himself. Women always wanted to leave a little piece of the hook in your mouth, even after they'd tossed you back.

"You weren't a cop," he said sharply. "You got your car? I'll walk you to your car."

"Our car's on the blink," she said. "I took a bus."

She stood up beside him as he tossed a couple of dollars on the table.

"I can take another," she said.

They walked out of the coffee shop, Lisa in front, Heath behind her, not wanting to look but watching the sway of her hips in spite of himself and remembering where he used to bite her under the covers.

He could feel her waiting for him to tell her that he'd drive her home, that he didn't want her taking buses and walking these streets after dark. She wanted more time to work him. If she got him alone in the small space of his car, she'd have him in her pocket again. She'd have him telling her how he'd never stopped loving her and maybe she'd give him a reward for that and maybe she wouldn't. Either way it would only end up with him getting run over again, and he'd decided that he wasn't going to be one of those cats squashed flat along the boulevard ever again.

He cupped her elbow in his hand and she went along with it, not knowing that he was going to hand her into a cab. Then it was too late. She didn't protest, she had her dignity. So she settled back as he handed the driver a ten-spot and told him to take the lady home.

24

The Styrofoam cooler was in the trunk so Sam could sit on the back-seat between Nadeau and Sam's Man, leaving his place on the floor to Checks, who was suffering every bump in the road and lurch of the wheel. Which happened often, because Machado was pissed off because the few beers that were left were getting hot in the trunk where he couldn't reach them.

"How come you put the asshole on the floor, the dog on the backseat and the beers in the trunk?" he finally blurted out.

"Whattaya want, I should put the dog in the hot trunk, he'd smother?" Pachoulo said.

"Put Checks in the trunk."

"He'd smother, too."

"So, what the hell, it'll save us the effort of doing him."

"Fachrissake, if he smothers who you expect to dig the hole? You want to dig the hole?"

"It's not in his job description," Sam's Man said, laughing through a barrel of phlegm in his chest. "This air conditioning's giving me congestion."

"Maybe you should dig the hole," Pachoulo said. "Get rid of your congestion. Get rid of that gut you're dragging around. Get rid of your fat ass."

"You're going to abuse me, you could go get somebody else to kiss Checks goodbye."

They were talking about the man they meant to kill as if he wasn't even there, Nadeau thought. Maybe that, more than any other thing, measured the depths of their depravity. He knew people who'd sell their mothers for a nickel and steal a dime from a blind man, but at least they'd have the decency not to tell the victims what they had in mind. Talking about it was, somehow, worse than doing it.

Checks stirred against his shoe. Nadeau could imagine how stiff the condemned man must be lying on the hard floor of the car the way he was, half curled up just like he was thrown, afraid to move for fear Sam's Man would get annoyed and kick his ribs in or bust his balls. It'd been an hour or more and Checks must have cramps in every muscle and pains in every bone.

His own leg was numb, being in one place all that time the way it'd been because he, too, was afraid to shift his legs and body around so he could get more comfortable. Afraid to draw attention to himself, hoping that by silence and inaction he could convince them—convince himself—that he wasn't even there. That he was just imagining the whole goddam horror.

There was no reason for him to be there. There was nothing about laying a bet on a horse, playing a little poker, bucking the market, that should find a successful man like himself sitting among thieves and murderers. A jolt of adrenaline hit him in the heart like a fist. If they went through with it, if they weren't just talking to hear themselves and to scare the shit out of Checks, he'd be an accessory to murder.

He heard somebody moan, and for a second he thought the protest had escaped from his own mouth. Then he realized it was Checks, unable to help it, crying out in pain and anguish.

Nadeau moved his foot away, trying to give Checks some room.

"You ever dig a hole, counselor?" Pachoulo said.

"What's that?"

"You ever dig a hole? You ever do a day's work in your life?"

"My share. I've done my share."

"Yeah, like what?"

"I was up at five o'clock when I was a kid, delivering bagels for my old man's grocery store."

"What the fuck you think of that, Carmine?" Pachoulo asked.

"I think that's admirable," Sam's Man said.

"But you ain't said if you ever dug a hole."

"Well, no, I don't think I ever had to do that."

"So, you'll learn. It ain't hard. Manny'll teach you."

"Look, Puffy," Nadeau began, "I think you've terrified Benny Checks enough."

"Is that what I smell?" Pachoulo asked.

That seemed very funny to Sam's Man and Machado, who jerked the wheel from side to side in his glee, sending the Cadillac swerving in and out of the lane. A trucker hit his air horns and blasted by them, creating a wake of turbulence that rocked them from side to side.

"Fachrissake, you watch how you're drivin', Manny, or you don't got to worry about teaching Al how to dig a hole. I'll make you dig a hole and jump in it."

"I could use a cold beer," Machado said.

"The man's suffering," Nadeau said, the fear pumping through him all mixed up with a growing rage. "At least let him change his position, make himself more comfortable."

"You making a demand?" Pachoulo said, turning around and staring at Nadeau with his dull, flat eyes. "Is this a negotiation?"

Somehow Nadeau knew he'd created a crisis for himself. How he handled it could have a lot to do with how much of his balls he'd have left when this ride was over. How well he could fight off Pachoulo's attempts in future to degrade him. It might also decide the fate of Benny Checks. It was suddenly very clear to him that Pachoulo had thrown down the glove and was watching to see what the kid who once got up at five o'clock to deliver bagels before school would do.

"I'm not making an appeal, Puffy. I'm making a fair request. If you're going to kill this man, there's no reason to grind him into the dirt first."

He moved his foot so that Checks could know he wasn't throwing him away but was trying to start a dialogue that might save his life. Checks laid his cheek on his shoe and Nadeau knew he'd gotten the message across.

Nadeau thought he saw a flash of something like respect in Pachoulo's eyes.

"A man in your position doesn't have to pull the wings off flies. That's for punks and two-bit gonnifs. That's for faggots wearing silk shorts and purple shirts."

"Hey, I got a purple shirt," Machado protested.

"Shut up," Pachoulo said. "Go ahead, Al, make your case."

"My case is made. So is your case. The man's lying on the floor and the dog's sitting on the seat. We all got the message."

He made it sound like what Pachoulo did, just because it was his nature to do the worst, was something grander, something symbolic. That the shy was some kind of old chieftain from the Sicilian hills, laying down the laws by which men would live and the signs by which men would know that Pachoulo's justice had been pronounced.

"What do you prove if you kill him? You already turned him into a dog under your feet."

Sam's Man looked down at Checks in surprise, as though that thought had never even crossed his mind, and he moved his feet to give Checks another inch.

"What does it get you?" Nadeau went on. "He's already learned his lesson. He's already out of business, without you having to pull off the road somewhere you don't know too well. Someplace where somebody could be hunting for snakes, picking up aluminum cans . . ."

"Screwing in the bushes," Machado said.

"Who wants to dig a grave on a hot day like this? Who wants to risk sunstroke, maybe a heart attack?"

Pachoulo glanced down at Checks.

"Make yourself comfortable," he said. Then he turned around and stared out the window.

"Well, what do you say, Puffy?" Nadeau ventured after a time.

Pachoulo didn't say yes, he didn't say no. Checks turned onto his back and stared up at Nadeau gratefully, already forgiving him for giving him the Judas kiss.

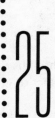25

Helena Nadeau never woke up much before noon. When she did come to, it was usually because she had to take a pee. She lay there on her back in the two-thousand-dollar bed, in the fifty-thousand-dollar bedroom, in the two-million-dollar Brentwood house, with her hand cupping herself between her legs, thinking of sugar-butter bread.

It was the sweetest of her waking reveries, a reminder of her childhood back in Wilkes-Barre, Pennsylvania, when her Aunt Cecilia would give her a slice of Wonder bread slathered with soft butter and sprinkled with sugar as a treat for being a good girl and staying out of the way while Cecilia plied her trade.

She captured and held the image of the sugar, glistening and white as snow. Like her tits. Like her belly. Like lines of cocaine, also white as snow, marching along a mirrored tabletop.

The sadness in her chest and belly was like a fist. When Aunt Cecilia had been in such a mood she'd curl up in the corner of a tatty chaise like a cat and tell Helena to leave her alone because she was suffering from a hairball and it might take some time before she could cough it up. Gin or whiskey was the medicine she took to kick it loose. During her earliest years Helena really believed it was a hairball that her aunt finally got rid of, kneeling on the worn bathroom linoleum with her head in the toilet bowl, retching out her cure for the blues.

Sometimes Cecilia would suck on a fat cigarette, drawing the sweet-smelling smoke down into her lungs and holding it there until hardly a wisp of it came back out when she puffed her cheeks and blew. Helena would stand between her aunt's knees and wait for what little smoke there was to reappear, gazing in wonder at Cecilia's painted mouth, her own small head filled with cotton, silly with a contact high.

When Helena was older, ten or twelve, Cecilia performed secret rituals with spoons and needles in the john, alone or in the company of one of an ever-changing roster of men friends, rough-handed men with withdrawn smiles and secret hungers glistening in their eyes.

It was one of them who took Helena's maidenhead when she was thirteen while her aunt laughed in narcotic pleasure and held her down.

The next morning Cecilia was all tears and self-recrimination. She even grabbed a pair of scissors and poked herself in the chest several times, hard enough to draw blood, while Helena screamed forgiveness and struggled to get the blades away.

Later, she thought it a little strange that she didn't hate her aunt for letting her be abused by the man, but felt a lot of contempt for her because, even while she was fighting to wrestle the scissors from her, Helena had known the suicide attempt was all an act. Cecilia's show of remorse, like the sugar-butter bread, was just something meant to reward Helena for being a good girl.

Her bladder was full and the demand for relief urgent. For a second she thought about letting go and wetting the bed. That, at least, would give her a real reason for getting up.

She kicked her legs and thrashed the covers aside. Jumped out of bed naked, her white skin spiderwebbed with thin red lines because she'd slept so soundly.

Sitting on the toilet, listening to the function of her body, shivering from the release, she touched her nose and found it sore.

A hot shower followed by a cold one kicked her body into second gear, but her head was still turning over like an old car's engine on a cold winter morning back in Pennsylvania. It needed a little choking, a richer mixture, a couple of red devils, a spur of coke.

She swallowed a couple of bennies taken from the stash in her stocking case, then laid out short lines of coke on her mirrored vanity table, shaking out the tracks, one for each nostril, building the little railroad she'd ride to the daylight moon.

Lisa Ray was alone in the Golden Comb Beauty Shop waiting for her one-o'clock.

If she quit her job and got another as an operator in a salon up in Beverly Hills she probably wouldn't have to postpone her lunch break for a customer. There was a way of running things in a beauty *salon* so that women worth plenty willingly endured the haughtiness of receptionists and the temperament of hairdressers, believing that it was proof of excellence on the one hand and their own generous humility on the other.

But when you worked in a beauty *parlor* in West Hollywood you were selling a different bag of goods, a sense of the commonplace, a little of the old-fashioned friendliness of the small towns a multitude of displaced women had left behind.

Lisa sat on her operator's stool, legs crossed, foot kicking, elbows on knee and cigarette in hand, thinking about her one-o'clock, thinking about her husband, thinking about Eddie Heath and his soiled panama hat that made him look like Bogart coming out of the shadows in a dangerous foreign city. Well, not really like Bogart. Panama was pale-haired and pale-eyed, sweet-faced and quiet-eyed, more like that actor —what's his name?—in *Star Wars*. Not the little one, the big one who was a space tramp or something like that.

What would it be like to be in bed with *that* stud, she thought, shaking her head right away at the foolishness of that way of thinking. Wasn't that what dropped her in the soup when Billy Ray came along with his snappy stories, good looks and dreams as big as the Ritz? He'd heated up her imagination and got her thingie longing for conversation with his thingie. If a man's cock had no conscience, like they said, she'd found out that a woman's pussy had none either. Men didn't know that. It was one of her sex's better-kept secrets.

She should have taken Billy Ray on as a one-night stand, or even two, but should never have let all the lessons her mother taught her persuade her to make something more of it. She should have done it with Billy and kept it secret from Panama. Worn out the letch for the cabbie who dreamed of being an actor and held on to the cop who was steady and solemn and not all that bad a performer, even if he couldn't carry her up to the top of the mountain and send her sliding down to the valley below.

When she'd talked it over with Sheila, who'd worked another chair in the Golden Comb and was, at the time, what could have been described as Lisa's best friend, she'd been told to think twice about the cop. Because cops went into dark places, carried guns, worked funny hours and had easy access to whores. And cops got killed.

Well, that was true. But cabbies went into dark places, worked funny hours and had access to women. They didn't get killed as often, but maybe that was because there wasn't much that really mattered about them that could be killed.

Panama was a steady man who'd made her feel safe and protected no matter what. And that had to count for plenty in the long, dark hours of the night.

"If he's got a brother, send him over to my place," Helena said.

Lisa spun around in surprise. She hadn't even heard the bell when the door opened. Helena was standing there looking a million in a white slacks suit with a champagne silk blouse, flashing peeks of her tits almost to her belly button.

Lisa wondered why a rich, flashy piece like Helena Nadeau patronized the Golden Comb when she could easily afford the poshest shop in Beverly Hills. She could flatter herself and think it was because she was a superior operator, but she had a suspicion Mrs. Nadeau wasn't born to money and wasn't used to money and felt more comfortable coming to a neighborhood beauty parlor. Or maybe it was to remind herself where she'd come from.

Helena was staring pointedly at Lisa's hand and grinning.

Lisa became aware that her hand was on her breast inside her starched uniform and her thumb and finger were teasing her nipple, working herself up, making her daydreams come true.

"Oh, my God, I was giving the whole street a show," Lisa said.

"Do it in the window and advertise unisex haircuts," Helena said as she shrugged out of her jacket. "You'll double your business."

"Wash and a color rinse?" Lisa said, standing up and picking up a barber's bib. She took Helena's jacket with her free hand and hung it up on the brass clothes tree.

"I just want it highlighted," Helena said as she walked back to the shampoo basin. "And trim the ends."

"If that blouse's real silk it might get water-stained," Lisa said.

Helena glanced toward the window fronting on the street. Lisa tied the bib around her neck and Helena unbuttoned the shirt the rest of the way, shucking it off and handing it to Lisa.

Carrying it back to the clothes tree, Lisa put the silk to her cheek to feel how cool it was. She flashed on something she'd read once about how marble was always ten or eleven degrees colder than the air around it. She wondered if the same could be said of silk.

When she walked back to the shampoo station Helena was already sitting in the chair. Lisa tilted it back and wet Helena's long hair with the spray nozzle, then started to work a glistening dab of gel into thick suds. She could feel the fine bones of Helena's skull under her fingers, no bumps, no hidden scars or blemishes.

"Are you reading my future?" Helena said.

Lisa looked down into Helena's beautiful upside-down face, chin tilted up, nostrils exposed, small tunnels to the brain, eyelids blinking up instead of down. For a minute Lisa saw a monster, and stepped back in confusion, startled out of her trance.

"You daydreaming or seeing ghosts?" Helena asked.

"I'm sorry."

"No reason to be sorry. I do it all the time. Only it costs me."

Lisa didn't ask her what she meant by that. She sprayed the rinse water through the blond hair turned dark and heavy, wrung it out as though it were a rag mop, and wrapped a clean Turkish towel around it turban-fashion. She kicked the lever and pulled up on the back of the tilting chair, bringing Helena upright in a hurry.

Blood gushed from Helena's nose all over the bib. She stood up screaming, bending her head forward, terrified by the carmine soaking the bib, tearing it from her neck and tossing it on the floor.

Lisa grabbed up another towel, shouting to Helena to sit down and put her head back. But the sight of her own blood had Helena in a frenzy. Her breasts and belly, the pure-white slacks, were spattered and spotted. Lisa grabbed her from behind and slammed her into the chair, avoiding her flailing arms and legs as she ran the cold water and wet the towel before putting it on Helena's face.

"Hold this. Hold this while I go get some ice."

She ran to the service hall at the back where management kept a small refrigerator for face masks and other beauty products, and in which the beauty operators kept iced tea and sodas. She tore off the folded handkerchief pinned to the front of her uniform and filled it with ice cubes, then ran back to Helena.

"Here, let me have the towel."

Helena gave it up. Lisa replaced it with the ice cubes folded into the handkerchief.

"Put your head back."

After a few minutes she took the pack away.

"It looks like it stopped. But you better keep the ice there for another minute."

"Jesus Christ, isn't this something?" Helena said. "I never had something like this happen before."

You keep snorting coke and burning out your nose and it'll happen again, Lisa thought.

She got another towel and spread it over Helena's nakedness as she lay back with the ice cubes jammed against her upper lip, eyes closed, tears puddling and running down her cheeks, her nerves screaming for a fix.

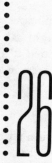

Pachoulo owned a piece of a chop shop on Alameda, near Olive Avenue Park over in Burbank, where stolen cars were dismembered with acetylene torches and the parts parceled out for sale. He'd picked up a junior partnership when the owner, Lou Varecka, got into him for five bones and couldn't make the payments. It was a legitimate body and fender shop when Pachoulo became a partner; now it was a chop shop and Varecka was practically working for the shy with a crew hired by Pachoulo.

It used to be work was done during the day. Now it was done at night and the cavernous garage lay empty during the daylight hours, a handy place for all sorts of illegal and illicit transactions.

That was where Pachoulo told Machado to drive the car.

"Pull the car right inside," Pachoulo told him when they got there.

"Who's going to open the doors for me?"

"What the hell, you crippled?"

"I'm driving the car. The least somebody could do is open the doors for me."

"Jesus Christ, nothing's easy with you, is it? Hey, Benny, you get out there and open the doors for Manny. Okay? Let Benny out, would you, Al?"

Nadeau opened the door and Checks crawled out of the car onto the oil-stained gravel, then staggered to his feet.

"Don't you try to run, Benny," Machado said.

"I can hardly move."

"So, that's good. Go open the doors."

"Wait a second," Pachoulo said. "How's he going to open the doors, he ain't got a key for the padlock."

"Well, I ain't got a key to the padlock."

"Who'd trust you? You got the key, Carmine?"

Sam's Man tossed around in the back of the car feeling in his pockets and came up with a ring of keys like some old-time jailer might carry. He handed it to Nadeau who handed it to Machado who handed it out the window to Checks who stood there with a terrible expression of expectation on his face.

"Why are we stopping here, Puffy?" he asked.

"We still got things to talk about."

"Whatever you say's okay with me. I already said that. Didn't I already say that?" He looked at Nadeau, seeking confirmation, seeking assurance that everything would be all right.

"Puffy, I thought we'd decided on an arrangement," Nadeau said. "I thought we'd already cut a deal."

"Oh, we cut a deal. That part we don't have to worry about. I take back what Benny Checks tried to steal from me. But now we got to consider repo . . . repo . . ."

"Reparations?"

"Reparations and whatever else I got to do to wash my face with my con . . ."

"Constituents?"

"I like the way you read my mind, counselor. I like the way you help me improve my vocabulary."

"I think it's admirable that you want to improve your vocabulary."

"Sure, I want to talk good like you so that people don't think I'm an asshole. It's important for my business that people don't think I'm an asshole."

"Jesus, nobody would think that, Puffy," Checks said like a fawning dog.

"You thought that or you wouldn't have done what you done. Go open the fucking garage doors. We still got some business."

Checks shuffled off to do as told. Pachoulo started to struggle out of the front seat of the car and Sam's Man struggled out of the back. Machado pulled the keys out of the ignition and put a leg out. Nadeau stayed where he was, hoping he'd be asked to participate no further.

"Don't get out of the car, Manny. You get out, Al, and come inside with Carmine and me."

"Why don't you want me to get out of the car?" Machado asked.

"I want you to go over to Benny Checks's house. Get his wife, bring her over here."

"Suppose she ain't home?"

"She's always home. She ain't home she ain't far away. You just hang around and wait for her, then you bring her back here. Al? I asked you to get out of the car."

Nadeau felt numb and sick. The flesh of his cheeks felt like wax about to run down his neck. "What do you want with Ana?"

"You call her Ana?" Pachoulo said, doing some business with his eyebrows. "You getting a little of that, Al, while you're helping her with her real estate deals?"

"For God's sake, Puffy, there's no reason to talk like that."

"Don't get your ass in an uproar. I was just making a joke. Come on out of the car, Al."

Nadeau got out and stood there as Machado kicked the Cadillac into gear and took off, spraying gravel, pissed off that he was always the one who was sent out on errands when the fun was about to start.

Pachoulo regarded Nadeau as though he was wondering how much he would take. Here he was pushing the asshole around like he was some schmucky two-bit grifter into him for a hundred, two hundred, ready to eat dirt just to get out of the weekly ten or twenty he had to pay up in order to stay even. All Nadeau had to do—all *he'd* do if somebody tried to pull the crap on him that he was pulling on the lawyer—was tell him to go fuck himself and walk away. What the hell could he do to a customer like Nadeau who just told him to go fuck himself and walked away? Oh, maybe he could see he had an accident, maybe bust his nose or break a leg, but he couldn't waste the sonofabitch. Not when the gamoosh was in to him for twenty bones plus vigorish. Shit! The man had no sense. No sense of proportion. Also he had no balls.

Pachoulo turned his back and started walking toward the garage doors, where Checks stood with the padlock in his hand and Sam's Man held on to the end of the leash while the dog took a pee against the wall. Pachoulo reached a hand behind him and snapped his fingers without turning to see if Nadeau would get the message. He was pleased when he heard Nadeau's step on the gravel.

"Open it up," Pachoulo said. Checks did as he was told. They stood piled up at the doorway for a minute, then Pachoulo tapped Checks on the ass and they all followed him inside.

It was cool in the garage. Pachoulo shivered.

"Jesus, I got a chill. Go over there and turn the heater on."

There was a big old-fashioned space heater against the wall. It was constructed out of one-inch pipe, bent into flat coils, standing on end, with a hot-water reservoir in the center of it. The protective cover had long since been thrown aside or torn apart to make some repair or other. There was a thermostat on the wall five feet away. Sam's Man went over and turned the dial to the top. The heater kicked on with a whoosh that made Checks jump.

He was hyper. He knew he was going to get it, but he didn't know how and he didn't know when. He wondered where Machado had been sent. Maybe that was a good sign that Pachoulo had sent his number-one punisher away. Maybe what it was going to be was just a little talk, a little scare, a little begging on his part. Maybe that's all it was going to be. Maybe.

27

About fifteen miles away from the chop shop, down along Ventura in Encino, where the car lots lined up for a mile, keeping the air popping with hundreds of flapping pennants, Heath and Missy were walking along like a couple with no place special in mind.

"You wanna buy a new car?" Missy asked.

"I been thinking about it."

"Wha' have you got in min'?"

"Maybe a Beamer. Maybe a Porsche."

He stopped in front of a silver 944 Turbo.

"You got tha' kind of money?" Missy asked.

"I'm not married. I save my pennies."

"Take ten tons of pennies to buy a set of them wheels."

"Wouldn't be enough."

"How many pennies you think in ten tons of pennies?"

"I wouldn't want to count."

He laid his hand on the hood, then pulled it back fast.

"Pistol," he said. "That car's hot as a pistol."

A salesman had come out of the glass-and-aluminum palace that was the showroom. He kicked his feet in front of him and lifted his elbows high as though he were strutting in front of a marching band. His sport coat was stylish but not loud. His tie had a smallish knot. His hair was cut conservatively, like a banker's. Nothing flashy about this man. Sporty, yes, but not flashy.

"I do that all the time," he said, cheerfully.

"Do what?" Heath said.

"Burn my hand on these beauties. How can you forget about the sun in sunny California? How can you forget about it in San Fernando Valley? Well, I forget about it. Or maybe I just can't resist patting the little darlings."

"Like they was horses?" Missy said.

"Hey, that could be it. I mean horses are in the national blood, aren't they? Every man a Westerner. Every man a loner out there under the stars."

"Every man?" Missy said.

"Well, I wouldn't know about women, would I?"

"Whattaya mean? You ain' got a wife? You ain' got a mother?"

The salesman grinned at Heath and said, "Well, you know what I mean," answering Missy, but really talking to the man of the pair.

"You mean a car's like a horse?" Heath said.

"A motorcycle's like a horse, maybe," Missy said. "I don' know about a car."

"Not just any car," the salesman said, "a Porsche. Power under the hood. Small. Built for speed. My name's Phil Doohan." He plucked a card from his jacket pocket and flicked it out as though he were dealing a hand of poker. "What interests you about this Porsche?"

"I just wanted to see how hot it got," Heath said.

"It's hot. It's very hot. It is, in fact, the hottest little buggy on the road."

"It ain' a horse no more?" Missy said.

"You're having fun with me, little lady. I know that and I don't mind. I don't even mind if all you're doing on this beautiful California sunshine day is window shopping. I wouldn't mind if you asked me for a demo, even if you haven't got the slightest intention of buying. I'd still be happy just to show her off. You want to get behind the wheel?"

"Look, why shouldn't I be straight with you," Heath said. "Who could afford a car like this?"

"You ever hear of easy credit? Well, as one of the owners of this enterprise I can guarantee you easy credit. I'm sure you're credit worthy. What do you do for a living, you don't mind my asking?"

"I'm a cop."

"This the little woman?"

"This is my partner."

"So you're on the job even as we speak?"

"That's right."

"I like that. I like the fact that I didn't make you. That means you'll do a good job for me if I ever suffer a criminal attack. Because who could guess the nice young couple in the peasant blouse and panama hat are a couple of cops."

"We do our best."

"So you're cops. You mean detectives, don't you?"

"That's right, detectives."

"Who make out a little better in the wages department than cops in uniform?"

"A little better. Not much better. Just a little better."

"You want to take a spin in this little beauty? I'll take you around the block," Doohan said with considerably less enthusiasm.

"No, that's okay, we were just passing by."

"How come you ain' tryin' to sell this horse to us no more?" Missy asked.

"My God, forty thousand dollars. Hey, I only drive one because I'm a dealership." He spotted a two-year-old Lincoln pulling up at the curb. A white-haired man and a redheaded woman half his age got out. "Excuse me. Look around. Enjoy yourselves," Doohan said and hurried over to the better prospect, elbows and knees pumping, two-toned loafers kicking out, showing the world what just being around a parade of Porsches could do to a man's energy.

"Shit," Missy said, "that man forgot all about givin' us a free ride."

"That's okay," Heath replied. "Nothing's ever free, anyway, you should know that."

28

Machado walked into the garage holding on to Ana's elbow. She was white-faced but composed, the expression on her face revealing very little. Her eyes fixed on Pachoulo, who was sitting on a fifty-gallon drum, his legs dangling, kicking his heels in a soft tattoo like some kid on a milk box. They flickered once toward Sam's Man and the dog, which had lifted its head and was sniffing the air in her direction, attracted by the perfume she wore. They flickered once toward Nadeau, who stood aside, trying to find shadows in the cavernous shed of concrete and corrugated metal. They never flickered toward the white, naked shape of her husband crouching on his haunches, chained by the wrist to a construction of pipes against the wall.

"Mrs. Checks?" Pachoulo said, very polite as though he were about to welcome her to a tea party.

"Ana Chempenovsky," she said, formally introducing herself, refusing to be addressed by a street name. Refusing to be intimidated by a fat man who squatted on the drum like a toad. Refusing to acknowledge that it was her husband who crouched on the concrete like an animal, shielding his genitals from her as though she were the only one who had no right to see him exposed.

She stared at Pachoulo and he stared back at her, both unblinking, fighting a battle of which the others had no part.

"You feeling good, Manny?" Pachoulo asked.

"Tip-top," Machado said.

"You in the mood for a little exercise?"

"Whatever you say."

"I say show me how's your batting arm."

"I ain't got no bat."

"Go see if you can find something. Look over there in that pile of hoses. See if you can find something what fits your hand."

Machado went over to choose a length of hose.

"Would you like to sit down, Ana?" Nadeau asked.

"Mrs. Chempenovsky," Ana said.

"Pick a pew. Take a load off," Pachoulo said.

Nadeau picked up a paint-stained folding chair nearby.

"Leave it alone," Pachoulo said. "She wants to sit down, she can walk over and sit down."

Ana didn't move a muscle. She just stood there like she was standing at a bus stop, thinking her own thoughts, deep inside her own head so that she wouldn't send any brain waves out which might attract attention. Thinking about what she was going to get for dinner maybe. Should she get the blue dress she saw in the window of MayCo maybe.

Machado walked over to Checks, swinging a two-foot piece of radiator hose in his fist.

"So go ahead, show me what you got," Pachoulo said.

Machado swung the hose. Nadeau winced and Checks grunted. The dog got up on its haunches, terrified, understanding punishment, smelling terror, afraid some of the violence could slop over onto him.

"That was nothing but a puny roller down to third," Pachoulo said, never taking his eyes off Ana, who never took her eyes off him.

Machado struck again and Checks cried out.

"For God's sake, Puffy," Nadeau said.

"Pop fly to center field. Gimme a base hit, Manny. Show me a little something."

"The goddam radiator's heating up the chain around my wrist," Checks said. "It's goddam burning me."

"Two out, Manny. I got money riding on this next pitch."

Machado laughed and swung hard enough to break bone. Checks screamed and started pulling frantically on the chain that tied him to the steaming radiator.

The dog started barking and pulling on his leash. He fell into a frenzy, heaving on the chain Sam's Man held wrapped around his fist, shaking the big man with the power of his lunges. Trying to get at

Checks. Wanting to join in the savagery as Machado swung again and again and again, his arm rising and falling like someone beating a rat to death out on some empty lot along the bay.

Checks's bladder and bowels let go.

Nadeau had tears streaming down his face.

Checks was moaning and crying steadily, with a high, keening note to it like a woman in great pain and anguish.

"Let Sam go, Carmine," Pachoulo said, never looking at the beaten man, fighting his fight with Ana Chempenovsky. Enraged because she wouldn't cry and beg. Wouldn't promise him anything if only he'd stop beating her husband, groveling on the floor all bloody and wounded, blood streaming down his face, piss and shit staining his legs.

She never budged.

For God's sake, Nadeau thought, she'll stand there forever, she won't give in even if Pachoulo kills Benny. She won't call it quits and bend the knee even if the mastiff tears out Benny's throat.

"Let the dog off the leash, Carmine," Pachoulo said again.

"You don't mean it, do you, Puffy?" Sam's Man said. "Not with the lady in the room."

"Let the fucker off the goddam chain, you stupid sonofabitch!"

Sam's Man shrugged and unsnapped the leash from Sam's collar. The dog lunged at Checks, who fought him off the best he could with his legs and arms, until he gave up and curled up on the floor, trying to protect his throat and balls and belly. Not even screaming anymore, not even moaning.

The tin walls gave back the dog's feral snarls magnified a dozen times.

"That's enough!" Pachoulo yelled above the din. Still he stared at Ana. Still she stared right back, white as a ghost, impassive, a wax mask. No expression there. No pain. No fear. The face of a corpse. "Get Sam the hell off him!" Pachoulo screamed.

Sam's Man struggled to get his dog off the attack and back on the leash.

Nadeau, thinking it was over, hurried over and knelt alongside the brutalized Benny Checks.

"Hey, we'll get you to a doctor. It's going to be all right. We'll get some antiseptic on those bites. It's all over, Benny. It's all over, isn't it,

Puffy?" he said, turning around where he crouched to look at Pachoulo, who hopped off the drum like the neighborhood fat boy. He walked over to Checks and unzipped himself, looking back at Ana. He took out his cock and pissed all over his victim's naked body.

"I got to take a leak, too," Machado said.

The smell of beer was sharp.

"Unwrap him from the radiator," Pachoulo said, as he put himself back in his pants.

"You want to walk over here, lady?" Pachoulo said.

Ana stood unmoving.

"You're very stubborn. You don't want to sit down. You don't want to come over here, help your husband get on his feet. Okay. Grab an arm, Manny."

He stooped down and grabbed an arm himself. Between them they half lifted Checks off the filthy concrete and carried him, feet dragging, over to where Ana stood. Dropped him there like a bag of rags.

"So all right, Mrs. Chempenovsky, I give you back your husband."

Everybody watched her, wondering if she would finally show something. She just stared at Pachoulo. He was the first to break it off and walk away, telling Sam's Man and Machado they were getting the hell out of there, they had things to do.

Nadeau was left alone with her and Checks. He couldn't believe she'd let it all happen without protest. That she hadn't at least tried to save her husband. That she'd just stood there throughout the whole thing, staring only at Pachoulo, as though the beating and savagery had nothing to do with her. He was about to say something, to make some protest or ask some question, but she finally looked at him, right in his face.

There was the strangest little smile on her face. Then she went straight down on her knees and picked up her husband's head and cradled it in her lap.

"Leave us alone," she said.

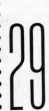

29

That evening when Helena and Nadeau came face to face in the living room overlooking the city, it was a toss-up who looked the worst, Helena, from the loss of blood and the scare the gushing nosebleed had given her, or Nadeau, with his knees still trembling from the terror of seeing a man beaten and humiliated the way Benny Checks had been and the shame of standing by and watching it without making a protest.

His distress registered on her before hers registered on him. She was glad of that, because it gave her a chance to be tender and sympathetic over whatever it was that was stressing him out. So if and when she had to speak up about what was scaring the hell out of her she would get some sympathy in return instead of one of his rotten rages.

But it didn't work out that way. He wouldn't answer her questions about what made him look the way he did, just saying that it had been a lousy day and he didn't want to talk about it, but, as long as they were on the subject of lousy, how come she was in her nightgown at five-thirty looking like she'd been dragged through a knothole.

She found herself in the pickle she'd been in a thousand times when she'd been a kid, wanting to tell about some misfortune that had befallen her so she might get a little comfort, and not wanting to say anything about it because that way she wouldn't have to give any of herself away and listen to a scolding.

Finally she told him about the nosebleed in the beauty parlor. In fact, when she warmed up to telling it, she made it sound twice as dramatic and dangerous as it had been.

"You had a nosebleed as bad as that?" he said.

"It was all over me. My slacks are in the tub soaking right now."

"You see a doctor?"

"I went over to see Jerry."

"What did he say?"

"Well, he said I had a nosebleed."

"What did he charge you, sixty-five bucks, to tell you that? He tell you what caused the nosebleed?"

He stood there pretending to be interested and concerned, leaning forward a little on the balls of his feet like a middleweight about to strike out with a right. He knew what had caused the nosebleed. Pachoulo had told him his wife had an expensive nose. Helena knew that he was just fucking with her head but there was nothing she could do but go along.

"Well, no, he had a look at it—"

"He had a look up your nose?"

"That's right."

"He didn't ask you to take your clothes off and have a look up your twat?"

"Why would he have to do that if I had a nosebleed?"

"I didn't say he'd *have* to do that. I just thought Jerry wouldn't want to miss the opportunity."

"If you're going to talk dirty for no reason . . ."

"You want a reason for me to talk dirty? I'll give you a reason for me to talk dirty. You've been snorting coke. You been snuffling that crap up your beak again after you promised—after you *swore* on your mother's grave—"

"I didn't."

"You didn't fucking what?"

"Swear on my mother's grave."

"You swore you were finished with that shit."

"I was feeling bad," she said in a small little-girl's voice. "I just had a taste."

"Don't give me with that fucking *taste*. You sniffed a headful of it."

"You do a line."

"Every now and fucking then. I've got it under control. It doesn't control me. I haven't got a nose that wants to smell it twenty-four hours a day."

"Jesus, don't exaggerate."

He took two steps toward her and she jerked back against the pillows of the couch, tightening her folded arms against her chest, afraid he'd hit her.

"I'm not exaggerating you've got a problem, a very large problem. What are we going to do about it?"

"I'm not going to snort coke anymore?" she said, using her smallest voice.

"That's a promise, is it?"

"That's a promise."

"But your promises aren't worth a plugged nickel, are they? Got any more ideas?"

"No."

"Well, I got some ideas. I'm cutting off your allowance. I'm locking up whatever jewelry you've got in the house. I'm putting your furs in storage. I'm going to keep you broke."

She turned her head away so that he couldn't see the little smile that jumped onto her mouth. He was such a smartass, thought he knew it all, knew how to put her in a cage, keep her barefoot and ragged without a penny in her jeans.

He came two steps closer. Now his knees were touching the couch. He leaned forward, putting his hands on the back of it, leaning down in close to her face and grinning like a shark.

"And don't bother going to that fat guinea shylock. I cut off your water there. I told that greaser sonofabitch he'd better close his fucking bank to you because I'm not going to pick up your obligations when you default. Now get your goddam clothes off and get ready for me."

"What are you talking about?"

"I'm talking about I had a really lousy day and I want a little comfort, a little exercise, a little something to take my mind off."

"Go play a game of racquetball," Helena said, with a show of spirit. "You closed my bank? Well, I just closed yours."

But she didn't really mean it.

While she lay back on the bed, Allan working like a country plowman above her, she thought about how she should take this opportunity to kick the habit, not because Allan wanted her to or was making it hard for her to keep it up, but because it surely would be the best thing for her health, especially after the nosebleed gave her such a scare.

She'd read about cocaine eating out the septum of a person's nose, causing more damage than she'd care to suffer, and she'd heard about other effects as well which she didn't even want to think about, so there were plenty of good reasons to stop using. She'd think about cutting it out, or at least cutting down considerably, maybe taking just a maintenance hit every now and then to keep herself steady so that she wouldn't go looking for something else to fill out the long days. He could lock up her jewelry and furs so she couldn't hock them. He could cut off her cash flow. But he'd have one hell of a time monitoring her credit cards or counting the sweaters and nightgowns in her drawers. Hell, she could supply herself for six months just by taking her extra cashmeres down to the Nice Twice shop.

He thought he was so smart, but he wasn't so smart.

Erin's Boy had come in second, beat out by Whacko in the stretch drive by a neck. There'd even been a protest posted for five minutes, the leader might have bumped Erin's Boy coming around the far turn, but it was disallowed and the numbers came up with Ray's horse paying ten-eighty for place.

If he'd said fuck it to his reputation as a go-for-broke buckaroo Billy Ray'd've walked away with a nice win. As it was he was down the two bills.

He lost ninety bucks out of the hundred he'd saved out for Lisa's gift playing liar's poker with three other cabbies. And that made him feel so low he started dickering with one of the hookers on the stroll to see if she'd do him in the parking lot for the ten.

"Fachrissake, Pidge, you got to show a little mercy," he said. "All I got's a sawbuck. What'll it take? Ten minutes?"

"Don't be such a bragger. I could make you pop in two."

"So okay, let's make a bet on that. You make me pop in two I pay you twenty. I last five minutes—"

"What's this all about? You think my mother had a foolish child? My price for a head job is twenty in the first place. So what am I gettin' if I make you pop in two and you pay me my regular price?"

"Okay, I'll pay you forty."

"If you got forty why don't you just pay me the twenty and forget about all this bettin'? It'll only take your mind off your pleasure and you'll waste your money thinkin' about the wrong thing."

"I ain't *got* the twenty. I just said. Didn't I just say?"

"Well, if you ain't got the twenty where you going to get the forty?"

"I'll owe you."

"Hell, I ain't no credit office. I'm strictly cash for Larry."

"You mean cash and carry."

"No I mean cash for Larry, my fuckin' pimp, who'll beat the shit out of me I go givin' out blow jobs half price."

"Okay, so that won't work. How about you do me for the ten, forget all the bullshit about popping off in two, who needs that anyway, and you don't tell Larry."

"Larry always knooooows."

"Okay. You tell him it's public relations."

"Everything I be doin' is public relations."

"Any rides ask me where they can get a little of this a little of that I give them to you for a week."

"Shit, I don't know."

"How about if I promise not to enjoy it?"

She laughed. "Two weeks?"

"What the hell."

Pidge worked on him and worked on him in the back of the cab where he'd parked it under a tree in a restaurant parking lot that wasn't getting much early-evening action. She did it every way she knew how and he resisted.

"You know how to do it New Orleans style?"

She paused to ask what the hell was New Orleans style.

"You mean you don't know?"

"I never heard of it, there's no such thing. Besides, I was born in Kansas City."

"So maybe that's the trouble."

She went back to work for another five minutes, then straightened up.

"You smear your cock with coke?"

"You think I got coke to waste on my pecker?"

"Well, my mouth's gettin' numb."

"You going to do it, you ain't going to do it?"

"I give up."

He zipped up and got out of the cab, Pidge scrambling out behind him demanding that he pay her for her efforts because how was she to know that his thing had turned into a bratwurst.

He told her he wasn't about to pay her ten dollars for such bad service, then walked down the street to the drugstore where he bought a bottle of cologne, nine twenty-one with tax, gift-wrapped.

"Does your Billy still got the cast on his arm?" Flo asked Maggie.

They were sitting, the three of them, Maggie, Flo and Essie, plus Mr. Armitage who lived upstairs in a corner room, in what amounted to one of the last boardinghouses in Hollywood. It was back behind the Chinese Theater.

Maggie's was the only room that was almost like an apartment because there was a private bath and toilet and something like a narrow sunporch which had been converted into an efficiency kitchen. Everybody else had to go out to eat. At least that's what they were supposed to do, but nearly every tenant had a hot plate for frying a chop or boiling coffee water.

Mr. Armitage even had a little microwave oven. He said he wouldn't put the fast-food crap some of his neighbors ate into his belly.

"Of course he's got the cast on his arm. What do you think, a broken wrist heals up just like that?" Maggie said.

"I suppose it kept him off the rest of the picture?" Essie chimed in.

"Well, it would do, wouldn't it? Sometimes I wonder about you two."

"Wonder what?" Mr. Armitage said.

"Wonder why they never want to believe anything nice about Billy."

"Maybe that's because we never seen him do anything very nice for his mother," Flo said.

"For me? My son never did anything nice for me?"

"Ever since I've known you that boy's given you nothing but trouble, nothing but heartache."

"What kind of trouble? What kind of heartache?" Mr. Armitage said, as though he'd been hired just to play straight man for the ladies.

Maggie had her mouth set, ready to attack her friends with a siege of silence. Flo took a swallow from her coffee cup and stared out of the windows into the tiny backyard. Essie looked at the back of her hands and started counting liver spots.

Mr. Armitage didn't act annoyed when nobody answered his question. That's the way it usually happened among the three women who sat around every chance they got quarreling with each other, punishing each other with the same questions asked a thousand times and always greeted by the same silences, so they wouldn't wither away.

"When did you come to Hollywood, Mrs. Ray?"

"Nineteen fifty-six it was. My husband was killed in the war."

"The Korean War?"

"No, no. The big war. He went down with his ship in the North Atlantic somewhere. I never knew exactly where. He never even got to see his little boy."

Flo let go a sigh.

Maggie looked at her sharply, waiting to see if she was going to make some comment meant to hurt her, but Flo was merely settling down to hear the story she'd heard a hundred times, like a kid settling into the pillows for another retelling of a favorite fairy tale.

"So how come you took such a chance, traveling all the way across the country with a small child?" Mr. Armitage prompted.

When his daughter and son asked him why he didn't move out of the boardinghouse, an anachronism that hung on for God only knew what reason in the face of the facts, a neighborhood no longer small-townish and safe as it once had been, he said he liked the people who lived in it. Not those foolish yappity old women, his daughter would say, Well, I'm a foolish non-yappity old man, he'd say, and when I close my eyes and listen to them quarrel they sound like young women and when they tell stories of the days gone by when they were young, I can dream that I'm young again.

"You know what a good-looking boy my son is?" Maggie said.

Mr. Armitage nodded and closed his eyes.

"If you think he's a good-looking boy—"

"Boy? The lazy lunk's forty-two, going to be forty-three," Flo said, her lips moving but no sound coming out.

"—you should have seen what a beautiful child. It took your breath away. He had lashes longer than Irene Dunne's and cheeks like roses. Everybody back in Newark—"

"The whole city?" Flo mouthed.

"—said he was the most beautiful baby they'd ever seen. Prettier than Shirley Temple at the same age."

"But could he dance?" Flo said silently to the windows.

"When he was ten I decided it was time to give Billy his chance. It was the most frightening thing I ever done—"

"But you done it," Flo mimed.

"—but I done it. I came out here and got myself a job selling tickets nights right down the street at Grauman's Chinese."

"Mann's," Essie said.

"It'll always be Grauman's to me," Maggie said indignantly.

Mr. Armitage settled himself more comfortably on the bridge chair. Now came the part about how she took the public transportation out to the studios in Culver City and the Valley, day after day, attending casting calls. And when she wasn't doing that, how she went to one agent's office after another looking for the right one, the one who'd make her beautiful Billy a star. And how she spent every penny she could spare on dancing lessons and singing lessons and recitation lessons. Now came the part that made him believe he was young again for a little while.

The door opened up and Billy Ray came breezing in like a tornado, waving his cast around his head like a club, pinching Flo's cheek, making Essie blush with a hug, greeting Mr. Armitage as though the old man was his best friend, kissing his mother on the cheek, making a big show of it, handing her the bottle of cologne all wrapped up in silver paper and pink ribbon.

"What's this, Billy?" Maggie laughed, beside herself with pride and pleasure, unwrapping the gift very carefully, folding the paper and wrapping the ribbon into a little curl which she could use again.

"It's a present," he said.

"What is it, somebody's birthday? It's not my birthday."

"Does it have to be your birthday I want to buy a present for my best girl?"

"Your wife should be your best girl," Maggie said, giddy with generosity and pretense.

He put his face into her neck and she screamed her delight as Flo and Essie smiled as hard as they could and envied her.

"Your mother was telling us about when you came out to Hollywood," Mr. Armitage said.

"Those were yesterdays," Ray said, remembering a line from a television show he'd seen once upon a time. He made it sound like those yesterdays had been filled with great events, stardom, fame and fortune, lost but soon to be restored again. "Hey, Ma, can I have a minute of your time and a piece of your ear."

"Oh, the things you say, Billy," she said, struggling out of the wicker chair which was the only piece of furniture in the place worth anything.

Flo tossed a look to Essie, knowing what was coming next in his little game. Mr. Armitage carefully looked away so he wouldn't be part of their disloyalty.

Billy moved Maggie as far back in the room as he could move her, over by the bathroom door, and turned his back to her guests.

"Ma, I'm in this little bind."

"For God's sake, Billy," Maggie said, all the joy draining out of her. "I just lent you a hundred dollars a few days ago."

"The way it happened was this," he said. "The people over to the emergency hospital wouldn't wait for the workmen's comp. Don't ask me why."

"You didn't tell me this when you borrowed the money."

"What was I going to do, get you all upset? You know how you get when somebody does something wrong to me. What was I going to do, tell you and then what'd you do, call up the doctor and raise hell? What could you have done?"

"Nothing."

"Right, nothing. So that's why I was a little short. I figured I'd make it up driving extra shifts but it's so goddam hard with this cast. I drive a regular shift and already it's throbbing and aching like a sore tooth."

"How much you need?"

"Fifty?"

"Oh, my God."

"Okay, whatever you could spare."

She went for her purse and came back again behind the shield of his body so her friends wouldn't see her giving him money again, though she'd tell them herself before the week was out, when she was feeling used, lonely and put-upon one afternoon. But right now, after the gift, after the bottle of cologne, she didn't want them to be witnesses to her humiliation.

"Where did you get that cologne?" she asked.

"I bought it," he said, moving back a step as though she'd slapped him across the mouth. "You don't think—"

"I'm sorry, I'm sorry."

"Jesus, I wanted to buy you a present. I didn't realize it was my last ten. But even if I did I'd've bought you the perfume anyhow because that's the way I was feeling and I was going to work another shift until my hand began to ache like a sore tooth."

She found a twenty, a five and six ones, all she had in the world. She stuffed them into his hand, not even holding back a dollar bill so that when he counted it he'd know she'd given him every last dollar she'd had and maybe he'd feel ashamed of himself.

"There can't be any more. Not for a while," she said.

He put his arms around her.

"Aw, Ma, don't you worry, I'll get it back to you by the end of the month. You can just bet I won't forget."

She watched him go out the door, bending around the edge of it so that his grinning face was the last thing she'd see before it closed.

Then she turned around and went back to her friends.

"Is Billy's hair getting a little thin on top?" Flo asked, pushing her own stringy hair back in place.

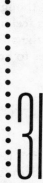31

With fifth squad gathered from all over the sprawling city and no one place to gather at end-of-shift except Rampart, which was a hell of a long way from the Valley, Sergeant Becker had made a command decision the third day into the operation and declared a coffee shop on the corner of Ventura Boulevard and Coldwater Canyon their unofficial headquarters.

The first time they'd walked in two by two, local uniforms, suspicious that the Valley arm of organized crime had moved in on their comparatively quiet beat, called for some motorcycle backup and went over to have a conversation. Mandingo and Poke Kopcha had been ready to shine the blues on and even risk a little fisticuffs, but Becker quickly flashed some brass, when it looked like the cops in leather were ready to try busting heads, and the threat of civil war subsided.

Now, at the end of day four, they crowded into the big double booth meant to accommodate large families, ordering up burgers, fries, spaghetti dinners, shakes, beers and coffee. None of them happy. Nearly all of them forlorn.

"Who ain't here?" Becker asked, not even bothering to look around and count heads.

"Monk and Kelly ain't here," Mandingo rumbled.

"Maybe they out on a date," Missy said. "Maybe they gettin' to know each other."

She was trying to make a little joke but nobody picked up on it.

"I hate it out here," Kopcha complained. "Over to Harbor you always got the breeze coming in off the ocean."

Everybody took a minute to think about their regular territories, the streets and alleys where they felt comfortable.

"They don't even like each other," Becker said, a beat behind, still thinking about how his pairings were going to work out, particularly with an asshole like Monk deciding for himself where he'd work his tours.

Then he saw Kelly and Monk walking past the windows from the parking lot, the freckle-faced Irishman waving his arms around in the air, talking a mile a minute, Monk just lumbering along with his hands in his pockets acting like he had a bad case of constipation.

When they came into the coffee shop and walked down the aisle toward the back, they could all hear that Kelly was talking about some basketball game.

"Monk hates basketball," Heath remarked.

At the table, Kelly sat down, shoving up against Missy, who gave his ass a little shove right back, nothing mean, just friendly. He caught it, shut up about basketball and turned to her with a big grin.

"Hey, my little tamale, how about we save our appetites and split a plate someplace away from the crowd?"

"I ain' your little tamale and you think you gonna do what I think you think you gonna do, I might as well warn you. I turn you into Irish stew."

Kelly moaned, tossed his head around and said, "I wanna die. I wanna die."

"So sit down," Heath said to Monk, who still stood there, a concerned expression on his face.

"I think I got to use the john."

"For chrissake," Heath said, starting to stand up.

"No. I don't mean a conference. I mean I think I got to use the john. I ain't had a dump in two days. The food you get out here in the Valley is awful stuff."

He shuffled off toward the rest rooms.

"What we got here is a lot of upliftin' conversation," Missy said.

"Monk's really got a very sensitive digestion. Everything upsets him," Heath said.

The food came, and Monk finally came back looking lighter, not exactly smiling but not frowning anymore. He sat down and ordered the spaghetti dinner.

"I hate this. I hate everybody sitting around in a goddam restaurant every night like one big happy family."

"We could report into Rampart after shift the way we're supposed to do," Becker said, immediately offended.

"I was just saying," Monk murmured.

"I'm just trying to make it easier on everybody," Becker went on. "So listen."

Everybody stopped in the middle of a chew or with a forkful of pasta dangling halfway to their mouth.

"Directives are starting to come down from Fitzsimmons's office about targets and objectives."

"Small-time bookies, hookers and drug dealers," Kopcha said.

Becker shook his head.

"No?" Kopcha said, surprised. "With these commissions it's always bookies, hookers and pushers."

"Loan-sharking, gambling and labor racketeering. One, two, three," Becker said.

"Somebody's getting serious," Kelly said.

It's no mystery. The way it works in any society, particularly in any city where the rackets and racketeers loot the union treasuries, buy the cops and courts, feed on legitimate businesses, intimidate and terrify the weak, is that there's a handshake deal between corrupt politicians, greedy businessmen and brutal mobsters. Once upon a time they took turns on top according to the times and the condition of the city. Now there's no way to tell them apart. Like that lady said, there's no white hats and no black hats. They all do business.

"You ain' tryin' to tell us they give us marchin' orders to take down the crooked politicians, crooked union leaders, crooked businessmen and like that," Missy said.

When there's a drive to clean up a town, usually it's the little fish that get netted. Back-pocket bookies get their pockets picked, hookers and Cadillac pimps get herded off the streets, the needle parks and shooting galleries get swept.

When the reform intentions are real, the law goes after other fish. They go after the racket bankers, the men who have the kind of cash it takes to finance any crime from a hijacking to a multimillion-dollar company takeover. They go after the sources of revenue that fatten the wallets of the bankers.

"I don't know about how deep and how high, but we're supposed to go out there and target high-powered gambling schemes and loan-shark operations."

"Somebody's gettin' smart," Mandingo said.

"That's right. They want to turn off the water," Becker agreed.

"So whatta we do?" Missy asked.

"We do what we do," Heath said, "except we're friendly to hookers, pimps, cabbies, fences, burglars, muggers..."

Kelly picked it up. "...bartenders, B-girls, forgers..."

Mandingo said, "...pornographers, hijackers..."

Kopcha chimed in with "...crooked judges, forgers, hookers—"

"Panama already said hookers," Missy said.

"They deserve another mention," Kopcha said.

"We turn the whole city into a bunch of finks," Missy said, as though just getting the news.

"Maybe somebody really means it this time," Becker said again, hopefully yet doubtfully. Somebody had pretended to mean it so many times before.

Becker was finished talking and everybody, except for Monk, was finished eating, so they started to slide out of the booth and stand up and say goodnight.

"Hey, Jesus, Panama," Monk said, looking up from his plate, "ain't somebody going to sit with me while I finish my dinner?"

Heath rubbed his eyes with the heels of both hands.

"You want to sit while he finishes his dinner?" he asked Missy.

"I got to go home and wash my hair. I'm worn down to my socks."

"While you're down there..." Monk said.

"Ah, when you grow up to a big boy you come aroun' an' ask me again."

"I'm not feeling it," Heath said. "I got to go, too."

"So, all right," Monk said, hurt and angry.

Heath started to say something, but thought better of it and just waved his hand before following Missy over to the register, where she was paying her check.

Outside on the street, they walked around to the parking lot where everybody kept their own cars so they could go straight home to wherever they lived right from the Valley.

"You ought to do it, Panama," Missy said.

"Do what? Go back there and listen to Monk moan about his constipation and the lousy food?"

"Go sleep with that woman who came to see you in the coffee shop over in Hollywood."

"What makes you think she wants to do that?"

"I got eyes, ain' I? I'm a woman, ain' I?"

"She's married."

"I unnerstan' that. But she's the love of your life, am I right?"

"We were pretty close."

"I like it about you men. You have a woman once, you tell all the boys how you do it to her upside down, over the kitchen table, in the bathtub, what a big macho man you are, on the freeway going seventy miles an hour. You have a woman many times and she picks somebody else you don' say nothin' except oh, yes, she use to be a fren' of mine. We shook hands. Maybe I pat her on her sweet patootie. You give me a laugh."

"What are you mad about?"

"I ain' mad. I'm jus' thinkin' you got your min' on this woman. You want to see if you still got that ol' black magic in bed with her. So why don' you go do it an' fin' out one way or the other."

"I haven't got a clue what you're talkin' about."

They were at her car. She unlocked the door on the driver's side, opened the window and slipped in behind the wheel.

"Jesus Christ, Missy, you're very hard to work with. I'm trying to keep personal things out of the work and here you are dragging it in by the heels."

"Maybe you want personal things out of it don't say I do," she said, starting the engine. "You goin' home an' get some rest?"

"I guess I'll go back inside and sit with Monk while he finishes his dinner."

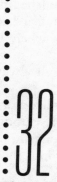

32

Phil Doohan was the middle brother out of five, born and raised in Bayonne, a town in the New Jersey iron belt just south of Jersey City, across the bay from New York.

His father, Mike, had been a fireman. He retired out to California when the oldest brother, Joseph, after getting a taste of the sunshine state during the Vietnamese war, decided to travel west and make his fortune, dragging the rest of the family, except for Paul, the next-oldest, who'd been killed in Vietnam, along with him.

Their sister, Mary, the only girl, married a Jewish boy, an accountant, and stayed back East. Most of the family never forgave her for that. Phil was the only one who wrote to her since his mother, Dot, passed away from a cancer in 1981.

Joseph, the eldest, the pathfinder, had red hair already going orange at forty-two, a skin that looked like it had been waxed and polished and white teeth as big as those of a horse. Whenever he laughed, which was often, a person flashed an image of a bear trap, ready to chomp down and grab you by the throat.

Everybody said that Joseph was the funny one. Whenever he invited you out to dinner and you laughed at one of his jokes he'd say, "You don't have to laugh. I'll pay for the dinner anyway." When you kept on laughing he'd say, "Pie for you."

Joseph thought he was funny, himself. He liked to tell the story about when they were kids and some guineas beat up on Paul and how they all went looking for the perpetrators and found them in a pool hall and how they dragged their asses out of there, sending the message that if you messed with one Doohan you messed with them all, and how this one asshole told Joseph that he'd just punched his brother in the mouth and how Joseph had said, "Don't feel bad, here's one for you," and cold-cocked the sonofabitch right where he was standing.

"Them fucking guineas make great straight men," Joseph always liked to say when he ended the story.

"Watch your mouth," Big Mike would say, as he laughed and dry-washed his red face with a big hand all chopped and charred from a thousand fires. They all laughed then and said the same things in the same way every time he told the story, although they'd heard it a thousand times.

It was a sort of family ritual, a reconfirmation of their tribal identity, and the acknowledgment that Joseph was their chief.

It was Joseph who picked North Hollywood for the business he'd decided on, figuring everybody liked a funny story and who could tell funny stories better than he could, and what better thing was there to do than tell funny stories all day and sell automobiles?

It was Joseph who found and rented, and later persuaded the rest to buy, the two houses, side by side, across the street from North Hollywood Park.

Then the youngest, Mike, moved up to San Francisco and opened up a coin shop, saying how he couldn't stand the sun shining all the goddam time.

Then Pat married Marsha and moved out to Thousand Oaks over the objections of his father and brother, who believed families should live in each other's pockets.

Then Phil got married to Angie and moved way the hell out into a waterfront condo in Oxnard.

So that left Joseph living all alone in one house and the old man living alone in the other apparently because each one was too stubborn to make the move. But, actually, Joseph liked it that way. He'd just as soon his father didn't know the type and number of the women that came into his house through the side door. Unmarried didn't have to mean celibate, though he was getting more and more choosy who he conned and joked into his bed what with the AIDS business scaring everybody back into their underwear.

It was Joseph who had the great ambition, who'd moved them from a used-car lot on Magnolia to the Porsche dealership that occupied a full block along Ventura Boulevard.

And it was Joseph who always came up with some new trick of the trade, some new scheme for expansion. He held what he liked to call "skull sessions" around the table in Big Mike's kitchen.

"What we got here," Joseph said, "is an opportunity to own, not lease, a garage, showroom and facility in the newest auto village in this part of the state."

"Way the hell up beyond Thousand Oaks. Somis is way the hell off the beaten track over by route one-eighteen," Phil objected. "We're looking at an hour commute."

"What's the matter, your air conditioning in the Porsche break down? I'm talking about a chance here to own a very big piece of a multimillion-dollar operation."

"At least," Big Mike said, as though he knew what the hell he was talking about.

"Potential several million dollars down the line," Joseph said.

"You're talking about going into a deal with a bunch of guineas who we all know, ever since back in Bayonne, are not to be trusted," Pat said. "Who brings this deal to you?"

"A lawyer by the name of Allan Nadeau."

"There you go."

"There I go, what?"

"Doing business with a guinea."

"Nadeau ain't Italian. That's French Canadian. Something like that."

"Fucking Canucks. Worse than guineas."

"What about our customers? We built up a nice list of customers," Phil said, wanting to get off the ethnic crap since his wife, Angie, was half Italian and he got enough bullshit about that as it was.

"We got customers for cars, remember. What we sell them is cars. They drive the cars from wherever the hell they live to wherever the hell we are because they want the type of cars we got to sell and they like the type of service we got to give them. The customers we got'll follow us no matter where we go. And we tap into all the money up there around Oxnard, Ventura and maybe even Santa Barbara. It's all moving up that way."

"How much are we talking here?" Big Mike said.

"Two hundred thousand for openers."

"For openers!" Phil practically screeched, his voice climbing up the scale like somebody had just clutched him by the balls.

"For Christ's sake!" Pat yelled, matching Phil scream for scream. "You out of your fucking mind? What does this mean, this openers? What the hell does it mean two hundred thousand for openers?"

"We see how the deal is structured. Maybe it takes another two hundred, two hundred and a half, before construction is completed. That's our end."

"And what do we get for half a million?"

"We get a ten-year lease fixed at one dollar a square foot, plus we get twenty percent of the total rental income from the entire project, which will occupy, when it's all done, the equivalent of four city blocks."

"When it's all done?"

"What the hell, you think you get twenty percent of a project like this for four hundred and a half? That's one-fifth. You figure the whole construction, four city blocks—"

"The equivalent," Big Mike said.

"—costs a lousy two million? More like two mil a section."

"How many sections?"

"Four blocks, four sections, for Christ's sake. The profits from the first section helps finance the second. The second helps finance the third. Do I have to spell out the whole goddam thing to you?"

"Well, yes, I think you should spell out the whole thing to us if you want us to get into a deal like this with a bunch of guineas and a Canuck shyster," Phil said.

"Well, I can't spell it out to you dollar for dollar. What this is is a skull session, we should think about going into this wonderful opportunity that somebody drops into my lap."

"This Canuck? This Nadeau gamoosh?"

Joseph leaned back from the table. His eyes flickered sideways toward Big Mike who was sitting next to him, sending the word that the answer to that wasn't for their father's ears.

"Hey, Pop, you got something to wet the old whistle?"

"I got some beer. I got a little gin and maybe some whiskey."

"Scotch?"

"Well, no, not scotch. You know I hate that stuff. Got a little bourbon whiskey."

"Jesus, I got my mouth ready for a scotch and branch water."

"Well, you'll have to distill your own out of your sock, because I ain't got any."

"I got some down in my car. In the glove compartment."

"You run around with a pint in the glove compartment?"

"In the demonstrator. For medicinal purposes. In case some customer gets a little faint. Gets a little sunstroke on a hot day, you know what I mean?" He stretched his legs out and searched for his keys in his pocket. "I'll just run down," he said, but because he wasn't standing up, Big Mike was on his feet first.

"I'll go out and get it."

"You don't have to. I can get it."

"I don't mind. You sit here, talk about the deal. You can tell me what you decide when I get back."

The brothers waited for the father to go, happy to have an errand and get away from the talk of such big money, just like he was happy to come down to the lot and wash the cars although Joseph always told him, "We got spicks and niggers to do that."

"So what's the secret?" Phil said. "Who brought the deal to you?"

"This Nadeau's wife."

"How come she's so good to you?"

Joseph grinned and ran his hand over his face as though keeping his pleasure from spilling over.

"Because I'm good to her."

"Jesus Christ," Pat said. "What does she look like?"

"You wouldn't fuckin' believe. Marilyn Monroe was a plain Jane compared."

"Why the fuck she giving it away to you?" Phil, asked, jealous right down to his toes, right into his bones.

"She ain't *giving* it away. She's got a habit and she doesn't want her husband to know she hasn't given it up."

"Back up, back up," Phil said. "What kind of habit?"

"Do I have to write it out in neon?"

"You mean she blows a little dope?"

"No, she snorts a *lot* of coke."

"You mean to tell me you want to put us in hock on a deal which some kokomo feeds you while she's laying on her back?"

"Well, she wasn't exactly on her back. More like on her knees."

"Jesus Christ," Pat moaned again.

"So while this sniffer's giving you head she just stops in the middle and tells you about a commercial real estate venture?"

"It wasn't like that. It wasn't exactly the *minute* she's doing it that the subject came up. It's sort of after, when I give her a hundred bucks, which upsets her very much."

"This whore gets upset because you paid her?"

"She isn't a whore. She's a legitimate woman who has this little problem."

"Where did she pick you up?"

"It wasn't exactly a pickup."

"Where'd you meet her?"

"She's walking around the lot, looking like a million, looking the Porsches over."

"She's looking to buy a Porsche and she don't have a hundred bucks to buy a snort?"

"I don't know why she's looking around. Maybe she has nothing to do with herself. Maybe she's restless because she needs a little something, so she's going here and there. Doing a little shopping. Keeping her mind off. She has some packages in the back of her car."

"What kind of car?"

"Jaguar."

"She's driving a Jaguar but she can't raise a hundred bucks?"

"I told you, her husband cut off her water. She finally admits to me that's why she's out shopping, why she had the packages from Magnin's and Bullock's in the back of her car."

"I missed that boat," Phil said.

"Me, too," Pat chimed in.

"She needs some money for a couple lines and she's got no cash. So she figures she'll buy some sweaters and blouses and like that on her credit cards, maybe her husband hasn't called up and canceled them yet. So that's what she does."

"She buys some clothes?"

"She buys some clothes and she figures she'll peddle them to some of her girlfriends."

"So she can buy an ounce?"

"That's right."

"So why don't she do that?"

"Because she figures it'll look very strange if she tries to sell new clothes to any of her girlfriends. Besides, whenever she wants to get rid of any sweaters, blouses, things like that, she always just gives them to her friends. Now all of a sudden it'd look very strange she wants to get paid for them. Even though she'd make them a very big bargain on new clothes."

"So now we're getting down to it. She's not only a hooker with a fancy gift of gab, but she's a booster wants to sell you stolen goods."

"You buy anything?" Pat asked. "I mean besides the blow job."

"For Christ's sake. She asks me do I want to buy something nice for my wife. Cheap. I says I haven't got a wife. She says that must be very hard for a big, good-looking guy like me."

Pat was grinning from ear to ear. Phil was looking cock-eyed, looking wise.

"I says it gets hard at times."

"And she asks is it hard at the moment," Phil said, "and you say you're feeling a little stiffness and she says, well, maybe she can take care of that. Make a little money and keep her brand-new sweaters and blouses."

"Where'd you do it?" Pat asked.

"In the closing office."

"Schmuck," Phil scolded Pat. "The closing office is the only one without half windows. Where else could he do it?" He went back to questioning Joseph. "So after she does you, she wipes her mouth and just happens to mention this commercial enterprise?"

"She was nervous and upset because of what she just done. She's making conversation while I'm counting out a hundred. She sees I'm in the automobile business so she just naturally asks me if I heard anything about this big automotive park they're going to put in over to Somis."

"What could be more natural?" Phil said. "Our smart big brother got hustled good."

"I wouldn't have minded," Pat said, still grinning at the thought of that million-dollar babe down on her knees doing it.

"I knew my asshole brothers were going to come up with something like this when I tell them what I glommed on to."

"Surprise, surprise," Phil said, laughing and waving Joseph away as he reared back in his chair. "Where the hell's Pop with that bottle of scotch?"

"So I ask her where a person like herself would hear about a deal like she mentions and she tells me her husband puts such deals together," Joseph went on, ignoring the hilarity, "and is presently doing a package with the Nicoletti brothers."

They stopped laughing.

"I heard of the Nicoletti brothers," Phil said. "They've done some big shopping malls."

"That's right. So maybe that would be enough for you, but it's not enough for me. I find out from Helena—"

"That's her name?" Pat asked.

"That's right. I find out where her husband eats his lunch."

"She just tells you that so you can maybe go over there and spill the beans to him over his steak and fries about how his wife went down on you?"

"Don't be an asshole all your life. She doesn't just tell me what I want to know. She tells me after I offer her another hundred for the name of the restaurant and I say that I want to meet her husband by accident and maybe get a little more of the skinny on this construction deal."

"What kind of accident did you arrange?" Pat asked.

"He drives a Lamborghini. I sell cars. I tell him the kid in the parking lot describes the owner of the Lamborghini to me. I strike up a conversation and tell him how much I admire his vehicle. We get to talking cars. He asks me to sit down and have a cup of coffee, a dessert, with him. That's just the way it happens."

"So, then, he just ups and offers a perfect stranger a chance to get in on a deal like this?"

"Why the hell not? He can check me out and see we got some expertise. Just like I check him out and see that he's got plenty doing what he's doing, putting these deals together. He makes the offer to somebody he figures has got an interest. What's so funny about that? For Christ's sake, you think investors with two hundred thousand dollars up-front money grow on trees?"

"Who's got two hundred thousand dollars up-front money?" Phil said. "Not us."

"Well, I mentioned that and Al said maybe he could help us with that."

"What's this? Now you're calling this fucking Canuck Al?"

"What the fuck you want me to call him, Shirley?"

"I mean you're calling this shyster Al, like he's an old friend."

"Like he's your asshole buddy," Pat chimed in.

Phil made a face like he smelled something very bad.

"You know what I think?" he said.

When Joseph didn't reply, Pat played straight man. "What do you think, Phil?" he said.

"I think our big brother Joseph here has been pussy-whipped by this Helen dame and—"

"Helena," Joseph said.

"Whatever the fuck. I think she'd been sucking your brains out your dick."

"Listen to me, you silly sonofabitch," Joseph shouted, getting up on his feet.

Mike came through the door with a large paper bag in his arms and Joseph shut up.

"Don't fight, boys," Mike said as though they were just kids again squabbling over who got the Sunday funnies first.

Joseph immediately subsided and sat down.

"What the hell," Mike said, setting the bag down on the table, "since we're all sitting around together, I thought I'd just go down to the market, get some bourbon for me, scotch for Joseph and a couple of six-packs to clear our throats. Also a couple bags of pretzels and potato chips."

33

The first couple of days after Benny Checks disappeared from the scene a couple of nervous horse players with winning slips trotted over to his house and knocked on the door, where they were met by Mrs. Checks, who paid off without a murmur. Hicky Demarra and Butcher-boy Messino bragged about how they kited their betting slips, raising the wagers by a factor of ten, and getting paid off for the larger bet because what did Checks's pie-faced wife know about what their bets had really been?

When days went by and still no Benny Checks, speculation ran, as they say, rife. Finally word leaked out on the streets something very bad had happened to Benny Checks. The word hadn't yet hardened into fact. Some said Manny Machado had cut his throat and left him for dead in an abandoned warehouse down to Wilmington. Some said the beast that dragged Sam's Man around had chewed off his hand. Some said Pachoulo had cut his balls off with a rusty knife.

Blinky Dado, who had a curiosity greater than most, even camped out in his Cadillac across the street from the house where Checks lived, hoping to see some sign that the bookie was alive or at least that there was a crepe hung on the door to say that he was dead.

"For crying out loud, what century you living in?" Billy Ray asked, when Dado told him that. "Who hangs crepe on the door anymore?"

"In Chicago they hang crepe on the door in the old neighborhoods."

"Haven't you noticed? We're in Hollywood, California."

"*You're* in Hollywood, California. I'm in Downey."

"They hang crepe on the doors over in Downey?"

"Not that I've noticed lately."

"So there you go."

"I was just using a figure of speech," Dado said.

"So, anyway, you didn't see no sign of Benny Checks."

"Not a nose hair. But he's in there."

"How do you know that?"

"I see how big the grocery bags his old lady brings home from the supermarket is. She's feeding two people."

"So that's all you know?"

Dado shrugged.

Ray got into his taxi and drove over to see what he could find out about Benny Checks the easiest, fastest way. He just parked in front of the house, walked up to the front door and rang the bell. When Mrs. Checks came to the door he said, "I heard that Benny wasn't feeling too good. I came to say hello."

"Who will I tell him came to say hello?"

"Couldn't I see him? All his friends would like to know how he's doing."

"They would?"

"Yes ma'am," Ray said, liking the way he delivered the line all humble and friendly like a character out of some forties moving picture when people still believed in the milk of human kindness and bought it by the quart.

"All right," she said, as though she'd just that second decided something she'd never thought much about before. "Come in."

He followed her through the hallway, taking a peek into the living room as they walked by. It looked like a room in a store window. Not a thing out of place. Gloomy as hell though with the heavy drapes drawn.

"So the hot sun doesn't fade the carpet and the slipcovers," she said as though she had eyes in the back of her head and could read his mind.

"I wasn't commenting," Ray said.

"It doesn't matter. Who cares about a well-kept house nowadays? Everything is to make more and more money. Husband working. Wife working. Children coming home alone from school."

"You got kids? Benny never said."

"No, we haven't got any children. But if we had, they wouldn't be coming home to an empty house." She stopped in front of a closed door and looked at Ray again. Very carefully as if she wondered if he would react properly to what she was about to show him. He made an innocent face like he made for his mother when he wanted to hit her up for a twenty.

That seemed to satisfy because Ana knocked gently on the door but opened it right away as though she didn't expect a response.

Benny was sitting in a rocking chair by the window, staring out through the lace curtains. He had on an old bathrobe and was hugging himself.

"A friend has come to visit, Benny," Ana said.

Checks didn't move. It was as if he hadn't heard her.

"Benny?"

He rocked the chair a little as though that should be enough to tell her he wanted to be left alone.

"Don't you want to see who it is?"

Benny suddenly jerked his head around, face startled, eyes stretched wide. Ray took a step back. Checks looked twenty years older, his jowls all slack, his neck stretched thin like a turkey's, his hair suddenly thin and unable to cover the bald parts.

Ray felt Ana's hand on his back, gently urging him to go inside the room. He felt like a kid being pushed into dancing with his cousin at a family wedding reception. He took a couple of steps because he didn't know how to resist. He had a feeling Ana was the kind of woman who'd never raise her voice or make a fuss but would always get her way. So why fight back? Then he grabbed himself by the scruff of the neck and started to turn around to say that as long as Benny didn't want to say hello, there was no reason for him to say hello. The door was closing. The latch snicked. So he had to turn back to look at Checks, who was still staring at him but not in such terror anymore.

"Hello," Ray said.

"You come to see me?" Checks asked.

"The word on the street's that you haven't been feeling too good. Ain't you been feeling too good?"

"I've had a touch of something."

"The flu's going around. Everybody's getting it."

"You think I got the flu?" Checks asked as though Ray was an expert and could put his mind to rest with a quick diagnosis.

"Jesus, I wouldn't know, Benny. You think you got the flu?"

"No, I don't think so. You know what I got?"

Ray waited to hear Checks say what it was he had, but Checks turned away and looked at the curtains again. After a long wait, Ray said, "So what have you got, Benny?"

"I got a case of the yellows."

"What?"

"I got a case of baby shit in my shorts, you know what I mean?"

Ray thought he knew what he meant but didn't want to say he knew. "You making a joke, Benny?"

"It's no goddam joke," Checks said in the voice of a dead man. He whirled around again, grabbing hold of the rocker's arm with one hand as though he needed the support just to sit up. "Pachoulo and those two scumbags of his stole my balls."

For a second Ray's eyes flew down to Checks's crotch to see if there were actual signs that the stories about the castration with a rusty knife were true.

"Oh, for Christ's sake," Checks said, his face all screwed up in pain and rage, dragging his robe aside, tearing the fly on his pajama bottoms open and dragging out his cock and testicles. "You want to see if I mean actually? There's actually. I got my nuts in my hand. But I ain't got my balls in my head and my belly. You know what the fuck I mean now?"

Ray glanced around and spotted a footstool half concealed by the drapes. He grabbed it and dragged it over in front of Checks. When he sat down they were practically knee to knee.

"Ah, Jesus, put them away, Benny. You don't want to catch a chill in your condition."

"My condition?" Checks said, covering himself, ashamed all of a sudden for revealing himself the way he had.

"You had a run-in with a fucking animal. Three animals."

"Four. That fucking dog chewed on me like I was a bone." Tears ran down his cheeks. "You want a cup of coffee? You want some cakes? My wife makes wonderful cakes."

"Who wants to snack at a time like this, we're talking about important matters? We're talking about your well-being. We're talking about your future."

"I got no future."

"Hey, babe, look at it this way. A welterweight goes up against three heavyweights and a fucking beast. How's a man going to win against odds like that? You take it easy. You rest. You get the old spring back in the legs and then you go out there as good as ever."

Checks wiped his eyes, moved to fresh tears because here was a friend—he hadn't known was *such* a friend—giving him a pep talk.

"Ah, Jesus, you're a real friend, Billy," he said, reaching out a hand.

Ray avoided that by passing his hat from one hand to the other. There was a little fumble and it dropped on the rug. He bent to pick it up and when he straightened up Checks had his hands back on the arms of the rocking chair, the tender moment past.

"So while you're resting what do you think about your other friend?" Ray said.

"What friend is this?"

"The lady in the pink stucco house up on the hill."

"She hasn't been asking for any action lately."

"Maybe she's heard some news. Wait a second, wait a second. Maybe she heard the wrong news, you know what I mean? Maybe I should go tell her what really happened."

"Why would I want her to know Pachoulo and that fuck Machado worked me over, pissed in my face?"

"You don't. That's what I'm saying. I go over and tell her you fought off some criminal types and you're recovering from some honorable wounds, you know what I mean? I tell her you'll be back better'n ever, maybe another week, maybe two."

"You want to get a little New Orleans head? That's what I'm hearing."

"No, no. I've got a wife at home."

"So do I."

"I love my wife," Ray protested, realizing the instant he said it that he was putting his foot deeper into the shit.

"So do I."

"I wouldn't saddle another man's horse."

"You'd saddle another man's fucking greyhound if we was at the dog tracks down in Florida."

"All I want to do is help you save your business. I take any bets she wants to lay down." Ray stood up. "This is the thanks I get."

"You want to run for me while I recuperate?" Checks said, his eyes drying up fast.

"I don't know about being a runner. I thought more like a temporary partner."

"Just with this old whore what gives great New Orleans head?"

"I wouldn't expect a share of that. What do you think? But the betting. I mean if I take bets from one why shouldn't I take bets from all?"

"You and me? Partners in my book?"

"Something like that."

"Like you take twenty percent?"

"I was thinking a little more."

"Like a third?"

"How about a half? Fifty-fifty like they say in the books."

"I don't know what the fuck books you read, Billy Ray. Must be books about Africa where the vultures come flapping down out of the sky when some poor goddam animal's been wounded and looks like it's about to keel over."

As he spoke the anger that had been chilled out of him by the awful beating and humiliation he'd suffered at the hands of Pachoulo and his musclers started flaming up again. His kishkes, nothing but water since that terrible hour, started turning solid.

This schmucky gamoosh, standing there with a half-assed grin on his face, this magimper with the pretty face who couldn't even make a living so his wife wouldn't have to shampoo and curl other women's hair, this know-nothing fucking loser who couldn't tell the eating end from the shitting end of a horse wanted to be fucking *partners* with Benny Checks?

He looked at his hands and saw they were trembling with repressed rage and that, he knew, was good. His balls were growing even as he sat there deciding what more to say to the asshole before he threw him out of his house.

"I ain't keeled over yet, Billy Ray! I ain't fucking dead yet! And even if I was dead and rotting in my grave you still wouldn't be man enough to take my coat and shoes and walk away pretending to be me. I stick my own fucking self in danger just so I could help you out with that guinea shylock, he shouldn't bust your arms and legs, he shouldn't put a couple of peas in your head and leave Lisa a weeping widow without a nickel in her shoe. I took the beating that should have been yours."

Neither one of them knew it but Ana was standing right outside the door taking it all in, smiling in the tight little way she'd smiled when she'd stood there and watched her man abused, pissed on, dragged across the floor and dumped at her feet.

"I did that for you, you rotten little sonofabitch, and this is the thanks I get for it? This is how a little low-life gonnif like you are, Billy Ray, pays off a friend like me, Benny Checks, what done what he done for you?"

Ray let him rave on, let him have his fun, let him hear himself telling lies about how what he did, lending him the bone and a half to pay off Pachoulo, was an act of charity and not a chance to stick him in his own pocket. He waited until Checks had to take a breath.

"Hey, Benny," he said, "you mind I use the toilet? I got to piss so bad I'm afraid I'll do it right where I'm standing and splash all over you."

He watched, triumphant, as the healing anger blew out of Checks's mouth in one long sigh.

Outside the door, Ana stopped smiling and walked off down the hallway toward the kitchen with a tray of iced tea and little cakes in her hands.

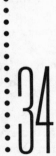

They could have come in one car, maybe the utility Ford station wagon they kept for lugging this and that around, but instead, they arrived in front of Benito's Italian Restaurant in three brand-new Porsches. One, two, three. Different colors. Red, white and blue. A one-hundred-and-twenty-thousand-dollar motorized stretch of enameled-steel bunting.

They gathered at the curb in front of the door and argued about which one of them was going to park the three vehicles now that they'd made their show. They didn't trust the kid in the red monkey jacket standing by ready to provide the service.

It was finally decided that Pat, being the youngest, should park the cars while Joseph and Phil went inside to start the handshakes.

"Does this mean that because I'm the youngest I'm always going to get the dirty end of the stick?"

"You don't want to park the cars, don't park the cars. Let the kid here park the cars. Gets a dent in one of them so what, we just take three more out of inventory. Take them right off the showroom floor."

"Do I need a speech?" Pat said, slipping behind the wheel of the lead Porsche.

"How come every time you do business with a guinea you got to do it in a guinea restaurant?" Phil asked, staring at the neon above the entrance.

"The food settles their stomachs. What are you asking me for?" Joseph said.

Joseph handed the kid a five-dollar bill. "You don't have to worry we're going to stiff you."

The kid put the fiver in his pocket without looking, staring at the sleek marvels, ready to kill for one if there was a way. Then he ran to hold the door for them as Joseph and Phil started for it, one adjusting his tie, the other shooting his cuffs so the gold links would show.

Walking in from the Valley heat the cold air hit them like a sledgehammer.

"Jesus. Hot, cold. Hot, cold," Phil complained. "Gives my sinuses hell."

It was bright toward the front of the restaurant where the big plate-glass windows let in the light, but it got darker and darker toward the back.

They heard their names called and walked toward the booth near the kitchen doors where Pachoulo, Sam's Man, Iggie Deetch and Nadeau sat. Nadeau was half standing up, holding his hand in the air as though his glittering pinkie ring was a beacon. He stood up all the way when Joseph and Phil reached them.

"So," he said and started the introductions, almost leaving out Iggie Deetch, who leaned back into the shadows with a calculator in his hand.

When Pachoulo leaned forward, Joseph said, "Don't bother standing up."

"I wasn't going to stand up," Pachoulo said. "These plastic seats give me a sweaty ass."

"A man shouldn't put his ass on anything less than leather and wear nothing heavier than silk," Joseph said, doing his hearty Irish poet act.

"I don't know can the owner afford leather. I don't know if I can afford silk," Pachoulo said. "A man can't afford something, he should do without."

"Everybody thought like that, we'd be out of business," Joseph said as a waiter appeared from somewhere carrying a captain's chair in each hand.

"Al here tells me you push a very expensive item," Sam's Man said.

"Porsches cost a couple of dollars."

The chairs were ready for them but neither Joseph nor Phil sat down.

"So go ahead, take a load off," Pachoulo offered.

They smiled, but still they didn't sit down. Then Pat walked out of the bright into the gloom and all three brothers were standing shoulder to shoulder.

"Sorry to keep you waiting," Pat said politely. "You got another chair?"

"Don't feel bad. Here's one for you," Joseph said, as he shifted over so he could slide in next to Nadeau. A look passed among the brothers that said seems like old times. They were up for it. They were ready to scramble.

So now they were all sitting there like a bunch of lodge brothers, squashed in shoulder to shoulder and ass to ass. Sam's Man on one end of the semicircular banquette and Joseph on the other with Deetch in the middle and Pachoulo and Nadeau surrounded. Pat and Phil sat in the two chairs, taking up the entire end of the table.

"Fachrissake, I feel like I'm being crushed to death," Pachoulo complained. "Hey, Carmine, why don't you go over to the next table there with that pet gorilla you got on the leash? Why don't you do that?"

Sam's Man dragged himself up out of the booth and sat down at the table nearby, giving Pachoulo and everybody else a little relief. Deetch shook his hands as though getting the circulation back into them.

"So what have we got?" Pachoulo asked, looking at Nadeau.

Nadeau slipped a few sheets of paper out of his inside breast pocket and spread them out, but he started outlining the deal without referring to them.

"The Nicoletti brothers are doing an automotive park—"

"What's that?" Pachoulo asked.

"It's a shopping mall for cars and automotive services. Everything in one spot behind a screening wall. Very attractive. An improvement instead of a blight to any community."

"They still got flags?" Sam's Man asked from the next table.

"What's that?" Nadeau responded.

"They still going to have them little flags on strings all around the lots? You know."

"Oh, advertising pennants. Well, I don't know. The dealers don't have to shout for attention in these automotive parks. That's the whole idea."

"Who gives a fuck these little flags, Carmine?" Pachoulo asked.

Sam's Man looked offended. "I just thought I'd ask," he mumbled. "I like them little flags." He leaned over with a great deal of effort and scratched Sam's ears, annoyed that his contribution to the predeal conversation hadn't been appreciated.

"Where was I?" Nadeau asked.

"You was talking about the Nicoletti brothers," Deetch supplied. "They the same Nicolettis used to wholesale Mexican beer out of Wilmington?"

"No, they've always been in construction as far as I know. You happen to know, Puffy?" Nadeau asked.

"What am I listening to here?" Joseph said, looking at Nadeau and leaning into him a little. "Is this a vaudeville act? How long is it going to take to lay this proposition on the table?"

"You getting antsy, Mr. Doohan?" Pachoulo asked.

"Out in Somis," Nadeau said abruptly.

"What?" Pachoulo and Joseph said at the same time.

"Out in Somis is where the Nicoletti brothers want to build the automotive park."

"Where the fuck's this Somis?" Pachoulo asked.

"That's the first question I asked, Mr. Pachoulo," Phil said.

Pachoulo stared at Phil for a minute as though wondering what the hell *that* was supposed to mean, then he grinned his toad's grin and said, "Hey, *goomba*."

All of a sudden the atmosphere was changed. All of a sudden they were all feeling very loose. They had this thing in common. Pachoulo and Phil both thought of the same question. Where was Somis?

"It's about forty miles southeast of Santa Barbara," Nadeau said. "About the same northwest of Hollywood."

"Out in the boonies," Sam's Man remarked.

"Anything more than six blocks from Hollywood and Vine is to you the boonies," Pachoulo said. "How come the Nicolettis choose a place fifty miles from nowhere?"

"Forty," Nadeau said. "And not nowhere. The best somewhere for a deal like this when land prices and population densities are factored in."

"So what do I know about where anybody should sell automobiles?" Pachoulo said. "What do think about the location, Mr. Doohan?"

"I think it's perfect," Joseph said. "If I didn't think it was perfect I wouldn't be here talking a loan. I'd be sitting in my beautiful showroom with my ass on leather."

"So you're talking a loan?"

"My assumption."

"How come you don't go to a bank?"

"We've used up our credit line to build up inventory for the new model year. One hundred models. Thirty thousand dollars a copy average dealer's cost. Delivery in fifths. Three million dollars, give or take a hundred-thousand-dollar bill."

"You got that kind of credit?"

"That's what we got."

"What have you got for this automobile park?"

"We've got our good credit, our inventory, our lease and a hundred thousand dollars cash."

"What is it you ain't got?"

"We haven't got the second hundred thousand dollars. It's the beginning of the model year. We always suffer a little cash-flow problem for a couple months."

"How long you want to borrow this large amount of money?"

Joseph looked at Nadeau.

"Nine months should see the project at the stage where bank financing can be secured for completion."

"Also the Doohan brothers would've sold a couple cars?" Pachoulo said, grinning his frog's smile again.

"That's it," Joseph said.

"Do me some numbers, Iggie," Pachoulo ordered.

Deetch fooled around with the calculator.

"They take a hundred, they pay back a hundred and forty over twelve months."

"A little elbow room we give you there," Pachoulo said amiably.

"That's forty percent interest," Phil said.

"You think I can't count?" Pachoulo said, throwing away the smile. "Can you count? You're in hock up to your eyeballs. I don't care you got three million in inventory, it's what you owe I think about. You got a hot deal what's going to make you a fortune but you can't get into this hot deal without you come up with a hundred large which you ain't got."

"We're talking short-term money here," Joseph said.

"A year could be short-term to you, it ain't short-term to me."

"Nine months. We only need it for nine months."

"So say thirty-five percent then. You take a hundred, you pay back a hundred and thirty-five in nine months."

Phil put his hand on Joseph's sleeve.

"You want to talk this over private?" Pachoulo said. "There's plenty of empty tables. Go pick a table and go talk it over private."

The brothers got up and walked over to a table half in the light, half in the shadows.

Sam's Man lumbered to his feet and came over to sit next to Nadeau again. "I don't know about dealing with the Irish," he said.

"What the hell's that supposed to mean?" Pachoulo asked. "Iggie Deetch here's a mick. Ain't you a mick, Iggie?"

"On my mother's side."

"So who ever said I trusted Iggie Deetch?" Sam's Man said.

"Go fuck yourself, fat boy," Deetch said amiably.

"That's the last time I ever let you feed dollar bills to Sam so's you can win a bet," Sam's Man said. The dog whined at his feet, sat up on his haunches and gave his master a look.

"That dog's got to take a pee," Pachoulo said. "Take him for a walk before he does it all over my shoe like he did the other day."

"He didn't pee on your shoe, he spit on your shoe a little bit," Sam's Man protested.

"So take him for a walk, he should wring out his sock, anyway. I don't want to take any chances."

Sam's Man got up and walked out toward the kitchen with the dog prancing joyfully beside him.

Pachoulo, Nadeau and Deetch turned their heads to look at the brothers as though they could hear what they were saying as long as they kept their eyes on them.

"I don't know if I want to do business with these guineas," Phil said. "You look at the face on them slobs, that one, Pachoulo, and the other one with the goddam beast, and what you see is a couple of very mean people."

"Since when does dealing with mean people bother us?"

"This isn't back when we were kids, beating up on the yids and ginzos," Pat said. "This is serious business, we don't pay up."

"What's serious business is this deal we got a handle on. Nine months, maybe less, we cash out these assholes and we're sitting pretty," Joseph argued.

"I'd like to know why this Nadeau steers us to this shylock," Phil said.

"He don't steer us. Helena happens to mention to me that isn't it a coincidence—"

"While she's going down on you for a hundred bucks?" Phil said.

"—that her husband's involved in building this automobile . . . what's that supposed to mean, while she's going down on me?"

"Here's this housewife turning tricks for a hundred bucks and she's got a lawyer for a husband who's into these big deals."

"So what's the question?"

"Why's she selling her ass?"

"He's a mean sonofabitch won't give her an allowance."

"Hey, Joey, I'm just saying you'd believe anything she told you."

"I'm not stupid."

"So maybe your cock's stupid is what I'm saying."

"Is that what you're saying?"

"Also that it's possible she was sent out to set you up."

"Jesus, you got an imagination."

"It's possible?"

"Anything's possible," Pat said.

"It's also possible you haven't got the balls for a deal like this. It's also possible you two want to suck nickels and dimes even though I've tried as hard as I could to make you think big, think successful."

"We got a Porsche dealership," Phil protested. "That's not successful?"

"It's small potatoes to what it could be if we got into this deal."

"It's such a good deal why don't this lawyer borrow the money from his guinea friends, keep it all?" Pat said.

"Everybody's got expenses, everybody's got money tied up in this and that. Look at us. We're going to have millions of dollars' worth of cars passing through the showroom but we still haven't got the two hundred thousand to snap up a sweetheart deal like this. So Nadeau hasn't got the scratch either. Not where he can get to it just like that."

"I don't like how easy it is for Nadeau to line us up with his friends who just happen to have that kind of scratch."

"What friends? What friends? He's a lawyer. He knows some types."

As if on cue, they looked toward Pachoulo and Nadeau and found them staring back. They waved. Pachoulo, Nadeau and Deetch waved.

"What the fuck they waving at," Deetch said.

"Somebody said something got them all thinking was we trustworthy," Pachoulo said. "So they decided to take a gander. Maybe the answer would be written on our kissers."

Nadeau was always being surprised at how acute Pachoulo could be, how accurately he could read the odd glance and gesture.

They watched the three brothers get up from the table and come back to where they were sitting. The brothers sat down.

"We borrow a hundred, we pay back one hundred thirty in twelve months," Joseph said.

"Nine months," Pachoulo said, "and you pay back one thirty-five."

"Give me a little elbow room. Split the difference."

"One and thirty-three thirty, ten months, and if maybe I want a new car you'll get me one wholesale?"

"Ten percent off suggested retail."

"Dealer's cost and ten."

"Hey, *goomba,*" Joseph said.

"You like guinea food?" Pachoulo said. "You want something to eat? A glass of wine? At least a glass of wine to baptize the deal."

While Pachoulo poured the wine with his own hand, Sam's Man came back with his dog's lead in one hand and Billy Ray's arm in the other.

"Look what I found out on the street," he said.

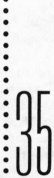

When Billy Ray came crawling up the front steps of the court cottage where he and Lisa lived, he looked like he'd just been in a wreck. Half his teeth were missing, one eye was swollen shut, and a broken rib gave him hell every time he took a breath. He could hardly pound on the door hard enough for her to hear.

When she finally did hear him she thought at first it was a passing wind rattling the door or maybe a neighborhood cat punching at a moth. When she looked out of the peephole there was no one to see but the pounding went on and even got louder.

"Who is it? Who is it?" she called out.

Somebody said, "Me," in a voice she didn't recognize. Maybe it was a druggie out there looking for targets of opportunity. If she opened the door he'd push her back inside and rape her, stick his thing in her everywhere, some stranger she didn't know and would never see again. He could beat her up for the money she didn't have. Kill her for the television set.

"Who?" she said, raising her voice.

"It's Billy."

She opened the door a crack without taking off the night chain though she knew she shouldn't even be doing that, a man could put his shoulder against the door and break the screws out of the rotting wood like the jamb was made of paper. At first she didn't see anybody, except the taxi standing half on the driveway, half on the burnt-out grass, its lights on, door open, motor running. Then the movement of a bloody hand reaching up toward her made her look down and there he was, her husband, lying on the steps like a wounded dog.

She closed the door and slipped the chain, opened it up all the way and bent down to grab his arm as he moved painfully and slowly across the threshold on his hands and knees. Together, they managed to get him up on the couch, Billy moaning and whimpering and giving out little cries with every move.

"What happened? Have you been in an accident?"

He shook his head, tears coming down into his ruined mouth, mixing with his blood, lips battered and twisted in grief and pain, reaching for her to be held and rocked in her arms.

"Your teeth, your beautiful teeth," she said. She backed off, feeling sick, feeling ashamed because the man she was supposed to care most about disgusted her. "I'll go turn the motor off and put out the head-lights," she said, then ran out of the house.

When she came back she was calmer, the first shock over with. She closed the door and stood off half a dozen steps.

"There's nothing wrong with the cab."

"Pachoulo did it," he tried to say, but it came out garbled and slurred, the single word, the hated name, turned into a comedy phrase. He reached out for her again and it almost made her laugh the way his clown's face with the black-and-blue greasepaint on the eyes and the red scrawls around the mouth looked at her so longingly and pleadingly. A child's face. A toothless baby's face.

So finally she went to him and held him for a minute and let him lay his head on her breasts and cry his heart out because all there'd ever been to Billy Ray was hope and there was no hope left anymore. She felt pity, but she didn't feel any love. Not a trace of it. It had all turned to dust and blown away.

They talked in the small hours. Lisa writing on a little pad of paper all the things they had to do to repair the damage Billy had done their lives as best they could. Billy answering the questions she asked, the suggestions she made, with one hand covering his mouth and the other holding a towel filled with cracked ice cubes on his swollen eyes.

"We've got to wreck the cab," she said.

"What the hell?"

"You've got to see a doctor. There could be something broken inside. You got to see a dentist. I mean that's what you got to do, take care of the damage right away. Get started putting yourself back together. You'll have to take some time off. You can't just take the time off without getting paid. We'd starve to death."

"We got to find three thousand dollars."

She acted like she hadn't heard him.

"So we have to make it look like you got in a wreck so you can get insurance. Workmen's comp."

"My bill with Pachoulo's up to three. He took back my loan from Benny Checks."

"I don't want to hear about it right this minute," Lisa said calmly, her practical tone of voice not changing one bit.

"Okay," he mumbled.

"We've got to take care of first things first."

"Okay. You think I could have a shot of something? I hurt like hell."

She foraged in the cabinet under the sink and came up with a third of a bottle of cheap brandy she'd bought once when she had the idea that making a special dinner with flaming sauce would put something back into the marriage. Afterwards she wondered why women did dumb things like that. She poured some of the brandy into a water glass. The smell of it had a sharp edge like the smell of kerosene.

He took a mouthful and started to cry, the tears welling up again and running down his swollen cheeks.

"My God, does that ever burn."

"You're going to hurt a lot before this is over," Lisa said.

He took another mouthful and shook his head as though that would keep the pain away.

Lisa took the bottle. "No more."

"Please? Why not? Maybe it'll help me get some sleep."

"You can sleep without it. For an hour."

"What are you talking about?"

"I'm talking about that's how long I hope it'll take for me to get somebody to help us."

"What help us?"

"I told you, we've got to wreck the cab and make it look like you had an accident. Otherwise there's no insurance benefits. There's no workmen's compensation."

"Christ, we can't do that. We could never get away with it."

"We better try."

"So what do we need anybody else for?" he asked, in fresh terror because he could see his troubles getting bigger and bigger, spreading out until he wouldn't be able to see the edges of this thing that was engulfing them, getting so big it'd turn back on them and swallow them up. If they didn't think about it, if they didn't *do* anything about it, maybe it would all go away. It was the trying to *do* something about it that was terrifying him. "Let it go. Let it go. Let things just happen the way they're going to happen."

She stood up and stared down at him, feeling so sorry for the guy that had been so good-looking once upon a time, but wasn't so good-looking now and might not be so good-looking ever again. It gave her a jolt. Made her think about what she'd done, marrying a man she thought was going to be somebody just because he had a pretty face. Caught up by that and his body, which had been so fine. Caught up in a moving picture. Pretty people, with heads twenty feet tall, Vaseline on their lips, light spraying through their hair from a phony moon, coming together mouth to mouth on the silver screen, living one of the corny tunes written by half a dozen writers with whiskey on their breath. And now that he wasn't pretty anymore did that mean she had to live out the rest of the romance? Did that mean she'd have to stick by him not because she needed or wanted him but because he needed her? Was that how it was going to be, living out dull lives because she didn't have the guts to walk up to the theater manager and ask for her money back?

"We've always let things happen the way they were going to happen, haven't we?" she said. "So look what happened."

She went to get her coat from the bedroom. When she came back he had the bottle in his hand. She marched over to him, tore it from his grasp and broke it in the sink.

"How're we going to make it look like a one-car accident banged you up if you blow drunk into the balloon? Are you crazy? Are you goddam crazy?"

"What do you mean, blow drunk? You expect me to drive the cab into a tree? Is that what you expect me to do?"

"I expect you to sit behind the wheel after I wreck it. That's all you've got to do. Just sit behind the wheel."

"This is getting out of hand," he said as though scolding her for taking some foolish risk.

She started to laugh, staring at him as if the sight of him was driving her crazy.

"You hear yourself? You goddam hear yourself? It's already out of hand. Our fucking lives are out of hand. Your fucking brain is out of hand. I'm trying to hold the goddam pieces together. That's all I'm doing, trying to hold the rotten fucking goddam pieces together."

She was ready to fly apart. He could see that. He kept on saying shush, shush, shush. It sounded like he was trying to be funny. Finally he said, "Who're you going to get to help?"

"Who've we got? Just who the hell do we got?"

"I don't know."

"That's right. You haven't got one friend who'd help us. We got your mother—"

"No!"

"Then all we got—maybe—is Panama."

Heath had lived in the apartment on Sweetzer for ten years. It wasn't great but it was all right. The manager kept the pool clean and there were a lot of transient women who came from all over the country looking for whatever.

He'd had some parties with more than one of them. Nothing ever came of the relationships. Sooner or later they bagged up their ambitions and loneliness along with their diaphragms and dancing tights and went somewhere else, great believers in new contacts. Working the crowd for what might be in it, coming up empty-handed, listening to clocks ticking. All kinds of clocks.

There was a clock in his living room, sitting on the table by the window. It chimed the hours and pinged the halfs and quarters. He'd promised himself he'd drown the clock a thousand times through long wakeful nights when he lay there staring at the shadows on the ceiling, trying to imagine sailboats and naked women, humming old show tunes under his breath, the goddam clock chiming and pinging his life away.

There was a long narrow window above his head, above the bed. You couldn't see out of it even standing up. It was up too high. Who wanted a view of the traffic on Sweetzer anyway? He tipped his head and stared at it, thinking about what Missy had said some time ago about doing it with Lisa. Trying to see how they fit after so long. If they'd fit at all, or if muscle, bone and flesh had shifted and remolded, so they weren't pieces of the same puzzle anymore. So he could put the pieces back in the box with the picture of what could have been on the lid and store it in the closet. The window was like the window in a cell. Cells just like it all over the city. People living in their little prisons.

The clock chimed, making it one o'clock. Did something else make a noise? He tuned his ears and heard a distant television set and the guy next door rattling around the bathroom. Then he heard the knock on the door.

He kicked his legs over the side of the bed and, in his shorts, walked into the living room calling, "Who is it?"

Two seconds before he opened the door he thought she might be there, coming to him. A second before, he thought what a crazy notion it was. A split second before, he knew for sure it would be her and he pulled the door open just as she was about to say, "It's Lisa." Saying it like she was wondering why he should even be asking who it was when it was her coming home again.

They'd fit like two halves of a whole. They'd fit like yin and yang, the Chinese symbol of completeness you saw everywhere in Chinatown, on the leathers of the gangs, on the boxes of lichee nuts in shop windows. They'd fit like two familiar hands coming together.

He lay on his back, his legs flung wide, her head tucked up underneath his ear, her breasts soft against his ribs, her hand cupping his balls, his hand on the swell of her hip, his thumb just reaching into the narrow valley below the bone leading to her center. He lay there listening to her quieting breath, thinking crazy thoughts about how they'd come together like a scene in a movie watched from the dark in the holy temple of the cinema when he was young. Irene Dunne and Cary Grant. Katharine Hepburn and Spencer Tracy. Ingrid Bergman and Charles Boyer. Shirley MacLaine and Jack Nicholson. Debra Winger and Tom Cruise. Marilyn Chambers and Johnny Holmes. Making love in the dark in the language of their time. Making love without a word of warning.

At first he didn't understand what she was saying. At first it sounded like more of her sighs and murmurs. Then the words started coming clear. Hesitant but very clear. First he dragged his leg away, though she tried to hold him against her with her knee. Then he drew his arm out from beneath her head and reached for a cigarette in the drawer of the nightstand beside the bed. Then he sat up and lit it, taking a long drag on the stale tobacco that had lain there drying out for six months since he'd decided to give up the weed.

He listened to her tale of woe and what she was hoping he would do for her and Billy Ray.

"Did you just pay me in advance?" he asked, his throat all clogged up with anger and rue.

She cried out softly as though in pain and touched his retreating back with her fingertips as he got up to put on his shorts.

"You're asking me to conspire to defraud the insurance companies. To destroy private property. To endanger the public right of way. To compound a felony."

"I'm asking you to help me."

He turned around on her, looking down at her, naked, not so much tempting as vulnerable.

"Why don't you just give up on him? He's a loser."

"I am giving up on him, Panama. But you can see I've got to get him out of this last one because it could kill him. I couldn't stand by and see an old dog kicked to death and not try to help."

"I'm a cop, goddammit. You really don't know what you're asking."

"Yes, I do. I know what I'm asking and I know what you're thinking."

He waited.

"You're thinking that if you do this for me I'll think it's because I spread my legs for you. You be just another asshole giving away the store for a piece of ass. You think I'll have you in my pocket again, like I did before, and that I'll take you out and hurt you anytime I want to."

"No, I don't think that."

"You're an old-fashioned man, Panama. Are you trying to tell me you don't think you owe me because I let you do it?"

He shook his head.

She smiled. It was almost sorrowful. "What an awful liar you are, Panama." She got out of bed, not trying to be graceful, letting herself be just the opposite. Nothing but what she was, a woman with a lot more miles on her than she'd had when last they'd come together in a bed. She walked around the room flat-footed, picking up her clothes, not sucking in her belly, not lifting her breasts.

"I'm not stupid, Panama, I know how hard it is, what I'm asking you to do for me."

"You going to say for old times' sake?"

She paused in what she was doing, half crouched over with her clothes bundled up in her hands, looking up at him with something hard and deadly honest in her eyes. "No. I wouldn't pull that shit on you, Panama. I'd never do that."

"Well, I'm going to do what I can for old times' sake. That's why I'm going to do it. Not for what we just did. For old times' sake."

Lisa drove Heath's car and he drove the taxi with Billy Ray sitting in the back. It was better that way. There were plenty of women driving hacks but one as pretty as Lisa behind the wheel of a cab at three o'clock in the morning could draw some attention.

His eyes flicked to the rearview mirror every few seconds, making sure she was following right behind him along the quiet streets as they climbed into the hills and the long stretch of Mulholland Drive, which rode the crest of the hills to the sea.

"You keep your trip sheet in the glove compartment?" Heath asked.

"Yeah."

"It in there now?"

"Should be."

Heath reached over and opened it up. He felt around and came up with some trip sheets under the jaws of a clipboard.

"This today's?"

"Let me see."

Heath flicked on the overhead, then held the clipboard behind his shoulder up against the plastic thief barrier.

"That's it," Ray said. "What do you want it for?"

"Your trip sheet's got to show a call. Otherwise what the hell would you be doing cruising Mulholland? You have any regular customers up around here?"

"There's one. I took Benny Checks up to this pink stucco once or twice."

"Recently?"

"Well, not recently. But I been up there myself a couple of times since Benny don't show around town anymore."

"This damned shield open up?" Heath said, whacking it with his elbow.

"No. It's not supposed to."

"When we get to where we're going to dump this hack, remember I want you to fill out a trip."

"Suppose somebody checks?"

Will you listen to that, Heath thought. Here's a guy with a face like a welter gone fifteen with a heavyweight, three o'clock in the morning, and his mind's checking out all the angles. Like a rat. As sly and crafty as a rat.

"Wait a minute. You're right. You get phony calls, don't you?"

"Sure. Wise guys call into dispatch, ask for a cab, nobody there when we get there."

"Can we say that happened?"

"Dispatch would know."

"Say you got the call and that's all you know. Some wise guy gives you a call, says he's dispatch. Why not? Nobody's going to care. Insurance makes a fuss you just stick to the story."

"What do I say about the time I was supposed to quit the shift and the time I take this call? Why is dispatch calling me when I'm supposed to be in the barn?"

"All right. You say you quit for the night, went home and got this call on your home phone from somebody you thought was this regular customer who wanted to make sure he got you to drive him."

"Her."

"Okay. It's more logical a woman would feel safer with a driver she knew."

"Who's going to believe it?"

"If anybody asks, you better give somebody your marker and make them believe it. I can't do it all. I *won't* do it all."

They rode in silence for a while.

"You been fucking her," Ray suddenly said.

"I haven't even seen her for two, three years until she came around asking me to get Pachoulo off your back."

"You been fucking her tonight," Ray said.

It was disgusting. Heath knew that Ray wasn't protesting. He just wanted to know who owed who and how much.

"Her ass for your ass, Billy Ray," Heath said, making it as nasty as he knew how, feeling a lot of contempt for Ray and not a little for himself.

They were quiet after that until they got to the spot along Mulholland south of Encino where houses are few and sheer drops off the road frequent. He parked the cab on the gravel shoulder at a spot wide enough for a turnaround, then got out as Lisa pulled in behind him. They stood face to face just out of the shine of the headlamps from his car.

There was a little twisted smile on her lips, lips that still looked swollen and bruised from his kisses.

"Hell of a way for us to get back together, isn't it, Panama?"

"Are we back together?"

The smile flew away and the moth wings of a frown appeared between her eyes.

"Oh, Jesus, won't you believe me? I came to ask you the favor. I don't deny that. What happened before I asked just happened because I wanted it to happen. I've been wanting it to happen ever since I laid eyes on your dirty old hat again. I didn't plan it. I didn't think it would happen but I wanted it to. You wanted it to just as much as me, didn't you?"

When he didn't answer right away, she turned aside as though she meant to run off down the black road. He reached out and put his hand on her arm.

"Sure I did. I've been wanting it to happen every minute, night and day, for six years."

She took a step toward him, looked over his shoulder, saw Billy looking at them through the back window of the cab, moved up against Heath's chest and gave him her mouth.

When the kiss was over, Heath put his hands on her shoulders and smiled, boosting her spirits but letting her know they still had a long way to go. "Let's get this over with. Kill your headlights and get my flashlight out of the glove compartment."

She went to do that, while he went over and opened the back door of the cab.

Ray got out, trying to look bold, trying to swagger, no longer feeling that the cop was doing him any favors because the cop had fucking been paid and was going to continue getting paid. Okay. He could live with that.

"Listen to me. I'm going to say it once," Heath said. "Even this hour of the night, you can never tell, somebody comes driving along even a lonely stretch of road like this. We're going to push the cab over the side and jam it against a tree. Then you're going to scramble down the slope and get in behind the wheel. We'll call in an anonymous citizen's—"

"I ain't going to crawl down the side of any mountain in the dark."

"You do it or I take Lisa home with me and leave you here to work it out any way you think you can."

"I don't know why we're even wasting the goddam time and effort," Ray said, starting to tremble all over, "just to get a doctor and a dentist to fix me up. Pachoulo's only going to have Machado and Sam's Man kill me next time, I don't come up with the three bones."

"Pachoulo's not going to do dick."

They both glanced at the scrape of her shoe as Lisa walked up. She handed Heath his flashlight and he tried the switch, snapping the beam on and off once.

Ray was still trembling. Heath was afraid he might be going into shock.

"You all right?"

"I don't feel good. What can you expect? You got anything wet in your car?"

"You've already had something. I can smell it."

"Cooking brandy. Just a couple. I'm not drunk."

"I know that. But you have any more they could maybe get a reading. We don't need that. Wait here."

Heath walked away, going over to the edge and shining the light down along the slope. He walked to his left and made a mark with his heel in the gravel. Then he paced off the width of a car the other way and made another gouge. When he got back to them, Ray and Lisa were facing each other. There was something in their attitude that told him they'd had words and Ray had lost the argument.

"There's a stand of eucalyptus about thirty feet down the slope, so it's going to be a cinch." He looked at Ray, trying to see if he was going to balk. If he was going to just say the hell with it and resist any attempt to help him.

"Okay, what do you want me to do?" Ray said.

"I told you. All you have to do is get behind the wheel and stay there until the emergency crew comes to get you."

"Oh, my God."

"It's not going to be all that long."

"Where will they be coming from?"

"How the hell do I know?" Heath snapped. "Don't jerk my chain, goddammit. Santa Monica. Hollywood. Maybe the fire station up on the ridge. You won't be sitting there more than an hour. Two hours tops."

Ray let go a wordless expression of deep distress and looked at Lisa as though she could figure out a way to make it better without making him go through all this. She stared back at him.

"Help me push it over," Heath said. He handed the flash to Lisa. "I'll take the wheel side and point it. You just help me push, Billy Ray."

Ray went to the passenger side and got ready. Lisa tucked the flash under her arm, went to the back and put her hands on the rear end.

"You stay away, Lisa. We don't need you," Heath said.

He opened the door and wedged it open with a good-sized twig.

"We don't want it jamming shut and locking you out," he said. "Okay, push!"

It was hard starting it from a dead stop but once it was rolling the cab acted like it wanted to jump over the side. Heath only just managed to point it exactly right so it went straight over the guiding marks he'd made. It went over the side, smashing through the undergrowth on the hillside to go crashing into the trunks of the eucalyptus trees.

"Give me the flash," Heath said.

He shone it down the hillside. The cab was cradled nose first into the trees, solid as a rock. Ray came up to stand beside him.

"Doesn't look like it even did much damage."

"We didn't need an end–over–ender," Heath said. "Can you get down there by yourself?"

"I don't know."

"I'll help you. Come on."

Heath took Ray's elbow and was surprised to feel how frail his arm seemed to be. All of a sudden a wave of pity and sympathy washed over him. What the hell had he been so goddam mad at all these years? Who knew what it was about one man that made it easy for him to steal a woman away from another man? How did he know there wasn't something very unsatisfying to Lisa about the relationship they had when Billy Ray came along to turn her head and talk her out of her underwear? Who the fuck knew? So what was there to have been mad about?

Heath helped Ray down the slope as if he had an old man in his care. They got to the side of the cab on the driver's side. The door was open. The damage was just to the front bumper, fenders and grill. The hood had popped open but wasn't even dented. The inside of the cab didn't have a thing busted. When he helped Ray into the front seat, the cab shifted a little bit and Ray clutched Heath's hand and cried out.

"Take it easy," Heath soothed. "It's not going anywhere."

Ray settled back and smiled weakly.

"All you got to do is take it easy."

"Suppose the rescue truck takes a hell of a while?"

"So you take a nap."

"Why can't we just go back up on the road? Why can't you just take off and I can walk down toward Sepulveda? Maybe somebody comes along and gives me a lift."

"The average citizen seeing a man walking along a deserted road this hour of the morning, all bloody and tore up, will just keep going. You want to take the chance the gamoosh that stops to pick you up don't knock out the rest of your teeth, maybe kill you when he finds out you've got nothing but loose change in your pockets?"

"Put in the call as soon as you can, okay?"

"The first public phone we come to. So, when somebody comes to get you, what are you going to tell them?"

"What?"

"You're going to tell them you were coming back from a no-show when a rabbit or a raccoon or something ran across the road in front of you and you cut the wheel without thinking and went over. Can you think of anything else we might've forgot?"

"I can't think of anything."

"Neither can I."

They stared at each other in the dark, trying to read expressions they could hardly see. Heath stuck out his hand.

"Good luck. Don't worry about it."

"You taking Lisa with you?"

"Sure. She's got to get back to town."

"I mean are you taking her home with you."

"No. I'm taking her back to your house. She's got to be there when the cops take you home."

"Oh, sure, that's right."

"Okay, then?"

"I'm not going to thank you," Ray said.

"That's fair. I'm not doing it for you."

"That's what I mean. I don't owe you."

37

Ana Checks tapped on the door and went right in. Her husband sat in his rocking chair, clutching the tatty bathrobe to his neck, staring out the window. Benny seldom spoke and rarely seemed to hear unless she sat in front of him, holding his hands, making him look into her eyes. There'd been a moment, when Benny had found his rage with that man, Billy Ray, when she'd hoped Benny was going to be all right. But it was like the last fruit of a dying tree, the last flaring up of a blaze before it turned gray and black.

For a while she'd hoped that the terrible humiliation could be healed under her loving hands. In bed she was more abandoned than she'd ever been even those few times before they'd been married. She'd displayed her still beautiful body like a whore, striking poses and grappling with his flesh in ways that she would never have otherwise dreamed of doing, offending her own sense of what a decent woman should do to arouse her husband.

Benny was able and willing in these nighttime encounters, but always afterwards, after orgasm, after release, he cried like a woman would cry, as though he was trying to get some strength from acting the part of the one who had surrendered. And in the morning, after a sleep like the sleep of the dead, a sleep that she knew was an escape into childhood and helplessness, he got up late and shuffled around like a hollow man until he finally sat down for the long watching and waiting at the bedroom window.

And, God forgive her, at first she'd almost exulted. Not in what had happened to her husband, but for what she thought might come of it. She'd been a thrifty housewife, saving every nickel and squeezing every cent, and there'd been weeks, even months, when cash just seemed to flow from an ever-running river of money out of Benny's pockets, a good part of which she managed to put away in bank accounts Benny didn't even know about.

She saw her dreams coming true. They'd sell the house and move away. North to a place where people didn't look over their shoulders and peer into alleys and start when a car slowed down even in broad daylight. To a smaller place where people were kinder to one another. Perhaps they'd purchase a small retail business of some sort. A little grocery. A baker's shop.

Now she saw what a foolish dream that was. There would be nothing good about taking a man away from the familiar sights and sounds and smells of a city he'd once loved, the people, gonnifs, pimps, whores and glad-handers, who were the people he called friends. Nothing right about going anywhere with a hollow man.

So she'd decided that what she had to do was protect what they had for a future that had to be postponed awhile longer. She started asking him questions, holding his hands and insisting he look at her, questions about how a betting book was managed.

She sat down on the footstool near his feet and took his hands.

"What do you do, Benny, when a certain horse or baseball team gets so much action it could wipe you out if it won?"

He looked at her with such an expression that she was afraid that he was slipping away from her so fast, day by day, that pretty soon he wouldn't be there at all. And then what would she do? She felt a great bag of tears pushing up out of her chest, filling her head, threatening to pour out of her eyes. Tears that were all black and red with fear and rage. She felt herself begin to tremble and was terrified that she would give way in front of him. Her hands clenched involuntarily and she saw his eyes widen as though her feelings had gotten through to him.

"What did you say, Ana?"

She repeated her question word for word.

"You lay some of it off," he said.

"What does this 'lay off' mean?"

"You got such heavy action on a horse, let's say, you're afraid he comes in you'll drown in winning slips, you lay off some of it with another book. You maybe even reach out to the biggest bookie you know who won't try to rope you in, make you one of his runners. An employee. You understand what I'm saying? Or maybe you reach out all the way to the Syndicate where the pool of money is so big it don't even make a ripple, the money you bet with them. So, then, you got the bet money spread around so no matter who wins you're still making your percentage on the odds."

"Just like stocks and bonds. Diversification."

"That's right," Benny said, and even smiled a little bit. "Why are you worrying about such things?"

"I don't know. I heard it on the television. On some story about gamblers. I wondered what it meant. Who would you go to when you had to lay some money off?"

"This one and that one. One Ear Caledrone. Tip Tobias." His face screwed up in concentration. He looked like a frustrated infant. "I don't know," he finished lamely.

"I hear about a man by the name of Iggie Deetch."

"He's not a bookie, he's a bail bondsman."

"But I'm told he knows everybody."

"He knows that sonofabitch Puffy Pachoulo is who he knows. Stay way from Iggie Deetch. Don't ask no favors from Iggie Deetch. I'll bet it was him whispered it into Puffy's ear that I was helping out a few friends with a loan, they should get off Pachoulo's hook."

She let go one of his hands and held the other in both of hers, patting it gently. He continued to grow more agitated, little flecks of spit thickening into a crust in the corners of his mouth as he raved on. She pulled his hand between her breasts and held it there, trying to soothe him with the softness of her flesh.

"Don't talk about that man," she said. "Don't talk about this Iggie Deetch, either. Just be still, be still. You want to come to bed and suck on Mama's tit?"

Every once in a while Maggie started to cry, dabbing at her splotchy face with a wad of paper toweling while Flo and Essie clucked and fussed and patted her hands, asking her if she'd like her drink freshened or her neck massaged, asking her if there was anything in the world they could do for her as they cringed inside themselves with embarrassment and fear.

Maggie had, just that day, gotten the word. They had to operate. The doctor wouldn't say but Maggie was old enough to read his eyes and mouth. There wasn't much hope for her, operation or no operation. The odds were a shade better if she went under the knife. Doctors held out hope like cherries on a stick leading you down the garden path. But when they wouldn't look too long or hard at you there weren't many cherries in the bunch.

"It's wonderful what they can do nowadays," Flo said brightly.

"Is it?" Maggie asked.

"Just last month my sister told me about a woman lives in her town got a cancer. Got cancer all over her body. In her breasts and ovaries and everywhere in the lymph system."

"That's the worse," Essie said. "Gets into the lymphatic it's all over."

"That's just what I thought until my sister told me about this woman," Flo said. "This woman went under the knife. The surgeon cut around her hairline and the front of her ear, down her jaw and along the side of her neck, under her arm and all the way down to her side and peeled her skin right back. Looked like one of those anatomical diagrams my sister said."

"She saw it?" Essie exclaimed.

"Saw pictures. Showed them to me. I saw them, too. You wouldn't believe. Peeled her back like a banana. Cleaned out every one of them whattayoucallems."

"Nodes," Maggie said.

"How did you know that?"

"The doctor said. He said the X-rays didn't show any cancer in the lymph nodes."

"Well, there you are," said Flo. "You're probably lucky."

"I'm sure you're lucky," Essie chimed in. "So what happened with your sister's friend, Flo?"

"The surgeon took out all the cancer and sewed her back up neat as you please."

"What about her breasts?" Maggie asked, wide-eyed, half enthralled by the medical horror story, almost on the table suffering what that woman had suffered.

"She had to lose them. Lost her uterus and ovaries, too. I mean the cancer was everywhere."

Maggie started to cry. Flo and Essie got up from their chairs and fussed around her, then settled back when her tears began to subside.

"I don't know why I can't stop crying," Maggie said apologetically.

"You got a right," Flo said.

Essie nodded. "You cry all you want."

"That's just it," Maggie said. "I don't want to cry. It'll only make me sick." She laughed sharply. "Listen to that. I'm so sick with cancer I got to have an operation—I might not even wake up—"

"Oh, no. Oh, no."

"—it's possible—and here I am worrying I'll give myself a stomach-ache from crying."

"You want a little more whiskey in your glass?" Essie asked.

"You think I should? I already had more than I'm used to."

"Well, I always say you got to have a little something to take the blues away."

"Well, maybe just a drop."

"I mean if a person who's got the kind of worries you got can't have a little drink, who can have a little drink?"

"What worries me most is how I'm going to pay for all this."

"Don't they have hospitalization down at the laundromat?"

"They used to have. But then it got so expensive they had to change the policy they had. The employees had a choice. They could take fewer benefits and not have to pay, or they could get extended coverage and pay half the premiums."

"So what did you take?"

"Well, I figured at my age I should take the extended coverage."

"That was smart."

Maggie stared at Essie wide-eyed. "Only I missed a couple of payments and they dropped me."

"You went back on the other policy without the premium, didn't you?"

"I tried to but they said I'd have to take another examination. That's when the doctor found the shadow."

"The cancer?"

"That's right, the shadow."

"So?" Flo asked, knowing something not so good was coming next.

"So the company wouldn't give me the insurance."

"Why not?"

"I had the shadow."

"You mean your doctor wouldn't give you a clean bill of health until you got your insurance?"

"He said he couldn't do something like that. It would be unethical."

"The money they charge is what's unethical."

"He said there are agencies will take care of the expense."

"What agency? What does he know about it?" Flo demanded as though the doctor were right there under her baleful glare. "My sister knew this woman—"

"The one they peeled like a banana?" Essie asked.

"This other woman. Had to have an amputation. Bad circulation from having the diabetes. She had to go to the charity ward."

"They don't call it charity anymore," Essie pointed out. "They call it welfare."

"I don't give a damn what they call it," Flo burst out, angry as hell and scared to death, seeing herself in Maggie's shoes, in the woman's shoes who lost her breasts, in the woman's shoes who lost her leg. "I call it charity. My mother died in a charity ward, swimming in her own pee and nobody to bring her a glass of water."

Maggie's tears rushed forth again, like turning on a tap in the sink.

She could have wrung out the sopping wad of paper toweling. Essie hurried over to the roller to tear off another handful and came back to give them to Maggie and tell her it wasn't that way anymore. They all sat there fearing that it was just that way and worse what with everybody having gone mad for money, doctors charging sixty dollars just to take your pulse, dentists charging two hundred to pull a tooth, hospitals charging five dollars for an aspirin.

"I got a little put away nobody knows about," Maggie said after the tears had let up for a minute. "Don't you worry about me, I won't be laying there in some ward like your mother had to do, Flo. That's not going to happen to me. Not if I can help it. I've got something put away. I've got thirty-seven hundred dollars put away. If I live through the operation, that should last me till I'm on my feet."

"My God," Essie exclaimed appreciatively, "how did you ever save up that much, the salary you make?"

"Thirty-seven hundred dollars," Flo said. "Hospitals cost seven hundred fifty dollars a day nowadays."

Essie made a face at her to shut up, then glanced sideways to see if Maggie had caught it. Maggie was looking fit to kill at Flo, hating her at that moment for taking the wind out of her brave sails.

"Well," she said, taking a swallow of her drink, *"Key Sara, Sara."*

Cowboy Frabotta was a bald-headed man with hands like hams, a voice like hail on a tin roof and a body without a neck. He'd driven taxis in New York, Chicago, Miami and Los Angeles for fifty years but he'd never ridden a horse in his life. They called him Cowboy because of his short bandy legs and his recklessness behind the wheel. He'd been lifted out of a five-car wreck on the Golden State Freeway three years before. They were willing to pension him off but he asked them what the fuck they expected him to do with himself all day, sit around and play with his pudding?

His way of expressing himself endeared him to everyone. The drivers all said that Cowboy liked to act like a sonofabitch but was a pussycat underneath. There was no real evidence that this was so, it was merely an article of faith. Actually, Cowboy was a narrow-minded, mean-spirited, bad-tempered bastard who held himself in check only because of a mitigating sense of stern justice.

He allowed his drivers their sleepers, their occasional journeys off the flag, their barters with hookers, their nighthawking, as long as they replaced the gas, when the cab was supposed to be in the barn. But he didn't allow them to think they were putting one over on him. If he braced anybody for his sins he expected a humble confession and a piece of the action if the action was spendable or hockable. He didn't, for instance, expect ten percent of a whore's services.

He couldn't stand a man trying to brazen it out with him.

"You think you got the highway cops bamboozled, Billy Ray?"

"What do you mean bamboozled? What's to bamboozle? I walk away from the wreck, so you're pissed off at me?"

"They make you blow into the balloon?"

"They don't ask me to blow in the balloon. I'm all bloody. My teeth are knocked out. They got more heart than that."

"They take you to the station?"

"They take me to emergency. You got it all there on that report. Why're you asking me what you already know?"

"I got this report. Now I want the story."

"There isn't any story."

Cowboy grinned because Ray sounded so funny without his teeth.

"What the hell're you grinning at?" Billy Ray said, though he knew very well what Cowboy was grinning at and merely wanted to make him stop doing it.

"I'm grinning at the wool you're trying to pull over my eyes."

"What the hell—"

"The way you're trying to snow an old snowbird," Cowboy said a little louder.

"—you saying? You saying—"

"I'm too old a cat to be fucked by a kitten," Cowboy said, his voice louder still.

"—I'm trying to . . ." Ray subsided.

Cowboy could see the wheels turning behind Ray's eyes. He sat there giving Ray a chance to cop, to tell him the truth, to throw himself on his mercy.

"I'm telling you exactly what happened," Ray said stubbornly.

"What were you doing on that end of Mulholland at that hour?"

"I had a fight with the wife. I went to sleep on the couch and I woke up in the middle of the goddam night. So I went up on Mulholland to take a ride to the beach."

"Maybe have a gander at the moon?"

"Yeah, maybe that."

"Then how come you got a false alarm marked on your trip sheet here?"

Sonofabitch, Ray thought, that's what he got for letting somebody else work his schemes for him. That goddam Panama Heath told him to make an entry to explain why he was up there that time of the morning. It was a foolish thing to do, because first of all who'd believe a customer called him direct at home and who'd believe the customer wasn't there when he showed up and who'd believe . . . Shit!

He made himself a promise then and there. He'd never let anybody make up his lies for him again.

"I can explain that," he said.

Cowboy waited.

"I have this argument with the wife and I go in to sleep on the couch just like I said and I can't sleep and I get to wondering what the fuck am I doing sleeping on the couch in my own house instead of in there doing boom-boom with the little woman and that gets me to thinking about this friend I got up on Mulholland, a retired whore what gives great New Orleans head—"

"What's the hell's New Orleans head?"

"If you never had any, I couldn't describe it. But I could maybe arrange for you to get a little sample."

Cowboy noted the bribe. Maybe Ray was getting ready to spill his guts. He waited.

Ray went through his story and found the spot where he'd left off.

"So that's why I was up on Mulholland."

"Why'd you mark it on your trip sheet?"

"I figured I wanted something in case a road inspector flagged me down and asked some questions. So afterwards I decide to go home but first I decide to get a breath of sea air and that's when this animal runs across the road right in front of me."

"You got instructions never to brake for small animals," Cowboy said.

"I know that. But I forgot. It was instinctive. I just jerked the wheel a little and there I was, going over the side. Jesus Christ. Am I lucky that bunch of trees was there."

"That's the story you told the highway patrol?"

"That's the truth."

"Okay, so you bamboozled the law but I don't know if you can bamboozle the insurance adjusters."

"How do you figure that? What's to get them in an uproar? There can't be twelve, fourteen hundred dollars' worth of damage to the hack, maybe two hundred for winching it up out of the canyon, maybe a hundred for the tow. You think they're going to send out a company dick for a bone and a half?"

"They might. Then there's the health insurance."

"I'm not kiting any bills. I'm not trying to make a score. What you see is the damage I got to claim. What the dentist says needs fixing'll all be on the up and up. Why would they question a true story and a legitimate claim?"

"Well, they might do when they find out you was fired."

Billy Ray sat there with his ruined mouth wide open. He couldn't believe his ears. Why would Cowboy want to do such a thing? Why was he sitting there with the little shit-eating grin on his face looking like Humpty Dumpty? Was he just playing cat and mouse, having himself a little fun? Goddammit, everybody had a little fun at his expense. What did he have? An acting career that was nothing, a mother that was always trying to cop little feels, a wife that was fucking the police force and a losing streak that had him three bones in the hole to the meanest sonofabitchin' juiceman in the city. Why should he keep on taking it? Why should he just squat there and let everybody shit on his head?

"You got any additions or amendments, Billy Ray?"

"I told you the way it happened. What else do you want me to say?"

Cowboy sighed. "Well, that's that. You better give me your badge."

Ray ripped the cabbie's badge off his hat and threw it on Cowboy's desk.

"Shove it up your ass."

"I wish you hadn't said that. I was about to say I was giving you a week's severance—"

"It's supposed to be two weeks."

"A week's severance. I was keeping the other week for not bringing criminal charges against you for illegal possession and abuse of a company vehicle. Now you can just walk out that door empty."

Ray wanted to let go and cry but he wouldn't give Cowboy that. He turned around and went to the door.

"Hey, hey, Billy Ray," Cowboy crooned softly, "you get any second thoughts, you get any ideas, you come on back and see me, you hear?"

Pachoulo was irritable. He'd been forced to leave his favorite booth in Benito's. That's not to say anybody physically took it over. Who'd be dumb enough or crazy enough to do that? No, he'd had to take a seat at the big round table closest to the kitchen where the owners, cooks, waiters, kitchen help and busboys gathered to divvy up the tips, have a glass of red and chew the fat at the end of a hard day, because there were just too many people to fit into the booth.

There was Sam's Man; Manny Machado; Iggie Deetch; the four Nicoletti brothers, Guido, Antonio, Benedetto and Ugo; their lawyer, Harry Spain; and their accountant, Gypsy Podhertz.

Also there was Taffy Boyd, Helena's candy man, who'd come early in the day to ask why Pachoulo wouldn't extend Helena any more credit and was still hanging around.

He giggled almost every time somebody spoke to him. It was a terrible habit for a dealer. It made him seem untrustworthy. A lot of people thought he was certifiable anyway. Some said that except for his brain stem, which moved his arms and legs and triggered the giggle, his mind had been burned away from sniffing, shooting, swallowing and shoving up his ass every substance known to man.

Ask him and he'd tell you about highs he'd had from packing red pepper or smoking dried bananas.

"So how come you don't let her have a little small change, Puffy?"

"What do you care, I squeeze off her cash flow?"

Boyd giggled. "We was in bed together and I was feeling tender and she asked me to ask you, so I'm asking you. But, tell you the truth, I don't give a rat's ass you don't extend her any more credit at the moment. But down the road, a week, maybe two weeks, her ass is no longer going to interest me—"

"It surprises me it interests you at all," Pachoulo interrupted.

"Hey, you know what she looks like. A woman like that could make a stiff get a hard-on. But down the line, a week—"

"Maybe two weeks."

"That's right. How'd you know what I was going to say? Jesus, Puffy, you're really something. I mean I can't take it out in trade forever. I can't pay the rent with her ass. I can't buy beans with her ass."

"Why not?"

"Why not what?"

"Why can't you turn her ass out on the street? You got her hooked, you got her in your palm. Tell her, she needs the price, to go out and shake it on the stroll."

"Well, I'll tell you why. I'm into pharmacology, I'm not a pimp, and I figure every dog should chew on his own bone. How come you don't turn her out? I hear you're spreading your wings."

"I got business with her husband, who's walking over here even as we speak. Do I got to tell you?"

"Introduce me as your cousin from Jersey. Introduce me as your corner druggist. You don't mind I sit around, have a glass of wine?"

"As long as you don't fucking giggle all the time or fall asleep in the spaghetti."

So Taffy Boyd was at the table when Allan Nadeau came to sit down. Then the Nicoletti brothers and their advisers came. So everybody had to move out of the booth to the round table by the kitchen.

When a bunch of guineas get together, Nadeau thought, you could either drown in the spray from so many mouths flapping or get your eye poked out with a gesticulating finger. That's not to say all Italians acted that way. Like there were Jews and kikes, Irishmen and micks, there were Italians and guineas. The Italians he'd worked with on construction deals before had been grand signores, impeccably groomed, soft-spoken and courteous. These Nicoletti brothers shouted at each other and slapped everybody on the back hard enough to crack a rib, ate as much pasta as Pachoulo, though not as much as Sam's Man, and generally caused an uproar.

"All right," Pachoulo said, "we all had to eat. Everybody's glass is filled? Okay. Now we talk about what we do next."

He looked to Nadeau, who had not originated this deal but had been called in by Pachoulo to steer the ship. His up-front fee was the write-off of his debt with Pachoulo and all that Helena owed the juiceman. He was also in for ten percent of the profits on the actual construction, Pachoulo not being so stupid as to be unwilling to pay for expert management.

The bad part was that Nadeau felt like Pachoulo's creature, bought and paid for. Not with cash. But the victim of his own corruption.

"So, counselor?" Pachoulo said, prompting Nadeau again.

"How is the permit process going?" Nadeau asked.

"The permits've been in our pocket before we even had the architects start the drawings," Guido said. "All this business with the planning commission and city council hearings is just waltzing around, you know what I mean?"

"We start the bulldozers the minute we got the down," Antonio said.

"You can't turn the engines on, dig a couple shovels, without you got all the up-front money?" Pachoulo asked.

"How does that work?" Ugo said, flat-eyed.

"You mean how do you turn on the engines?" Pachoulo asked.

"How do we turn them on we don't have any gasoline?" Ugo said, not cracking a smile, all his loud friendly talk and laughter tucked away in his vest pocket. "I think you're getting funny with us, Mr. Pachoulo. Before Mr. Nadeau puts us in touch with the Doohans, we was talking to the Christiano brothers about financing the whole deal."

"They'd want your pants."

"They wouldn't get our pants. They'd put up the money and we'd put up some buildings. Everybody makes out a little."

"So my friend Nadeau here shows you how to make a lot."

"We appreciate. But we don't appreciate all of a sudden you want us to turn on the engines without we got the first construction money in the bank. We come here thinking you wanted a piece of the proposition personally."

"I wasn't showing any disrespect," Pachoulo said soothingly, "I was just asking. It's no crime to ask this and that, is it?"

"No crime," Ugo said.

"So how much more do you need?"

"Three hundred thousand," Nadeau said.

"So, there you go. It's not that I don't trust Al here," Pachoulo said. "It's just I want to get the skinny from the horse's mouth before I lend any more of my money to these micks."

Nadeau hid his surprise. It was the first he'd heard about the Doohans borrowing any more money.

"Now I know," Pachoulo went on. "I trust what you say, Mr. Nicoletti. These micks come to me again, I got three hundred large they can have. For a price."

Nadeau saw it then. Pachoulo had no real interest in the automotive park. He'd asked for this meeting not because he wanted to see if maybe he could make a little investment of his own in the project, like he'd said. He was a juiceman, first, last and always, and that's what he understood and believed in. Usury he could understand. He was charging the kind of interest the Bank of America would kill for, and if the Doohans could be talked into another loan, larger than the first, they'd have to put up something substantial to secure it. Their business, their homes, their honor and maybe their lives. If they were greedy enough. If they took the cherry.

"It's too soon to go back to them for more," Nadeau said. "It would be easier for me to raise it elsewhere."

"You ask them," Pachoulo said complacently. "You ask them and they don't want to come to me for the loan, we do what you say."

"How come you don't invest yourself, Mr. Pachoulo?" Ugo said.

"It's not my business," Pachoulo said. He slapped Taffy Boyd on the shoulder and Boyd giggled. "My friend here was only just saying before you came that he thinks every dog should chew on his own bone."

After another glass of wine and a handshake all around, the Nicoletti brothers left.

"I hate these chairs," Pachoulo said, getting to his feet. "Now we can go back to the regular table."

"Can I have a minute?" Nadeau said.

"Sure. The rest of you stay here," Pachoulo said.

The two of them settled into the semicircular booth while the others stayed behind at the littered table.

Nadeau leaned across his folded arms and practically whispered, as though he believed the walls had ears.

"What's the hidden agenda?"

"Agenda? What is this agenda?"

"What's the game?"

"Why do you want to know what's the game?"

"I don't like to run around blindfolded."

"You got your game, I got mine. You got this automobile park, I got the Doohans' distributorship."

"What for? You don't want to be in the construction business, why do you want to be in the automobile business?"

"I know cars better than I know buildings."

"What else?"

"I need a laundry."

"Oh."

"So 'oh.' You think you know all about it now?"

"I don't want to know."

"You don't want a piece of the action?"

"I don't want anything."

"I always knew you was very smart. Maybe that's why I like you."

"Mr. Pachoulo," a woman's soft voice said.

They'd been so deep in conversation, practically nose to nose, they hadn't heard Ana Checks walk across the carpet.

Pachoulo started to get to his feet, nearly knocking over the candle in the wine bottle, momentarily forgetting himself, King Pachoulo, holding court, tossed back in a startled moment to when he was a child, fearfully polite to the pale-faced nuns at St. Rose of Lima Catholic school.

The way Ana Checks looked, Nadeau almost made the same connection. Black dress, hair almost hidden beneath a black pillbox hat with a narrow white band around her brow, hands folded beneath her breasts, white face, colorless lips that were as thin and straight as a blade.

Pachoulo remembered he wasn't a little boy anymore but, for some reason, still couldn't get himself to sit down. He crouched there, half sitting, half standing, trapped by the table edge, first sticking out his hand as though to shake hers, then gesturing with it when she failed to take it, inviting her to sit down.

"Mrs. Checks?" he said.

"Mrs. Chempenovsky," Ana replied.

"Would you like something? A glass of wine?"

"I am not here looking for hospitality."

"Sit down, sit down," Pachoulo said, but she just kept standing there. He finally got his legs working and sat down himself.

"What are you here for, Mrs. Chempenovsky?" Nadeau asked.

"I am managing my husband's business for a little while. He hasn't been feeling well." There wasn't the slightest hint of reproach in her voice. It was as neutral and unemotional as a still puddle of water in the street. "I am looking for a man by the name of Iggie Deetch. I was told that where Mr. Pachoulo was, Mr. Deetch could usually be found."

"That's Iggie over there," Pachoulo said, thrusting his chin out toward the table where Deetch, Sam's Man and Machado sat around while Boyd dealt out a hand of cards. She turned her whole body to look where his chin was pointing. "The one with the ears sticking out."

Pachoulo looked at Nadeau and made a face as though asking what the hell this woman was doing. She'd sat there while her naked husband had been beaten and pissed on without a flicker, now here she was waltzing into the place where the men who did that to her husband were sitting around and asked a dumb favor like Pachoulo should point out who was Iggie Deetch.

"You don't mind my asking," Pachoulo said, "what for do you want to see Iggie Deetch?"

"The horse players come to the house putting down bets on a horse they call Becalmed. Too much money for us to cover the bets on this one horse. If it wins we could be ruined, Benny and me. Everything we have worked for all these years could be in danger."

"Pardon me for saying so, but I hear stories around town that you've got property here and property there," Pachoulo said.

Ana looked at Nadeau, as though knowing him to be the one who would have told such tales, breaking the trust between lawyer and client.

She had no respect for him. Nadeau could feel her contempt flowing from her in thin, icy sheets, but she never copped. Her eyelids never flickered and her lips never curled. She just glanced at him once, like a small slap in his face, then turned her pale gaze back to the man who'd done horrors to her husband. Had stolen his manhood. Had maybe even taken his mind away.

"I've got property," she said. "I mean to keep it. That is why I am here to ask Mr. Deetch if he can tell me of a bookie who would like to share the bets."

"You don't got to bother talking to Deetch," Pachoulo said. "It ain't my usual game but I could help you out. I could take whatever you want to lay off."

"You don't even know how much it is."

"I can cover it, don't you worry."

"Ten thousand dollars."

"That's no problem. How much you want me to cover?"

She went into her black bag and came out with a stack of money wrapped in a brown paper band and secured with an elastic. She turned it over and they could see the white betting slips all neatly gathered on the other side, the money and the bets tied together face to face. She laid the bundle in Pachoulo's fat hands.

"You sure you won't have a glass of wine?" he asked.

"Perhaps another time," Ana said and suddenly smiled a smile that was sweet and tremulous, the smile of a young woman flirting just a little.

Pachoulo counted off a thousand dollars and handed it back to Ana. Her brows lifted and her eyes widened.

"Your commission."

"Win or lose?"

"That's the way it works. I always play fair."

It's a wonder his tongue doesn't fall out of his mouth, Nadeau thought.

Ana nodded and put the money in her purse. Then she walked away.

As she passed the table where Machado and Sam's Man were at their game of cards, Machado reached out a folded ten-dollar bill. "Here you go, sister," he said.

She missed a step, paused, took the bill, ducked her head as though in blessing and hurried on across the restaurant and out the door.

"You look at that? Manny don't even recognize her."

"Why would he recognize her?" Nadeau said. "He wasn't knocking her around."

Pachoulo scarcely heard him. He was still in a state of wonder at her appearance in his place of business.

"How can you figure?" he said. "I have her husband pissed on and she waltzes in here and hands me ten large, just like that."

"What about the horse?"

"It ain't got a prayer."

41

Francis Michael Fitzsimmons was on the front page of the newspaper more than the mayor, more than the governor. He was practically on the front page more than the president. Sometimes he shared photo opportunities with the mayor or the governor. Once the president shared a photo opportunity with him.

You didn't have to be a political maven to know that he was running hard for high public office. He just hadn't declared himself or identified the brass ring he was reaching for.

Whenever his face failed to appear in the *L.A. Times* for more than three days running, he called another strategy session with the top police brass or, when that failed to make the news, gathered the troops around him down at Rampart for what he liked to call skull sessions. As though they were his football team and he was their coach preparing them for the big game against a traditional rival. He'd had two of those so far and was in the middle of a third. After the first time, there was always plenty of media.

"I want to tell you people," Fitzsimmons said, "that we're making progress. You've been out there collecting the data and stirring up the pond. Let me tell you, some interesting creatures are floating up to the surface. It's becoming pretty clear that the drug operations, the mule running and the heavy dealing, the vice operations, the prostitution and the pornography, the crimes of violence for profit, burglary, hijacking and B and E, are financed by the profits from illegal gambling and loan-sharking."

"Do tell," Monk said under his breath. "All he had to do was come ask one of us, we could have told him."

"Gambling's a mess the state's going to have to get into sooner or later. They've got to figure a way to convince the consumers out there that the lottery's a better buy than half a buck put down on a number at the corner candy store. We'll give them all the information we collect and what help we can, but they've got the laws and regulations and they'll have to lead the attack."

"Shit, I didn't know it was that easy," Monk mumbled.

"But this other mess, the juice racket, is ours."

"I don't want it. You want it, Panama?" Monk asked.

"Oh, for chrissake, I got to listen to him and you, too? Button up."

"So, instead of working from the outside, hassling the runners, the pimps, the whores, the burglars and other assorted gonnifs, we're going to work from the inside out. We're going after the big juicemen, the *bankers of crime*."

"See, like that," Monk said. "You see how he took a little wait there, lifted his head up, and hit that last bit there? That's a line the reporters and TV anchors can do something with. It's got a ring to it."

"I hear' it before," Missy said.

"That don't matter. In fact if it's not original it makes it better. Everybody remembers it but they don't know where they remember it so they think maybe it's something they thought up themselves. Or if they do remember it, they said it so many times they *think* they made it up themselves. Like that line Dirty Harry said in that picture. 'Make my day.' The writer who wrote that line didn't think it up. He heard it somewhere. I heard it a long time before Dirty Harry said it. But he said it and then a hundred million people said it so everybody—"

"Jesus Christ, Monk, you're worse than Fitzsimmons up there," Heath said. "You two could give courses on how to talk for an hour and not say anything. What the hell you rattling on for? Something got you nervous?"

"More like something's got you nervous," Monk said.

"Well, now that you mention, something's got me a little nervous."

"Like what?"

When Heath answered, he was talking to Monk, his old friend, but he was looking at Missy.

"I got a roommate."

"You mean a live-in?"

"That's what I mean."

"Anybody I know?"

"Lisa Kubiak. Lisa Ray."

Heath saw Missy's eyelids flicker a little but that was as much as she showed.

"So you took my advice and it did the trick, huh?" she said.

"What trick?"

"Took care of your nerves."

"Well, goddammit, you don't have to make it sound like she's a dose of medicine."

"Hey, buster, I tell you go get the joy juice outta your system. I don' tell you to buy the whole enchilada."

"Why do you have to talk dirty like that? Joy Juice. I mean, for chrissake."

"You talk the way you wanna talk an' I'll talk the way I wanna talk." Missy moved away, squeezing herself between two big cops, one of whom looked down at the pressure of her body as she passed and widened his eyes.

"Don' you say it, wise guy," Missy growled, and kept on going until she was well away from Heath and Monk.

"What was that all about?" Heath asked.

"I warned you," Monk said. "You can never say I didn't warn you."

"Warned me about what?"

"You know goddam what. Missy's got the hots."

"For what?"

"For your hat, you silly sonofabitch."

Up on the platform, Fitzsimmons was finishing up.

"So all I can tell you, boys and girls . . ."

"That's cute," Heath mumbled.

". . . is to go out there and do more of what you're doing. It won't be long now."

He raised his arms above his head as though he were a political candidate on the campaign trail accepting applause and cheers. All he got was the shuffling of feet as the cops and detectives made it over to the coffeepot to see if they could wring out one more cup before going out on the streets and a rising din of conversation as they competed to tell each other about their troubles with the wife, the kids and their hemorrhoids.

"Do you think they're losing their enthusiasm, Buck?" Fitzsimmons asked Choola.

"I think you're keeping them inspired."

"I hope so. If the general doesn't show himself to the troops now and then they start to lose heart. You'll be at the party tonight?"

"I wouldn't miss it for the world."

"I'm glad to hear you say that. I admire your administration skills, Buck. I may have a proposition to put to you tonight. We'll see what kind of a crowd we get."

He waved a hand to the assembled cops, all of whom were either out the door or standing around with their backs to him, and charged off the platform as though problems of great moment awaited him.

"I thought the way that bit goes is the general's supposed to show himself out on the line where the troops are getting shot at," Gunnar Norenson said wryly.

"With that black streak in that white hair somebody could mistake him for a skunk and shoot him between the eyes."

"A skunk's white on black, not black on white, but I get your meaning. You think he means to announce?"

"Announce for what?"

"That I couldn't say. I don't know how high that sucker thinks he can jump."

"I think he thinks he's got springs in his knees."

"What do you think?"

"I think I'm going to that party tonight and be as nice as I can be."

"Me too."

"You don't have to sit scrunched up against the door that way," Heath said.

"I'm not your girlfrien'. Wha' you wan' me to do? Sit in your lap?"

"Why are you being so goddam unfriendly? You tell me to sleep with Lisa and find out where my head's at and then you carry on like this."

"Whatta you think, I'm Dr. Ruth? You think I tell you to do something, you're supposed to go ahead and do it?"

"Well, a pal gives you good advice—"

"What the hell's this pal? Nex' thing you know you'll be callin' me buddy. I ain' your pal an' I ain' your buddy."

Heath pulled the car over to the curb, set the brake and shut off the engine.

"You're my partner. You're the cop I walk around with. We're joined at the hip, babe, you like it or not. You don't like it, we talk to Becker and get him to team you with that Kelly. I'll get Monk back. That's the way it should have been in the first place. I don't know which bonehead dreamed up this business of splitting up teams that have been working together for years. Whoever it was should be put away. I can't work with a partner who's always got a wild hair up her ass—"

"Why you talkin' dirty?"

"See? Like that. There you go. You go talking dirty to me, it's okay. I forget myself and say something and you push out your tits to show me you're a lady. You grab me by the buns and give 'em a shake and tell me I should try it on with you someday, but if I grabbed you by the buns and started trying you'd go screaming rape."

"Why don' you try it an' see?"

"What's that?"

"You don' hear so good, either?"

"Huh?"

She slid across the seat. When she put her mouth on his a little spark of static snapped. He jerked his head back.

"Too bad," she said. "We could've been hot stuff."

42

It was one of those fund-raisers attended by a crowd that was, in the words of One-Potato Sharkey—who remembered the great days of Hague in Jersey City and Daley in Chicago—"small but cherce."

The mayor was the highest-ranking official in the room but wasn't getting much of the attention since his was clearly a falling star and this youngster, Fitzsimmons, was a star on the rise.

The purpose of the gathering was to raise some money and to give a good many people their first chance to meet the wonderboy from the smallest state in the union who'd decided to come live and play in their yard. To size him up. To see if he was a bet to put up against the Republican senator or the Republican governor and wrest the power away.

That's not to say that everybody in the room was nominally a Democrat. There were, in fact, more registered Republicans than otherwise. But these were all the folks who contributed to both parties and publicly embraced all philosophies in the sure knowledge that no matter which side of the street they ended up walking they'd still be picking up most of the loose change.

Nobody even seemed to mind that the rubber chicken, soon to be served, was costing them two hundred dollars a head, plus what they spent at ten dollars a copy at the no-host bar, and they hadn't even been told specifically what the Committee for Democratic Advisories, the sponsors of the shindig, was supposed to espouse. They just knew, without being told, that it would finance some educational project if Fitzsimmons failed to announce for public office and would be the beginning of a campaign war chest when and if he did declare.

Anybody at the party would have a lot of names to drop the next morning, but there were plenty of rank-and-filers and even some new-comers milling around happy to be there even if wondering why.

Plenty of good-looking and distinguished men. Plenty of beautiful and desirable women.

When Nadeau walked in with Helena, pausing briefly at the top of the three steps that led from the landing to the reception hall off the hotel banquet room while Nadeau looked around for Charlie Swale, president of the Historical Buildings Society, the man who had invited him to meet Fitzsimmons, the roar of conversation stopped for a second while everybody looked.

Her body was sheathed in a tube of glittering lamé neck to toes, with just her gorgeous milky arms and neck and her exquisite face rising up above the pillar of gold.

A hundred women turned green. A hundred men felt a twitch in heart or groin.

Fitzsimmons stopped talking in midsentence and stared.

Joseph Doohan put his hands in his pockets, rocked back on his heels and wished that his brothers had been invited to come along to see the unbelievable creature he was poking. He had started across the room toward the Nadeaus when Nadeau spotted Swale.

Nadeau took Helena's elbow in his perfectly manicured hand to make certain she could navigate the three steps without mishap.

Helena's eyes caught Doohan's and she gave an almost imperceptible shake of her head.

Fitzsimmons excused himself and, seeing that Swale was the target of the man escorting the vision, grabbed Swale's elbow and went to meet the woman he meant to fuck before the week was out.

When they met in the middle of the crowd, Swale did the introductions. The guests moved and shifted as though disturbed by a stone thrown into the center of a pond, rearranging themselves so they had a better view of the charmed couple, magically creating a space around them.

There were some who were amused to think that one day Charlie Swale might dine out on the story of how he brought Fitzsimmons and the beauty together. There were some women who felt disappointed while their husbands felt relieved that the white knight had found his lady and taken the possibility of competing for her out of their reach. There were a few who felt sorry for Nadeau.

"Mr. Nadeau," Fitzsimmons said, giving him all his attention as though he was afraid if he looked at Helena he'd knock her down on the parquet floor and take her then and there, "I've been looking forward to this meeting."

"I wasn't even aware that you knew of my existence."

"You underestimate your reputation. Charlie tells me that you're one of the principal developers in the city."

"I don't think of myself as a developer. I'm really no more than an expediter."

"How's that?"

"I bring land, seed money, financing and construction people together."

"Which category does Mr. Pachoulo fall into?"

"Mr. Pachoulo is involved in various enterprises," Nadeau replied without a flicker. "He was raised by a father who believed in confidentiality—"

"His father was a petty criminal. A minor thug."

Nadeau smiled. "I've heard those rumors."

"Rumors? He was arrested a dozen times. It's on the books."

"Charged but never indicted."

"Was he a client?"

"He was long before my time."

"But his son—what do they call him—?"

"Puffy."

"His son, Puffy, is a client of yours?"

"He's asked me to draw up a few contracts, assess proposals, and consulted me in other business matters."

"Doubtful business matters?"

"Every deal I've ever been asked to advise upon has been legitimate."

"Then you don't make a habit of consorting with Mr. Pachoulo's type?"

"He's an uneducated man. Self-made. Is that the type you mean?"

"I suppose your practice isn't entirely made up of Mr. Pachoulo's type?" Fitzsimmons went on as though Nadeau hadn't even spoken.

"Everyone is entitled to counsel," Nadeau said evenly.

"I know the principle, Mr. Nadeau. After all, I've been trained in the law myself."

"But no longer practice it."

Fitzsimmons smiled a smile white enough to match his hair. He turned to Helena, touching Swale on the back as he did so.

"This talk must be annoying to you, Mrs. Nadeau."

"Oh, no," Helena said.

Charlie Swale, old pol that he was, caught the signal and, grabbing Nadeau by the arm, moved him away and across the room on the pretense that there were several members of the society he wanted Nadeau to meet.

A gray-haired man standing next to Doohan said, "Nicely done."

"What did you say?" Joseph asked.

"I was admiring the way Fitzsimmons cut the heifer out of the herd right out from under her bull's nose," he said, gesturing with his head as Fitzsimmons walked Helena toward a side door to a private sitting room, his hand at her back, not touching but merely hovering there as though captured in a magnetic field.

Doohan could hardly keep from telling the man that the beautiful woman everyone was admiring was the woman who spent time with him in a certain hot-pillow motel at least once a week, sometimes more.

"Well, no harm, I don't suppose," the man went on. "The young woman's beautiful, the husband's intelligent and ambitious, I'm sure, and Fitzsimmons is soon to be a power."

They watched as Fitzsimmons disappeared through the door behind Helena.

Doohan glanced over to the group where Nadeau and the man who was holding on to his elbow had finally parked and saw Nadeau watching what he was watching. Then Nadeau looked at Doohan and something passed between them. Doohan couldn't say exactly what but the closest he could come was that Nadeau felt ashamed yet somehow triumphant.

Nadeau raised his hand and made a gesture, pointing to the entrance, then disengaged his arm, excused himself from the group and sauntered over that way, timing it so that he reached the three steps at about the same time Doohan reached them.

"I hope you don't mind, Joseph, I invited you here to talk a little business."

"Why should I mind you treat me to a two–hundred–dollar meal?"

"Don't thank me until you taste the chicken."

"So what's the business?"

"The Nicoletti brothers hit some unforeseen problems right after they started the excavation."

"They did? How come they didn't tell us?"

"They hit underground water sooner than they expected."

"The geologists didn't know it was there?"

"The geologists don't know everything."

"So what's it mean?"

"It means they have to raise more money before they can go ahead. The city and county permits hadn't cleared when they started. They were just formalities, but now they could be delayed."

"Except somebody gets paid off?"

"No, nothing like that. They have to prove to the commission that they have the funds to put in the necessary stanchions, sump and sump pumps and can successfully cap off the underground stream if that's what they find out is causing the flood."

"How much are we talking about?"

"Two hundred fifty thousand."

Doohan was tight–lipped and pale. He felt like you might feel when you walk into the dark hallway of your house and all of a sudden a light shines in your face, somebody puts a gun in your belly and tells you that he wants your money or he'll shoot you.

"Where you going to get the money? Those investors still lined up and waiting like you said?"

"That's a problem. Something like this flooding in the excavation happens, everybody puts his money back in his pocket and looks the other way. They figure who needs problems so early in the game."

"It could kill the project?"

"Well, the Nicoletti brothers aren't going to let that happen. They know how to fix it, whatever it is, no matter how bad it might be."

"So?"

"So it means reorganization. New loan applications. A restructuring of debt and participation."

"Cut to the fucking chase, Al."

"In the absence of other eager money it means the principal investor has to increase his participation."

"Meaning my brothers and me?"

"That's essentially correct."

"Nobody essentially told us we were the principal investors."

"You never asked."

"You gave us the idea. Everybody gave us the idea."

Nadeau shrugged.

"So now I'm asking," Doohan said, staring at Nadeau's throat, smiling a smile that said his guts were spilling out on the floor and a powerful rage was building up behind his heart.

"It's nothing to panic about," Nadeau said.

"It's not?"

"I've got it covered."

"You have?"

"I've already made inquiries on your behalf."

"To who?"

"To your lender, of course."

"Puffy Pachoulo?"

"He looked the situation over and said he'd be happy to increase your loan."

"Jesus Christ," Doohan said. It sounded more like a prayer than a throwaway. "Why didn't you call a meeting with the Nicolettis and my brothers?"

"The Nicolettis already know the situation. What do you think you'd get from your brothers?"

"What do you mean?"

"What would you get? I'll tell you what you'd get. Nothing but arguments. Your brothers are cautious men. Do I have to tell you? Your brothers followed you out here to California. They never would have done it on their own. Your brothers followed you into the used-car business and the new-car franchise. Without you and your ideas they'd still be switching new tires for old while the customer was in the office signing papers, and packing transmissions with foil to run another thousand miles before they turned to dust."

"I can't commit them to two and a half times what we've already got in it without at least talking it over."

"Let me get to it from another direction," Nadeau said. "Your nuts are in a vise. You don't back up your first bet, you lose the money already in the pot."

"A hundred and thirty-three thousand. Maybe we get a little something back from the Nicolettis when the deal's closed out. Maybe we—"

"There wouldn't be anything coming back from the Nicolettis."

"So we eat it. We tighten our belts and we pay it off on a schedule."

"That's not the way it works. The way it works is that you borrowed a hundred thousand dollars. You pay back one hundred thirty-three thousand in ten months, which would be one hundred fifty-nine thousand six hundred dollars if the loan term was one year, which means the interest rate is fifty-nine point six percent per annum or four point nine two percent a month. So, on a loan of one hundred thousand dollars your obligation is to pay four thousand nine hundred and twenty dollars a month or one thousand two hundred and thirty dollars a week interest."

"You got all the numbers right there in your head, haven't you?" Doohan said, feeling his anger finding a direction, focusing on the sonofabitch standing right there in front of him with his fancy tux with the wing collar and the red tie, red flash handkerchief in his pocket and red satin cummerbund making a splash across his trim gut. Doohan knew all at once that, in this crowd, he looked like an old-fashioned small-time New Jersey politician or mortician, attending a fish fry tossed by the neighborhood Knights of Columbus. Knew that he was out of his depth. That he wasn't and never had been smart enough or ruthless enough to play hardball with the big boys. Knew it when it was too goddam late.

"We'll double up until we got it paid," he said, not believing they could manage it but wanting to hear himself say there was a way out.

"That's not the way it works, Joseph," Nadeau said, looking slightly pained as though something sour had just repeated on him. "You can't pay down the principal a piece at a time. You've got to pay the principal off all at once. You pay the interest every week—"

"We haven't been doing that."

"Mr. Pachoulo understands you're new to this method of banking. He gave you a little grace period. Allowed you to pay by the month. Now the new schedule kicks in. He wants it by the week from now on. You miss a week and there will be penalties."

"We never talked about penalties."

"They're implied. Just like you take money out on a credit card. It's written in the small print."

"I never saw anything written. We never had any paper."

"On the subject," Nadeau said, and pulled a folded sheet of paper out of his pocket. "Here's a promissory note for the two hundred and fifty thousand you want to borrow. No time limit. You just have to pay eighty-three thirty-three a month interest."

"So this time it's by the month, not the week?" Doohan said, his jaws aching from trying to hold a pleasant expression on his face.

"That won't change. It's right here in the agreement."

"You got everything down pat, ain't you?" Doohan said, falling back on the language he'd used when he and his brothers had been the Doohans, terror of the neighborhood.

"I took the trouble to inform myself before bringing this offer to you. I'd never enter a negotiation without knowing all the facts."

Doohan knew that the lawyer was calling him an asshole. He'd roped him into a lousy deal and now he was calling him an asshole for not doing his calculations.

As though he was reading his mind, Nadeau said, "You came to me. I didn't come to you. I never made any business proposals. You asked to have a piece." He put his hand out and gripped Doohan's wrist. "Look, Joseph, for Christ's sake, the deal's still a good deal. All right, you have to walk the wire without a net a little longer than we figured. Who can predict water gushing up out of the ground?"

"How come this time it's on paper? I thought Pachoulo said his interest rates were high because he couldn't have the protection of paper."

"This isn't exactly a legal document. It's more like informal proof that everybody knows what they're obliged to do."

They stared at each other, Nadeau relaxed, Doohan as stiff as a corpse, his mind running around like a squirrel in a cage looking for a way out.

"What you have to do, Joseph, is take a chance," Nadeau said softly.

Doohan was looking over his shoulder. Nadeau wondered if he could persuade him to go along, because one way or another Pachoulo was going to have what he wanted out of Doohan. He already had the harpoon in his heart. All he had to do was winch him in, deck him, shoot him, slaughter and skin him.

"You have to take the chance," he said, "because if you don't you'll be down on your knees looking for pennies in the gutter for the rest of your life."

Something in Doohan's eyes changed. Nadeau couldn't read what was in them. He glanced over his shoulder to look where Doohan was looking, to see what had changed the expression in his eyes. He saw Helena walking a step in front of Fitzsimmons as they threaded their way through the crowd. Then they reached a wider place and Fitzsimmons tucked his arm through Helena's arm so that his hand rested against the side of her breast and he leaned in close to her hair and made some remark which made her laugh and look into his face as though they'd already made some future plans.

Then he knew what he saw in Doohan's eyes. Not the envy of a man who wanted a woman like Helena but thought he'd never have a chance of getting one but the jealousy of a man who saw another man poaching on his territory. He felt a suffocating dose of the same jealousy and almost overpowering rage. Then it was past. He was holding out the paper, apparently waiting to consummate the loan arrangement, cool and businesslike, above it all. He hoped Doohan wouldn't notice that his hand was trembling.

But he did, and a look passed between them that practically said it all. Now there were few secrets between them. They were locked into a dance and they knew it, no way to escape for either of them.

Some of the heat of the day was still left over as the night came down on the Valley.

Phil Doohan stood in front of the first rank of used Porsches, BMWs and Cadillacs, wondering if he shouldn't talk to Joseph again about

wholesaling out all the American cars they took in trade, even the luxury models. He thought it looked better for people to see nothing but
top-of-the-line foreign makes on the lot. Their dealership was Porsche,
their image was German. Okay, maybe the BMWs, a Jaguar, a Rolls
wasn't so bad. They made the point that their customers were very
special. But Caddies and Continentals should be shuffled off. They
ruined the look. The ambience.

He even hated it when a cheap compact or a standard make came
driving up to the curb. Like the goddam Chevy that was pulling up
right that minute. Ten years old. Almost a wreck. He started walking over, figuring out what he could say to get them on their way.
Tire kickers. Looky-loos, that breed of bird that made it an evening
out going around drooling over items they could never afford.

He pasted a welcoming grin on his face when he saw who it was
who got out of the car. "Hey, there, Panama," he said.

Heath walked around and opened the door for the woman in the car
with him.

"How's it going, Phil? Selling plenty?"

"By the dozens," he said, looking the woman over. Not bad. No
knockout but pretty enough. Looked tired though. "Out for some
fresh air?"

"Have to drive a hundred miles," the woman said.

"This is Lisa. Lisa, meet Phil," Heath said.

Pleased-to-meet-yous passed between them, Phil reaching out his
hand and squeezing hers.

"You're right. The air's been pretty bad. But I think a breeze could
be kicking up any minute now."

Lisa stood there smiling politely, looking at the line of glittering vehicles under the lights, just standing there as women do while the men
talk about a lot of nothing. Finally she wandered off and started peering
into the interior of this car and that.

"So that's the wife, then?"

"No. I'm not married," Heath replied. "Didn't I mention that?"

"Maybe you did. I don't remember. So you were just taking a drive
and saw me standing out front here and stopped to say hello?"

"Lisa needs a car. I saw you standing out here, like you say, and
thought I'd ask you did you know anyplace we could get her some
transportation."

"Well, it was nice for you to do that. I don't have to ask, you're not talking about an upscale vehicle? Nothing like a Porsche or a Beamer?"

"No, nothing like that," Heath said, and laughed.

"Nothing basic like the one you drove up in, either?"

"I think we can try for something a little better than that."

"That your undercover heap?"

"Something like that."

"I haven't got anything on the lot. You can understand that."

Heath nodded.

"I don't even want to keep the Caddies and Lincolns here. I'd rather push them out to other dealers. Joseph has a fondness for them. Don't ask me why."

"They're big."

"I'll give you that. And ride like a boat. Like driving around in an air-conditioned womb."

"Some people wouldn't think that was so bad." He was watching Lisa, who had stopped to look at a light tan Cadillac Seville. "That model's not too big, is it?"

Phil looked around. "No, the Sevilles are small. Plenty of luxury though."

"What year?"

"That little baby? Eighty-one. Only reason a car that old's even on the lot, let alone in the first rank, is that Joseph likes to drive it around. Likes it handy for quick errands."

"What kind of quick errands?"

"I don't know. This and that."

"Like going down to the X-rated motels on Lankershim in the afternoon?"

"I don't know about that. What are you talking about?"

"I'm talking about your brother's got a thing going with a woman by the name of Helena Nadeau."

"How the hell you know that?"

"For chrissake, I'm a cop, Phil. What do you think I do all day, hang around eating tacos with Missy and playing pocket pool?"

"Well, my brother doesn't tell me everything he does like what you just said, but he hasn't got a wife and I suppose a man'll go out and take care of what he needs one way or another."

"I don't object. I'm just wondering if he knows that this woman's married to a lawyer."

"I think he might've mentioned that."

"Who does business with a juiceman by the name of Puffy Pachoulo?"

"I don't know what is this juiceman."

"Don't fuck with me, Phil. You know what is a juiceman."

"Uh-huh."

"You heard of one by the name of Puffy Pachoulo?"

"I don't think so."

"You sure now, Phil?"

"I think I'd remember a name like that. What's it all about, Panama?"

"It's not about anything at the moment. I'm just looking here and looking there."

"The ways cops do."

"That's right. The way cops do. Pachoulo isn't a very nice man. We could be maybe picking him up and asking him some questions one of these days."

"Thanks for telling me."

"I'm not telling you anything you shouldn't know. I just thought, what with your brother seeing this lawyer's wife and him being the lawyer for this Pachoulo, your brother wouldn't want to get caught with his pants down in case we had to ask him some questions."

"About this lawyer's wife, you mean."

"About her and maybe about her husband which leads to Pachoulo, one way you look at it."

"Your wife—"

"I'm not married. Didn't I tell you?"

"Sure. What's wrong with me. It looks like your lady friend really likes that little Seville."

"It's a peach, but I was really thinking of something less expensive."

"I don't know what you can get less expensive than an eighty-one that'll give you any service. Five thousand sound like a lot?"

"Is that blue book?"

"Way below blue book."

"How about financing?"

"I could make that very easy. Why don't we go into the office and talk about it?"

44

Joseph Doohan had no opportunity to speak to Helena without somebody around for even a minute until after the dinner and the speeches were over. Until the gathering started to break up. Until Fitzsimmons squeezed Helena's hand and gave her a last good-bye that really meant later before walking off with his aides and bodyguards, already looking presidential, or at least gubernatorial. Until Nadeau went off to retrieve her wrap and left her standing beside a pillar on the landing checking the contents of her little purse.

"We didn't even get a minute," Doohan said.

"Oh, hello, Joseph. No, we didn't, did we?"

"I thought I'd be sitting at your table for dinner, seeing that your husband invited me."

"I wouldn't know about Al's arrangements, would I? You'll have to complain to him."

"I wasn't complaining, I was just mentioning."

"Oh. Well, that's okay, then."

"See you Wednesday?"

"Wednesday?"

"You know Wednesday? That's the day when you come out to meet me at the motel every week."

"I don't think so, Joseph."

"You can't make it this week?"

"I'm not sure I'll be coming out to the Valley any day. Not for a while."

"Afraid your husband'll find out?"

"Well, there was always that danger, wasn't there? I just don't think it's such a good idea anymore."

"That sounds pretty final."

"It could be final," she said, a little M of thoughtfulness appearing between her perfect brows, marking the flawless skin. "Yes, it is final."

"Mind telling me why?"

"Well, among other things Al tells me you went into some business deal that went sour—"

"And you don't think I can pay for your ass anymore?"

A skin of ice covered her face in an eyeblink. The girl from Wilkes-Barre stared out at Doohan.

"I don't know if you can afford it, you could be broke pretty soon."

"You Al's shill?"

"How's that?"

"He send you out to rope suckers in with your ass?"

"Grow up, Joseph. Learn how to take no for an answer."

"You going to give that white-haired asshole a no for an answer?"

She made a slight noise with her mouth as though spitting out something that had a bad taste.

"Or are you just upping your price?"

"Hey, Joseph, you got a bargain. Be grateful."

Nadeau came toward them with Helena's wrap draped over his arm like a battle standard.

"I see you two got a chance to say hello. Maybe we'll get together for dinner some evening soon so you can get to know each other better."

"I'd like that," Helena said and turned herself so that Nadeau could drape the cape of gold over her shoulders.

Nadeau stood there with his arm around Helena's shoulder, emphasizing his ownership. "I think you did the right thing signing the deal."

Doohan could feel the tears coming. If he didn't do something to relieve the pressure he'd start to cry in front of Nadeau and Helena and they could even think it was for all the wrong reasons. He took a step away as he turned, stumbled and hit the pillar with his shoulder. Nadeau, wearing a tight little smile, reached out a hand to steady him and Doohan punched him in the face, knocking him to the floor.

"There's something for you to feel bad about," he said, paraphrasing the victorious boy he'd been long ago.

45

It was long past Benito's closing hour. All the tables had been cleared, the chairs upsided off the floor, the busboys sent home. Even the after-hours gathering around the big table was over. Pachoulo watched the headwaiter and the manager clear a couple of empty wine carafes and half a dozen glasses, pick up the ashtrays, stuff the crumpled napkins under their arms.

There were some sounds coming from the kitchen, the last rattlings of pots and pans.

Bobby Eel was mopping the floor, moving backward toward the kitchen doors like a vaudevillian doing his exit bit.

Pachoulo and Sam's Man were the only two left. Machado was gone. Iggie Deetch was gone.

Pachoulo sat in his favorite booth picking his nose and watching Sam's Man feed his dog from his mouth. Sam's Man had his legs spread and the mastiff was up on his hind legs between them. Sam's Man was taking pieces of cold sausage and putting them between his teeth, then letting Sam take them from his mouth.

"That's disgusting, Carmine," Pachoulo blurted out.

"What's the matter?"

"You're letting that animal take from your mouth. You're letting that animal's lips touch your lips."

"A dog's mouth is cleaner than a person's mouth. You ask any doctor, he'll tell you. A human bite is the worst bite you can get."

Pachoulo let it go. He just sat there staring as Sam's Man kept on feeding the goddam dog from his mouth.

There was a long silence. The last pot and pan had been rattled.

Bobby Eel and the slap of his mop had faded and disappeared. Some-body said goodnight from the kitchen and the sound of locks being turned and thrown could be faintly heard.

"It looks like you're humpin' that fuckin' dog," Pachoulo said.

Sam's Man looked at him very mildly. "You got to get yourself a woman. Something's got you all upset."

"Nothing's got me upset. What could have me upset?"

Sam's Man just looked at him as Sam stroked his belly with his paw, begging for more sausage, more attention.

"Don't look at me that way," Pachoulo said.

"What way is that?"

"Like you're reading my mind."

"I can't read your mind, Puffy, but I can get ideas."

"About what?"

"About what could be maybe bothering you."

"Like what?"

"Like Benny Checks's wife coming here."

"I don't like that woman comes in here looking like a nun, acting like she's not even mad after we made her watch what we done to her husband. It ain't natural."

"See? I knew it was something about a woman what was upsetting you."

"I got a woman anytime I want a woman."

"I don't mean hookers. You should get yourself a girlfriend. Maybe a wife."

"You don't got a girfriend."

"I got Sam," Sam's Man said with a hint of triumph and deep satis-faction in his voice.

The restaurant manager was standing in the lighted doorway of the kitchen, his hand on the bank of light switches, waiting for the word that he could close up once and for all and go home.

Pachoulo stared at Sam's Man and his dog acting like they loved each other.

"How much would a puppy like Sam cost?" Pachoulo asked.

46

There's no doubt there's a Mafia, a Syndicate, a Unione Siciliana, an Outfit. Whatever people want to call it. But racketeering is not altogether organized under one handful of *capi* and there is no *capo di capi* of crime.

There are also the Hong Kong Triads, the Chinese Wah Ching gang, the United Bamboo exported from Taiwan, the Japanese Yakuza. There are Vietnamese syndicates, Korean organizations, not to mention the crime corporations made up of Mexicans, American blacks, Haitians, Cuban Marielitos and the Colombian drug traffickers.

Also the Aryan, the Latino and the Afro-American brotherhoods and gangs, originating in prisons but spreading out into the real world.

Plus the street gangs, boys and young men earning their chops bopping old ladies and holding up candy stores.

Organized crime is more like a business consortium, the result of family loyalty, neighborhood associations, old-boy networking not much different from the process by which a great number of automobile manufacturers became three giants and a couple of midgets that controlled the marketplace. Until the foreign imports came along. Not much different from the price-fixing oil companies or the way any number of enterprises chop up the United States into territories.

Not much different from one political party or the other gaining control of a city and filling the civil service jobs with their own people.

That doesn't mean there aren't plenty of independents out there running for office, pumping gas, driving cabs and trucks, filling in the empty spots the big boys don't bother to fill, fighting one another for the crumbs from the lion's feast. Some of them growing strong enough to defy the lion or invade the lion's den.

The newspapers are full, nowadays, of company executives pumping poison into landfill upon which houses are built and in which families with children live, just to raise their profit margins a penny a hundred, and CEOs who've managed companies nearly into bankruptcy and walked away with golden handshakes worth millions, and preachers who steal, and cops who murder, and politicians who sit down and eat with the devil.

Sometimes you can't tell the white hats and the black hats apart. Like the lady said, they all do business.

Criminals are always on the lookout for new ideas. Murder and mayhem may always be the most persuasive arguments they have, but it's innovation that gives them the illusion that they're more than thugs.

Forced bankruptcy is the newest golden pot. In some cities it's called scam and in some bust-out.

You find a legitimate business with solid credit. You get your foot in the door and your ass on a director's chair. You grab control and with the company's good credit you make heavy purchases from manufacturers or wholesalers and secure heavy bank loans. Then you sell off the merchandise to other discounters or to legitimate businesses owned by other criminals at greatly reduced prices. When the creditors start yelling for their money you go belly up.

If the company marked for looting has already used up its line of credit, you pay off a portion of the last shipment of goods, then order a larger shipment for overnight disposal.

Puffy Pachoulo was ready to step up in class. He was ready to try bust-out, and the Doohan Porsche dealership was the plum.

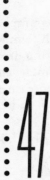

47

"What we got here," Pachoulo said, "is a difficulty."

The Doohans, Joseph and Phil and Pat, glanced at one another as though calling up the images of the five brothers that once upon a time could not be beat. But what they saw—which they had not allowed themselves to ever see before—were three soft, aging men.

Joseph, ruddy, well-scrubbed face showing cracks and sags, veins breaking on the nose and cheeks from too much booze, eyes gone a little yellow from too many long nights alone and too many frantic nights with whores.

Phil, all soft in the belly and growing wattles on his neck, the glad-hander with a touch of arthritis, the slick salesman with the oil drying up in creaking joints, the tomorrow man whose tomorrows had arrived and had no flavor.

And Pat, never the brightest of the bunch, grossed out on television, beer and baseball, with a wife whose body no longer stirred or satisfied.

"I don't see a difficulty," Joseph said. "We're a little late paying off the interest on our loans. We'll take an extension."

"Whattaya think, I'm a banker and you're a third-world country?"

"This is a hell of a place to meet," Phil said, looking around the garage.

A few cars were lying around in pieces. The radiator banged and wheezed trying to pump heat into the cave of concrete that would never be warm if it pumped away for a hundred years.

"How come you ask us to meet here in a goddam barn? What's the matter we don't meet at Benito's, have a little pasta, a little wine?

I'm getting so I really like your guinea food."

"We're in the garage because we got serious business to discuss. You didn't answer my question."

Manny Machado coughed so they would look at him and see him smile his killer's smile.

Phil tossed another glance at Joseph, who just sat there as though somebody had punched him dumb, as though he was so ashamed about what he'd done, taking out that huge loan behind the backs of his brothers, that he was giving up the leadership of the family. Phil looked at Pat and decided it was up to him.

"What question's that, Puffy? You were talking about a country?"

"And, on the subject, I don't like it you call me a guinea."

"We been calling you a guinea and you been calling us micks for how long now?"

"When we're friends. When we're sitting around scarfing the pasta you say you like. When we're having a glass of wine like honest men, you can call me a guinea, a wop, anything you want. Now we're talking business. What are you going to do about the money you owe me?"

"Haven't you heard? There's a recession going on. One of those recessions the president says isn't a recession. Everything's slowed down. On the subject. We should have been a lot further along on the construction than we are. I've been keeping an eye out ever since the problem with the water."

"So what?"

"So it doesn't look like the Nicolettis are doing the job as promised."

"What's that got to do with me? I lend you the money, I don't guarantee you when the job gets finished."

"I'm just pointing out the delay gives us extra expense."

"Which you think you can pass on to me?"

"I didn't say that." He was already sitting close to Pachoulo on a folding chair and now he leaned forward even closer. "What I said was that it's no fault of ours we missed a couple of payments."

Pachoulo turned his head slightly. It looked like all Machado did was lean forward over his shoulder, not making a big move out of it. He punched Phil in the mouth.

Joseph and Pat were on their feet right away.

Sam's Man said something and the mastiff came to attention.

Machado took a pair of thin leather gloves from his back pocket and started putting them on.

"I hear you tell the stories about what tough guys you was when you was kids," Pachoulo said. "I got a laugh about the one where the guy says to Joseph here, 'Hey, that's my brother you punched in the mouth,' and how Joseph here says, 'Don't feel bad, here's one for you.' Well, like that." His foot lashed out and the point of his shoe hit Phil in the shin. "There's one for you."

Phil howled.

Joseph took a step and Machado was there, hitting him once in the belly and once on each side of his face so his rosy cheeks grew redder.

"You're not kids anymore and I don't think you was ever very tough," Pachoulo went on. "Manny, show these fucking micks how tough they ain't."

The brothers were ready to fight back, but Sam's Man pulled a gun out from under his armpit and made Joseph and Pat back off while Machado went at Phil, bobbing and weaving, lashing out with stinging, cutting jabs and hooks, making jokes, making fun of Phil's clumsy attempts to counter.

When Phil was lying on the filthy floor, his cashmere sport jacket ruined with oil and grease, Machado started on Pat, who did better but not great.

Except for the three blows already struck, Joseph was left alone.

"What about me, Machado? You ready to start on me?" he challenged.

Machado turned his back on him, smiling at Pachoulo. Joseph made a rush for him, the tears rushing out of his eyes, blinding him. Machado stepped aside like he had eyes in the back of his head.

Joseph cursed and raged, the spit swamping down his chin as he went after Machado and then Sam's Man, who held the gun up out of the way so it wouldn't accidentally go off while he fended Joseph off with straight-arms. Sam pranced around and barked but didn't attack.

When Joseph went after Pachoulo, Pachoulo kicked him in the balls and knocked him down.

Joseph, on his knees, clutched himself and hung his head, tears, spit and snot dripping on the floor.

Pachoulo stood up. "So you owe two months' interest plus penalties.

That's too much. I can't afford it." He took a folded paper out of his pocket and held it out. "You got three days. You don't come up with the payment, you sign this paper."

He waited for one of them to ask him what the paper was for. When they didn't he shrugged and looked mildly surprised.

"You don't want to know what's on the paper? I'll tell you what's on the paper anyway. I had Al Nadeau write it up, so it's all legal. It makes me a partner. Well, it don't exactly make *me* a partner, it makes a company what I formed a partner. You don't mind I want to go legitimate? I always wanted to be in a legitimate business and I always liked cars. That's why I bought this garage, you understand? I don't want a piece for nothing. Besides I forgive the interest and penalties what you're late, I'm going to put some of my own money in our franchise. I think we need more inventory. That's what I think. So we pay off the factory part of what we owe on the last shipment and then, a week or so, we put in a big order. Take some of them cars they can't unload off their hands. They'll love us. They'll give us the dealership-of-the-year award."

He reached down and tucked the contract into Joseph's pocket.

"Hey, you shouldn't kneel on the floor like that," he said. "You'll ruin your pants."

Any good innkeeper sells discretion with the room. Any great hotel-keeper offers intuition and the utmost security as well. Such paragons become the confidants of presidents and kings.

When Fitzsimmons walked into the Barringer, a small luxury hotel tucked into a wooded area of Brentwood, with only two plainclothes-men at his side, Myron Derby, spotting the afternoon arrival from his office, came out and smoothly took over the desk, smiling softly, eyebrows raised, silently inquiring how he might serve this patron who his intuition told him was about to play a game of hanky-panky in which he would play a small but significant part.

"A room on the second floor," Fitzsimmons said.

"Overlooking the garden?"

"That would be nice."

"One night?"

"One day really. I need a private, discreet setting for a very important conference."

"You'll be requiring room service, then?"

"I'd like some refreshments laid on before the conference begins. Champagne, cold chicken, a bowl of fruit, a tray of chocolates, coffee and tea."

"For how many?"

"Wine for two. Coffee and tea for three."

"Will you require a waiter standing by during your conference?"

"I'd like the refreshments laid on before I occupy the room and then I'd like to remain completely undisturbed."

"I understand, Mr. . . . ?"

"Fitch."

Derby turned the leather case holding the registration card around so that it faced Fitzsimmons.

"Is that necessary?" Fitzsimmons asked.

"It's customary."

"But I'm not staying the night. If I understand the hostelry regulations . . ."

"I didn't wish to presume."

"About what?"

"Some patrons wish the evidence of business conferences to be a matter of the public record for tax purposes."

"And others do not?"

"I wouldn't presume to say when one thing or the other was wanted."

"You have a great future in the diplomatic service if ever you decide to give up innkeeping."

"Thank you, Mr. Fitch. If you wouldn't mind waiting in the lounge for fifteen minutes I'll see to it that your room is prepared according to your orders."

"When my secretary arrives..."

"I'll send her straight up."

"Give her the extra key."

"Would you like to settle your account beforehand so that you may leave without delay when your conference ends?"

"An excellent suggestion."

Derby had already made the necessary calculations in his head. Accommodations, wine, chicken, fruit and service—coffee and tea on the house—tax, privacy, courtesy and discretion added.

"Will you be using the phone for long-distance?" he asked.

"If the phone is used at all it will be for incoming calls only."

Derby nodded, taking such a valuable customer's word on it. "Three hundred and seventy-two dollars and sixty-nine cents."

Fitzsimmons reached into his breast pocket and withdrew a leather billfold, removed four new hundred-dollar bills fresh from a money machine and laid them on the counter, admiring the way the manager played the game, calculating a bill in dollars and change instead of rounding it off to the nearest ten or twenty in a way that would have seemed careless and cavalier.

Derby put the four crisp notes into the till and, selecting the newest, brightest penny, counted out the change.

"Receipt?" Fitzsimmons asked.

Derby hesitated only the fraction of a moment, then quickly wrote one out, tore off the original and handed it to Fitzsimmons.

Fitzsimmons pocketed the receipt, then picked up the carbon and the carbon paper, tore them up, his eyes on Derby's eyes, a smile on his neat mouth. "My option," he said. "I may not have occasion to use it for tax purposes."

Derby nodded and watched the cool, white-haired gentleman pick up his escort and saunter into the lounge. He called room service and ordered the refreshments for room 201. Then he went back into the till and took three of the hundred-dollar bills that would never appear on the books.

Fifteen minutes later Fitzsimmons left the lounge with only one of his men. They took the stairs instead of the elevator.

Room 201 was the last room at the end of the corridor. There was a back staircase leading down into a walled garden.

"Okay, Joe, why don't you go downstairs and smell the roses," he said, opening the door to the room with his key.

"I've got an allergy," Joe said.

Fitzsimmons grinned. "So hold your breath."

"Are you going to be that quick?" Joe asked, clearly in possession of joking privileges through long association.

Fitzsimmons went into his billfold and took out two twenties.

"Don't miss your lunch. Just be where I can reach out for you in three hours."

Inside the room a credenza against the wall was laid with a large terra-cotta bowl of fruit, a wine cooler large enough to hold two bottles of wine, and a roast chicken, carved but reassembled with colored toothpicks. On the coffee table was a silver tray with all the silver pots, bowls and pitchers necessary for serving tea or coffee, milk or cream, sugar or sweetener.

Fitzsimmons took off his jacket, tie and shirt. His skin was nearly as white as his hair, in sharp contrast to the sunburned ruddiness of his face, neck, hands and forearms. He kicked off his shoes and took off his socks and trousers. He wore pink boxer shorts with racing stripes down the sides.

There were two double beds that took up about a third of the room. The floor space adjacent to the French doors giving out onto a balcony was clear except for the coffee table and two small club chairs. Fitzsimmons moved the coffee table to the foot of the bed closest to the door and farthest from the balcony. He put the two chairs in the space between the bed and wall that separated the bed-sitting room from the bathroom.

He took the pillows from the beds and the cushions from the chair and made a nest of them on the floor by the French doors, stepping out onto the balcony for a moment to see that there were no buildings or high ground anywhere around that offered sight lines into the room. Even then he left the doors open just enough to invite a breeze and closed the sheer curtains.

He placed the bowl of fruit, the chicken, the wine and two glasses on the floor beside the couch he'd made.

Then he went into the closet and closed the door.

49

In the dream Panama saw himself lying in bed asleep. His sleeping self became aware of a presence in the room. He knew it was a shadow come to cut his throat. He waited until the shadow hovered above him, but when he tried to lash out a hand and foot he couldn't move.

Someone screamed. Himself in the dream? Someone in the bedroom? He sat straight up, the sheets tangled around his sweaty legs. Lisa stood by the chest, wearing nothing but her bra, her hands rummaging around looking for fresh underwear in one of the drawers. She looked at him with wide-stretched eyes, frightened by his outcry. The telephone rang again.

It was an old and familiar dream, almost as old as dreams of flying and walking naked down a busy street, almost as old as the wet dreams of his adolescence. An old dream that clung with determined claws.

When Lisa padded over, knelt on the bed and tried to cradle him in her arms, he shook her off and reached for the phone as it rang again. He'd been so long alone that such tenderness and concern challenged and embarrassed him.

He grunted into the mouthpiece.

"You don' wanna work, we don' gotta work," Missy said.

"I overslept."

"Don' I know you overslept? You got to stop this all-night jig-jiggin', Panama. You gonna give sex a bad name."

"Where are you?"

"Over at the taco stan'. Where would I be?"

"Half an hour."

"Bullshit, brother," she said without anger and hung up.

"Missy?" Lisa said.

He nodded his head and wiped the last shreds of the dream out of his eyes with the heels of his hands.

"She watches you like a hawk."

"The shift began an hour ago and I'm not even out of bed."

"She'll cover for you."

He got up and stood there naked, conscious that he had a morning hard-on, half wanting to see what she would do about it.

She reached out and cupped his balls.

"For chrissake," he said and went into the bathroom to take a shower, having proved to his satisfaction that she couldn't control herself.

Jars and bottles were scattered all over every flat surface. The two washrags on the bar and the one on the edge of the tub were smeared with mascara and eyeliner. Her panty hose and underwear were draped on top of the towel racks and over the shower rod. More of her clothes were on the floor, kicked into the corner.

He turned on the shower taps and stood outside the tub, testing the temperature of the water with his hand. When it was right he got in and pulled the curtain over so the floor wouldn't get wet.

He had his hands full of lather, washing his face, when he heard the curtain rustle aside and felt her hand on his shoulder as Lisa supported herself stepping into the tub.

He took his hands away and let the spray wash the soap from his eyes.

She embraced him from behind, her breasts soft against his back, her hips grinding into him with gentle provocation. Like it or not he got stiff all over again.

"I'm already an hour late, Lisa."

"You prowled all night every night this week. You go say you're washed out and then you get up and prowl all night."

"I'm not used to sleeping with anybody."

"I can understand. You want to get twin beds?"

"You breathe so quiet it makes me nervous."

"I can't help it how I breathe."

"It scares me. When you're asleep I watch you for a long time sometimes to see if you're still breathing."

"I feel you watching me."

"You hardly move when you sleep."

"I could learn to snore."

She reached around, her hand slick with soap she'd taken from his belly, and began to stroke his cock.

He manufactured a little laugh and said, "That won't be necessary. I'll learn to get along with it," as though she wasn't giving him another erection.

He turned around and faced her.

"You make it sound like a job that won't be too pleasant," she said, getting up on her toes and capturing him between her thighs.

"You've got to give me time," he said.

"It's not like we're strangers."

"We've been longer apart than we were together."

She moved his hands so they cupped her buttocks, then lifted herself up with her arms around his neck and maneuvered until he slipped into her.

Bodies doing what they want to do while the heads are doing something else, she thought.

It was a quiet fuck, almost without passion or excitement, thoughtful, even solemn.

She thought about the people they'd been. Only six years ago? That wasn't anything like a lifetime, yet here they were, two different people. Except they weren't hungry like new lovers were supposed to be hungry. Except each one knew the other one's body too well. It wouldn't be long before they'd just be using each other for pillows.

Sex was like drugs, Heath thought. After a while you did it just to maintain your balance. You didn't do it for the high it gave you but to avoid the terrible pains of withdrawal.

Lisa thought about how when the rockets stopped going off, when the earth, like they said, stopped moving, what you had was need and comfort. It had come to that with Billy. He needed her. She gave him comfort and that gave her comfort. She worried that Panama, who'd needed her once, didn't really need her now and might never come to need her again.

After all, add it up. Say two people got married when they were twenty. Stayed married for fifty years. Say they went at it hot and heavy the first year, five times a week. Two hours a go. Five hundred and twenty hours. Say five hundred so she could keep the calculation in her head. Say they slow down to three times a week, one hour a go average, the next ten years. Now you've got fifteen hundred and sixty hours. Say sixteen hundred. So now you got twenty-one hundred hours. Next twenty years, twice a week maybe but not every week. Twice a week for forty weeks. What do you know, another sixteen hundred hours. So that makes thirty-seven hundred. The next nineteen years, once a week for forty weeks. Forty times twenty equals eight hundred less forty equals seven sixty. Grand total forty-four hundred and sixty hours. Make it forty-five figuring in specials and holidays. Four thousand five hundred hours. A hundred and eighty-seven days. Twenty-six weeks out of a lifetime. Half a year out of fifty years. She giggled at herself.

Heath mistook it for arousal and increased the pace and vigor of his thrusts, puffing away like a fading runner, trying to keep his balance in the water-slick tub.

She bit him on the shoulder. It was the least she could do.

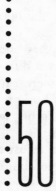

Helena stood in front of the door to 201 feeling a little bubble of anticipation rising up from her groin to her heart.

Hot and heavy was the name for Francis. He liked to go at it hot and heavy. But first there had to be surprises. Some of the surprises had hurt. She hoped this wasn't going to be one of those.

She inserted the key in the lock and turned it. She grasped the doorknob and turned that, too. She had the feeling that she could stop right there, never going into the room, standing there betwixt and between forever. Make herself feel just like she felt in the second before the rush of free-base took hold or during that funny pause right after she injected herself with a needle.

She put her shoulder against the door and pushed, sidling into the room like a cat burglar.

The sheer curtains closing off the French doors billowed into the room, pulled by the draft caused by the open door. She closed it and the curtains drifted back like a sigh.

She closed the door and double-locked it so no careless maid would come in by mistake. She saw the pillows and cushions on the floor, the bowl of fruit, the wine and the chicken, pierced with a hundred tiny spears, sitting on its plate.

When she walked over to the bed farthest from the door and started taking off her clothes, she heard the merest whisper of something dragged across the carpet as Fitzsimmons opened the door to his hidey-hole a little.

She knew he was peering at her from the dark cave of the closet. She could feel his eyes touching her naked back and bare ass. She turned around and released the cups of her brassiere and felt pinpricks on her nipples as though his eyes were biting them. She stepped out of her bikini panties and brushed her hands over her bush, fluffing it out, inspecting it for tangles.

It took her several minutes to finally get comfortable on the couch of pillows, making a great effort of twisting and turning, humping herself this way and that before finally settling down in a pose both comfortable and provocative. She peeled a banana and placed it between her breasts pointing toward her chin. She draped a bunch of grapes over her belly. They were chilly and her belly jumped a little at the shock, making her giggle. She wondered what Al would think if he saw her wiggling around a hotel-room floor turning herself into a fruit salad. She broke off two or three of the largest grapes and inserted them into her vagina.

Then she lay back against the pillows and peeled a plum with her long fingernails.

When Fitzsimmons, naked, finally came charging out of the closet and leapt upon her, making the gobbling noises of what he meant to be a ravening wolf, it came as no surprise to her, though she always found these attacks out of closets, from behind drapes or from under pieces of furniture a little exciting.

While he indulged in fantasies of eating her down to the bone she could engage in fantasies of rape.

He lay back with a smear of banana on his chin and grape skins in his teeth.

"Next time ice cream between your tits and whipped cream in your pussy," he said.

"Jesus, Francis," she said, "you're going to make a hell of a governor."

"President."

"Whatever."

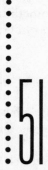

"You losin' it, Panama," Missy said.

"Losing what?"

"Losin' your edge."

"That's a hell of a thing to say to your partner."

"I got to call it like I see it. Your head is always someplace else. It ain' on the job."

"How can it be on the job? We been running around for weeks and what have we got? We got a line on a couple of small-timers dealing drugs to the high school kids. The local uniforms know all about them, busted them twenty times and they just walked through the revolving door. We got a list of maybe twenty hot-pillow joints sell rooms for sex by the hour. You want to bust a bunch of housewives out on a fling? Why would we even want to bother? We turned up maybe two, three shys doing a little business here and there."

"You keep goin' on, I'm gonna start losin' it, too."

They were walking along Ventura, because it was as good a street to be walking as any other, down where the Doohans had their agency. The sun blasted off the windshields and the polished paint jobs into their eyes. They had to turn away and close their eyes for a second against the painful glare. While their eyes were shut the flapping pennants sounded louder. Like the snap of beach umbrellas.

"We should go down to Redondo, Santa Monica, take a swim," Heath said.

"We gonna turn up something today. I feel it in my bones," Missy said.

They saw Phil Doohan up ahead, running a chamois over the paint-work on a red Porsche. He turned around, saw them approaching and started to hurry toward the showroom.

"Wha's tha'?" Missy said.

"What's what?"

"Doohan sees us an' runs away."

"Maybe he remembered a call he's got to make."

"Sure. Hey, Phil, what for are you runnin' out on us?" Missy shouted.

Doohan threw up a hand and waved, half turning his head. "Got to go," he called back. "Have a nice day."

"That ain' good enough," Missy said.

"Maybe he's got to wring out his sock," Heath said, showing no interest.

"Come on, come on," Missy said, and trotted across the lot between the cars on her little high-heeled boots, small ass swinging in her tight jeans.

Heath followed along for the fun of watching and for lack of anything better to do.

Inside the showroom the Porsches crouched like big shining beasts, beautiful, lethal and desirable when tamed. The smell of wax and leather made Heath sniff with pleasure. Funny how the smell of money could lift your spirits one time and make you unhappy another, he thought.

Missy was going here, going there, looking for Phil.

Heath stood in the middle of the floor watching her scurry about like a rat terrier, saw her shove against the door to the men's toilet and barge right in.

He ran in behind her, about to ask her what she thought she was doing.

Phil was using both hands to wash his face over the basin. He looked up and over as she slammed in.

"My God, Missy, what do you think you're doing coming into the john while a man's taking a pee," he said.

"Look at me. Look at me," Missy replied.

"Can't you see I'm washing my face? I ain't even zipped up my fly."

"How come you wash your han's an' face first, before you zip up your fly?" she asked, leaning against the toilet stall.

"That you, Panama?" Phil said. "Why don't you do something about this crazy partner you got?"

"Why don't you stop washing your face, Phil?" Heath said.

"Get the fuck out of here and let me do what I'm doing."

Heath went over and gently pulled Phil away from the sink with a hand on his shoulder. He turned him around and Phil gave it up. Stopped trying to hide it. His scrapes and bruises were two days old, a mask of indigo and yellow-brown.

"Who did it, Phil?"

"I got mugged. I was the last one to leave the other night. I was just closing up when these two gamooshes come in and try to rob me."

"*Tried* to rob you?"

"Well, robbed me. Whatever there was in petty cash."

Missy went over and got some paper towels from the dispenser and handed them to Phil. "Hey, you drippin' all over your nice jacket," she said softly.

"How much was that?" Heath asked.

"A hundred, two hundred dollars. Not much cash circulates around a dealership. Checks and credit cards. Not much cash."

"How come you didn't report it?"

"What for? What could the cops do? They'd come around here, take a report, cluck their tongues and that would be that."

"They beat the shit out of you, Phil."

"So next time they won't have it so easy."

"What do you mean by that?"

Phil hesitated half a minute, then he opened up his jacket to show

Heath and Missy a thirty-two snugged into a holster at his belt.

"Oh, for chrissake, Phil, what do you know about guns?" Heath said.

"I know how to pull a trigger."

"You got to have pulled a trigger a thousand times before it's second nature. Otherwise you hesitate and whoever it is takes it away from you and shoves it up your ass," Heath said.

"I'm getting in some practice."

"I don' like it," Missy said.

"I understand you don't like it," Phil said. "You want to lay a charge of possession on me?"

Heath let a rush of air out of his mouth and left the toilet. Missy tap-tapped out behind him.

"You believe that crap about the muggers?" she asked.

"No, I don't believe it. What you want us to do, give him the third degree?"

"Look. There's Pat over there. We could ask him."

Heath changed direction and walked over to the glassed-in office where Pat sat at the desk writing up paper. He knocked on the door and Pat looked up. His face wasn't nearly as bad as Phil's but it looked like he'd met up with the muggers, too.

"I forgot to tell you," Phil said at Heath's back, "Pat was here when those bozos came in with their pistols and banged us around."

"That right, Pat?"

"That's right," Pat said, his eyes looking at his brother for whatever else he could read there. He grinned. "Where were the cops when we needed them?"

"That the story you want to go with, Phil?" Heath said.

"I don't know what else to tell you."

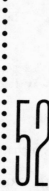

52

The coffee shop on the corner of Ventura and Coldwater had become like a second home for Becker and his squad. Except for Heath, who was playing house with his old squeeze and always acted like he couldn't wait to leave.

"He puts in his fifteen, twenny minutes jus' to show us he ain' pussy-whipped," Missy'd said one night.

"You're just mad it ain't your pussy doing the whipping," Kopcha said.

"Hey, your fly's open. I can see your pecker."

When Kopcha looked down, Missy said, "Sorry. It's jus' a piece of noodle you dropped in your lap."

So every day and every day they gathered at the coffee shop and insulted each other and talked about any one of them that left the table before the others were ready to leave. So that it got so that everybody hung around and hung around, waiting to be last so nobody could yank their chain if they weren't there to yank back.

They were well known to the employees on that shift. Regulars. Somebody to brag about to other regulars. Their own cops hanging around. Cop groupies got the word and came to sit at the next tables, asking questions, cutting a few numbers. One blonde had her eye on Kopcha for no reason the others could understand.

"I don' see your sweet patootie wit' the peroxide hair," Missy kidded.

"I wore her out last night. She's in the hospital. She's in intensive care."

"You couldn' wear out a turtle. Crush it maybe, but not wear it out."

Kopcha reached under the table, grabbed Missy's knee and gave it a little squeeze. She yelped.

They were all friends. They were all fellow cops. Except maybe Monk still held a jealous grudge against Missy because even now, with Heath bam-bamming Lisa Ray, Missy and him were still partners, leaving him with the fucking Irish comedian, Jimmy Kelly.

"What is it with you?" he suddenly snapped. "Whatta you got on your mind? You're pissed off Panama here's back with his old girlfriend. You're pissed off old Kopcha here's got a blond bomber wants to knock his nuts off. You're pissed off—"

"Ah, stick a sock in it, man," Mandingo said.

"What the fuck you mean stick a sock in it?" Monk was angry, nobody could exactly say why. He couldn't exactly say why. "You making a mouth at me?"

"I don't make a mouth. You keep on making a mouth, I'm gonna stick my twelve and a halfs in it."

Monk made a move like he was ready to get up and scramble.

"Sit down," Becker said. "Stop acting like a bunch of kids. What have I got here, a bunch of kids?"

"Our Gang Comedy," Kelly said.

"Well, it's not funny," Becker snapped back.

"Look, it's got you, too," Kelly said.

"What's that?"

"Failure. Failure's got us by the balls."

"Missy, too?" Kopcha asked.

"Missy, too. We been shim-shammin' around, asking here, asking there, working the turf, and what have we got?"

"Maybe Panama an' me got somethin'."

Becker looked at Heath. Then the rest of them looked at Heath.

She and Panama maybe had something, so who did they look at for the news after she announced it? They looked at the man. They didn't look at the woman so she could tell it, they looked at the man. So, how do you fight something like that? Sonofabitch.

Missy looked at Heath.

"There's these three brothers own a Porsche dealership over on Ventura..." He told all about how they saw two of the brothers looking like they'd been in a fight without raising their hands, and how the other brother wasn't around like he usually was.

"They're Irish?" Mandingo said. "Maybe they like to go out, have a few, get into a fight."

"Why's it got to be they like to have a few and fight because they're Irish?" Kelly said.

"Why you always asking me to teach you how to walk sly?"

"So, never mind that, never mind the jokes—all the time with the jokes—never mind. So what do you think? What does these two micks getting beat up say to you?"

"It could mean they got on the wrong side of a juiceman."

"One or the other," Mandingo said affably. "Got in a drunken brawl or the wrong side of a juiceman."

"It ain't much," Kopcha said.

"It's better'n nothin'," Missy rapped right back.

"Maybe it's nothing and maybe it's something," Becker observed.

"When you've got nothin', anythin' looks like somethin'," Mandingo said softly. "I hate this goddam task-force bullshit."

"Maybe Dan Piscaroon's got a little something," Becker said.

"Dan Piscaroon works North Hollywood?" Heath asked.

"He was teamed up and put over to Brentwood District."

"So?"

"So he was drifting past the Barringer Hotel who does he see walking inside but our fair-haired leader." The way he said it, a little sarcastic, making Fitzsimmons out to be an asshole—which he'd never done before—meant he was getting fed up with all the show-and-tell with nothing happening, too. "Piscaroon goes on in to see if there's maybe a conference or a meeting of some sort going on. Fitzsimmons's in the bar. Piscaroon sits down and reads a paper like he's waiting for somebody. Ten minutes later Fitzsimmons comes out of the lounge and the clerk calls him Mr. Fitch and Fitzsimmons goes upstairs. Then Piscaroon hears the desk clerk ask the kitchen if everything has been laid on as ordered, the chicken and the fruit and everything."

They were all getting wide-eyed, hoping for something here.

"So Piscaroon reads some more of the newspaper and the first thing you know this hooker—he's not sure she's a hooker—walks in."

"How come he ain' sure?"

"He says she's got the swing and the ass but she hasn't got the sass. He says a hooker like this hooker would cost a thousand dollars a trick."

"Fitzsimmons can afford it," Heath said.

"So?" Kopcha said.

"So she asked at the desk for Mr. Fitch and went on upstairs. Piscaroon took a walk because the clerk was starting to give him the old one-eye."

"That's an interesting story," Kelly said, "but what's it got to do with anything?"

"It's got to do with someplace down the line we put a foot wrong, we play the game a little free-style, and Fitzsimmons don't back us up the way he says he's going to back us up, maybe we got a little leverage."

"I got to go," Heath said.

"Finish your pie and coffee," Monk said, like a wife would say to a husband.

"I got to go," Heath said again. He slid out of the booth and went on out.

"He don't want it, I'll finish his pie," Kopcha said.

53

The evening had turned chilly.

Pachoulo waddled into the showroom looking like a fat gray duck. He was wearing a gray tailor-made suit with a light gray topcoat draped over his shoulders. His shoes were gray leather and had Cuban heels which lifted him up a couple of inches. A gray fedora rode his head at an angle, one side of the brim snapped down. You didn't have to be a historian to see the resemblance he was trying to create. Give him a scar on one cheek and Capone and Pachoulo could have been mistaken for brothers or at least kissing cousins.

Al Nadeau, who habitually wore a light gray topcoat with a baby-lamb collar, stood beside Pachoulo looking uncomfortable as though afraid somebody would see the similarity in the coats they wore and think they were the same breed of cat.

Pachoulo stood in the center of the floor and surveyed the whole layout. He examined the windowed salesmen's offices and poked his head into the more private office used for closing deals.

"These rooms ain't big enough," he said. "We'll have our meeting right out here."

"You want to sit behind the desk, Puffy?" Iggie Deetch asked.

"No, we'll all sit over there around the table."

He gestured toward the collection of couches and easy chairs where the customers were romanced while drinking tea or coffee. He walked over and took the big wingback as though he were the new owner of the establishment.

The Doohans, Phil and Pat and Joseph, said nothing. They arranged themselves on the longest couch.

Machado sat on the arm and even laid his hand on Joseph's shoulder like they were old friends. Joseph shrugged it off.

"Touchy, touchy," Machado said, and laughed.

Iggie Deetch pulled a club chair closer to the coffee table and laid his leather document envelope on it while Sam's Man settled into another chair. He sank so deep it looked like he'd never be able to get out of it again. Nadeau took the chair beside him and tried to slide it back, wanting to distance himself from the proceedings. The legs wouldn't slide on the rug and he was trapped there.

"What's this all about?" Phil asked.

"We want to look over what we bought into here," Pachoulo said. "Something wrong with that?" He glanced at Nadeau.

Nadeau leaned forward.

"Mr. Pachoulo feels that, considering the cash-flow difficulties this dealership is having, he'd like Mr. Deetch to look over your books."

"Deetch is a bail bondsman," Phil said.

"Also a CPA," Iggie Deetch said.

"I don't know if we want anybody poking around the books without we have our own accountant do a quick audit," Phil said.

"Let them look if they want to look," Joseph said.

Phil was about to put up a protest but took a look at his brother and changed his mind. "Okay, Joseph, if you say so," he said as though he knew his brother was terminally ill and wanted to preserve the illusion that Joseph was still a powerhouse.

"So what else?" Phil asked.

Iggie Deetch opened the envelope, took out a paper and slid it across the table toward Phil.

"What's this?" Phil asked.

"It's a hold-harmless contract which relieves you of any responsibility or liability for any transactions Mr. Pachoulo may initiate."

"That's what it does for us? So what does it do for Mr. Pachoulo?"

"It don't do nothing for me. It's just to take a load off your mind nobody's going to try to take away your houses, your personal vehicles, whatever else you got separate from the business."

The rims of Phil's eyes had turned red. He looked like he was just coming off a ten-day drunk. He shook his head and looked at his hands, the fingers laced together so hard the joints had turned white, and made a noise in his throat that wasn't quite a laugh and wasn't quite a scream but something in between.

"Why do you bother going through all this legal gobbledegook? Why don't you just come in here with your guns and bully boys and grab the business out of our hands?"

"Hey! I'd never do that. I ain't a thief," Pachoulo said with real indignation. "I'm a person what lends money to other persons what needs it or think they needs it. Is it my fault some people get themselves into bad deals? Is it my fault some people are bad businessmen? Somebody en . . . huh?"

"Endangers?" Nadeau said.

"Endangers three hundred and fifty thousand dollars of my money I'm supposed to say what the hell, be my guest?"

"You sucked us into a crooked deal."

"You want to take that to court? You want to put the Nicoletti brothers up on the stand, accuse them of setting you up, ripping you off, legitimate contractors built big buildings all over this town?"

Joseph put a hand on Phil's arm and said, "Don't argue, Phil."

Phil gave it up.

"Who acts for you?" Iggie Deetch said.

"I do," Joseph replied in the voice of a man already dead and buried.

"Sign right here."

"So that's that and that's that," Pachoulo said, laboring up out of the chair. "Now I want to go into the big office, have a look around, get a feel of the business. You know what I mean?"

Machado got off the arm of the chair and started after his boss. Sam's Man was stuck in the depths of his chair. He reached up for a hand as Machado passed.

"You got to lose some weight, Carmine," Pachoulo said.

He turned around and skirted his chair, his broad back looking twice as broad as the coat swung away from his shoulders.

Phil stood up and fumbled the gun out from under his jacket, almost dropping it. "Hey, Pachoulo."

Everybody looked at him, the way he said it.

"Turn around, you sonofabitch," Phil said. His voice was shaking and his hand was shaking.

Pachoulo heard the danger. For a second it looked as though he wasn't going to move. Then he shifted his weight and eased himself around as though careful that his coattails shouldn't knock over anything breakable.

"Phil, for God's sake, put it down," Nadeau said. "It's just a business difficulty. It isn't worth it. This is a death-penalty state."

"No jury would convict. They'd give me a medal."

"Think of your immortal soul."

"Listen to the man," Pachoulo said. "He's a lawyer, don't you know."

Joseph was standing up behind Phil. He wrapped his arms around his brother from behind and grabbed the wrist of the hand that held the gun, pulling it down so the gun pointed at the floor.

Phil could feel his brother's tears on the back of his neck. He let go and the gun dropped to the floor.

Machado started moving then, but Pachoulo said, "Hey, Manny!" and Machado stopped in his tracks.

"Don't do nothing to him," Pachoulo said. "I ain't even mad."

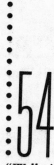

54

"Well, it's certainly a terrible way to treat your mother," Maggie said. "I ain't seen you in weeks."

"A week, Ma. Maybe a week," Billy Ray said.

"Two weeks at least."

"Ten days. Let's say ten days."

"What are we doing? Negotiating? Go get me my calendar off the wall and I'll tell you exactly when you was here last. What's wrong with your front teeth?"

"What the hell's going on? One minute you're talking about calendars, the next minute you're talking about what's wrong with my teeth."

"You're trying to get my attention off your mouth."

Ray put his fingers in the corners of his mouth and pulled his lips back. "So look at my teeth. There's my teeth."

"They look different," she said.

"I got to confess."

"What have you got to confess?"

"You know how I always felt funny about my crooked front tooth?"

"I never knew you felt funny about your crooked front tooth. What crooked front tooth?"

"This one right here."

"I never noticed it was so crooked."

"It overlapped the next tooth."

"A hair. Maybe a hair. Not so's anybody could notice."

"Well, maybe I never said anything but it always bothered me."

"So okay?"

"I'm having caps made. These are just the temporaries."

"Oh, my God."

"What's the matter?"

"You had such beautiful teeth and you're having them capped. I never heard of such a thing. Such beautiful white teeth you've always had. Why shouldn't you have beautiful teeth? After you got off the tit I always gave you the richest milk could be bought."

"Ma, let's not start talking about me breast-feeding and all that again."

"I was talking about the milk I gave you."

"That either. Maybe you didn't notice but lately my teeth was getting yellow."

"From all the cigarettes you smoke. Tobacco stains. There's a toothpaste—"

"Never mind the toothpaste. I had it done. Next week, ten days, the dentist's going to have the permanent caps ready. My mouth's going to look a million. I'll smile at you, you'll have to put on sunglasses or go blind. You hear what I'm telling you?"

"What you're telling me is that you need money."

"How come every time I tell you something, bring you some news, you think I want to screw some money out of you?"

"You shouldn't use that language to your mother."

"What language?"

"You know."

"You mean 'screw'? Jesus Christ. I don't mean screw like that, I mean like screwing a screw out of a piece of wood."

"You shouldn't take the Lord's name in vain, either."

"I should know better than to tell you anything."

"Don't get mad, sonny."

"Jesus Christ."

"How much money?"

"It's going to cost three thousand."

She put her thin hands between her breasts as though she felt a sinking feeling there.

"I don't understand. They advertise in the newspapers a full set of uppers and lowers for two hundred and forty-nine dollars."

"What are you talking about? Cut-rate butchers. They make teeth like that on an assembly line. Like you go to the five and dime and pick out a pair of reading glasses. Go to the five and dime and pick out a set of teeth. Might as well go down to the Salvation Army. You want me to go to a dentist who hangs around the Salvation Army?"

"I never said anything like that."

"This man I'm going to is the best dentist in Beverly Hills. He works on the mouths of stars. Danny Thomas goes to him, fachrissake. You think he does caps for two hundred and fifty bucks?"

"Three thousand dollars. I haven't got three thousand dollars."

"Look, did I ask you to give me three thousand dollars? Did I ask you to give me any money at all? I didn't even want to tell you about my caps. You had to make a remark about my teeth. You had to practically twist my arm so I'd tell you about my new caps."

"So where are you going to get the money?"

"I got a few pennies put away. So all I need is maybe two thousand dollars."

"How about a million?"

"You can't help me out, Ma, you don't have to make fun."

"I'm not making fun. I'm just saying it'd be just as easy for me to get you a million as for me to get you two thousand."

"You don't have to lie to me."

"What do you mean lie to you?"

"I know you've got a little in the sock. I know you always got a little in the sock."

"I like to keep a little just for emergencies."

"So, this don't count as an emergency? My good appearance don't count as an emergency?"

"I didn't say that. All I said was . . ." She turned away in her chair, putting her arm over the back, the ever-ready handkerchief wadded up and ready to soak up the tears.

"If you're going to cry, forget I ever said anything about my teeth."

"I got a cancer, sonny."

"Forget what I look like. What I'll do is I'll see if I got enough for a down. I'll pay the dentist off on time."

"I need an operation, sonny."

"The sonofabitch don't like it, I'll just walk around with these temps until I can work enough double shifts to make the scratch."

"If I even live, sonny, I don't know when I can go back to work again, if ever, and I got nobody to take care of me." She whirled around on him, her face screwed up in rage and anguish. "You listening to what I'm saying? You hear what I said?"

"I heard, Ma. I just didn't want to hear what I heard."

He got up and went to her, getting down on his knees, letting her hold his head against her breasts as he hugged her around the waist. It was the first time she could remember in a long time he'd ever come to her and embraced her without her asking, without his wanting something from her. She hadn't been so happy, she thought, in ages.

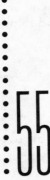

Heath and Missy were sitting in her car across the street and halfway down the block from the Doohan Porsche showroom. Missy had a big ribbon in her hair and was scrunched down so far on her side of the car that her eyes could barely see over the bottom of the window frame. She had a big lollipop which she waved around when she talked.

Heath was bareheaded. A false mustache adorned his upper lip and he was wearing granny glasses.

To anyone who cared to glance their way they looked like a suburban father with his daughter in tow.

"You know, Panama, I was suspicious there for a while you was bald."

"What gave you that idea?"

"Well, you never took off your hat, did you? So tha's wha' I figured. But you got nice hair."

"You keep waving that lollipop around and you'll have it stuck in my nice hair."

"Oh, oh, here they come again."

She straightened up a little to watch Pachoulo's big new limo pull up with Machado at the wheel. Sam's Man, the dog and Pachoulo got out of the back, Machado and Nadeau out of the front.

Heath reached back and grabbed his camera. It was an autofocus. All he had to do was point it and shoot. It only took a second. Little chance of anybody noticing. He lifted and lowered the camera four times as Pachoulo, Sam's Man and Machado milled around alongside the car, Pachoulo throwing his arms in the air, his face red with anger. Nadeau stood there looking uncomfortable.

"Wha' you think they arguin' abou'?"

"I think Pachoulo's mad because that dog did something to the upholstery in his new car."

"Either that or the dog peeded on his shoe."

"That's a possibility."

Their quarry started walking through the ranks of cars on display, Pachoulo shaking his foot every other step.

Missy giggled. "You're right. I like that dog."

Heath took one more shot.

"I think we got enough."

"There ain' a doubt Pachoulo's takin' over."

"Not a doubt." He started the engine and pulled away from the curb. A block away he took off the glasses and handed them to Missy, then reached back and got his hat. He put it on and glanced into the rearview three or four times until he got the angle just right.

"Hey, you really somethin', baby," Missy said. "I better get this ribbon outta my hair. Firs' t'ing you know some citizen'll be callin' in that a dirty white slaver is kidnappin' a little Chicana girl."

"You know," Heath said, his thoughts somewhere else, "what we got here could be the first real bite."

"Promotions, babe. You never know."

Becker looked over the photos.

"Where'd you have these done? Down to the police lab?"

"Where do you think?" Heath asked.

"I was hoping you'd say you had them done in one of those one-hour places."

"How's that?"

"You don't know?"

"Know what?"

"First, third and eighth squad all set up raids on this place and that. By the time they got there the cupboards were bare."

"You think somebody down at the police darkroom is giving away secrets?" Heath said, a note of doubt in his voice.

"I didn't say it was anybody at the darkroom."

"I thought that's what you said," Mandingo observed.

"No. What I was saying was that you don't know who you can trust. The fewer people know what the hell you got, the better off you are."

"Which is what I've been goddam saying all along, splitting up teams that worked together for years," Monk said forcefully. "You can goddam tell who you can trust when your partner's been with you for years."

"Monk, you going to start that again?" Kelly asked. "You're going to give me a complex you keep mooning over Panama here."

"Moony Monk," Missy said.

"Go fuck yourself," Monk suggested mildly.

"I do that it make you so jealous you kill yourself," Missy shot back.

"Never mind. Never mind," Becker said. "What I'm saying is we keep this to ourselves until I turn it over to Choola."

"I'm all for that," Kopcha said. "Let's all of us keep anything we find out to ourselves. That way nobody'll know anything and nothing'll get done."

"You got a wild hair?" Becker said.

"I got a sour stomach from all the crap I've had to eat in strange restaurants."

"You gettin' lonesome for familiar streets?" Mandingo asked.

"You jus' mad because this operation screws up your routine," Missy said. "Hey! The blonde tell you she don' wan' no more jig-jig?"

"Fuck the blonde. I just don't like getting indigestion for nothing."

"Well, maybe now it won't be for nothing. Maybe we got something," Becker said, waving the pictures around.

There was practically a crowd in the office they'd set up for Fitzsimmons down at Rampart.

Buck Choola, Howard Bradford, and Gunnar Norenson were there along with Fitzsimmons and one of his two bodyguards. Which was all right if you looked at it one way since they were all cops or at least law enforcement agents of one kind or another. But Heath thought that he would certainly like to know what the hell Charlie Swale, the ward heeler, was doing here.

For that matter he didn't know what he was doing here. He and Missy had told the story of their surveillance four times already. He was in no mood to make it five.

Somebody had requisitioned a desk, a leather chair for Fitzsimmons and a couple of wooden armchairs. They weren't enough.

There was no place to sit. Heath was jammed up against the wall and Missy's ass was jammed up against his groin. He was getting a hard-on in spite of himself.

There were a couple of floor lamps with sixty-watt bulbs in them. The desk lamp didn't work, so somebody had taken the shade off one of the floor lamps and brought it closer so Fitzsimmons and the other big shots could examine Heath's photographs.

Heath noticed there was a brass spittoon on the floor by the window. Wherever the hell that had come from.

Fitzsimmons's secretary had gotten cute and filled the old spittoon with daisies. Heath was drawn to it. He kept on looking at it whether he wanted to or not. It was as though that item symbolized the lack of seriousness and purpose which seemed to have infiltrated the whole operation.

He could see pretty well where the trouble lay. This Fitzsimmons was one of those gamooshes who were very good at laying down policy and sketching out broad programs but very lousy when it came to administration and execution. He thought he was being a clever manager delegating authority and responsibility all over the place but all that did was spread the word among so many people that security went to pot. Every lead and piece of evidence became common gossip. Then middle management like Becker started looking for excuses to save their asses. Some fucking darkroom assistant would end up under suspicion. They'd make a case that some underling like that blew the operation. It was all such bullshit.

He'd said it just the other night over at the diner. "You can't have it both ways," he'd said. "You can't shout about what you're doing in the media every time you let go a fart and then expect the crooks not to smell it."

He felt Missy jab her ass up against him.

"Hey, don't do that," he said.

She looked up at him and jerked her head toward Fitzsimmons, telling him to pay attention.

Heath saw that Fitzsimmons and the rest of the brass were looking at him expectantly.

"If you'd come over here, detectives. Give us the benefit of your on-the-scene observations?"

Missy simpered a little and started making her way through the bodies to a place at Fitzsimmons's shoulder. Heath sidled sideways trying to make his hard-on as unobtrusive as possible. Fitzsimmons was looking at him all the way, a little smile on his lips. One cunt hound to another, Heath thought.

"That's okay, take your time, detective," Fitzsimmons said. "I know it's a little crowded in here and that makes it hard."

Sonofabitch, Heath thought, the man's got a sense of humor. If I didn't think he was such an asshole I might even like him.

"Sir?" he said, leaning against the edge of the desk, bending over to look at the photo Fitzsimmons was pointing to.

"Who is this man, detective?"

"That's a lawyer by the name of Allan Nadeau."

"You know him, Fitz," Charlie Swale said. "Remember, you met him at the fund-raiser."

"I thought the face was familiar. Is he Pachoulo's mouthpiece?"

"He does work for Pachoulo," Heath said.

"You know this for a fact?"

"I've seen him in Pachoulo's company more than once. I'd say it's a bet."

"We'll have this lawyer in for an interrogation," Norenson said.

Heath caught something in Fitzsimmons's eyes, a momentary hesitation.

"I think that's the next step, Gunnar," Fitzsimmons said. He looked at Heath as though closing a book. "You did good, detectives."

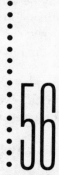

56

It was her day off. Lisa went back to her old house to get some more of her clothes and things.

She was of two minds. On the one hand she knew that it wasn't working out all that well, living with Panama. No matter what she did or how she did it, she couldn't help feeling that she was nudging him aside in his own apartment, crowding into his space. She could feel resentment break out all over him like a rash when she'd forget and leave a pair of stockings drying over the shower bar or he picked up a washcloth to wipe his face and found eyeliner on it.

She'd found out things like he didn't want to be asked if he wanted orange juice in the morning. To get himself started he'd maybe open the fridge, take out the juice and drink his fill right out of the carton or the pitcher. Or he'd guzzle what was left of a quart of milk or a flat Pepsi or whatever there was to take the dryness out of his mouth. Once she asked him why he didn't use a glass and he gave her such a look that you would have thought she was trying to act like his mother.

She'd found out he didn't like to be teased anymore. No tickling and biting his ear to get his pecker up. If she wanted to make love she had to go right at it. Come out of the bedroom bare-assed while he was reading the paper. Unzip his fly and go down on him. Maybe that would take his attention off the sports page right away, maybe it'd take a while.

Other times he'd be cute and play games to get her hot when she was feeling zero degrees centigrade.

Sometimes he wanted to talk, sometimes he didn't want to talk.

Once, when he wanted to talk, she asked him why he blew so hot and cold, was this way and that way, and he said that's just the way he was. And when she said that wasn't the way she remembered him, he said she was talking ancient history. Six years wasn't ancient history, she'd said, six years was only six years. And he'd said that was all she knew about it, as though she was silly and stupid.

It wasn't like a person having moods. Everybody had moods. She understood moods. It was like a person fighting with himself. Not wanting what he wanted. Not loving what he loved. Not trusting what he knew he should be trusting.

She'd have walked out, if she'd had any pride. She hated the way he made her feel like a charity case. Sometimes when they had sex he made her feel like she was paying room and board. She should pick up and walk the hell out but that would mean sharing with some girlfriend or moving back in with Billy and sleeping on the couch until she could find someplace of her own.

That was the other hand. If she was around Billy on a steady basis, sooner or later he'd break her down with his jokes and grins and pitiful glances. Sooner or later she'd listen to him sing the blues and tell her how the good days were just around the corner. Sooner or later, in some lonely hour of the night, or when she'd had a beer too many, or when his whining made her heart feel soft and generous, she'd let him into her again. And then she'd feel so bad about being easy that she'd convince herself she should give the marriage one more try, throwing good money after bad, until he got himself into one more mess too big to fix. A mess that would kill him or kill her. At least then she wouldn't have to worry about it anymore.

She didn't expect him to be there when she opened the door with her key and stepped into the living room. But he was there, sitting on the couch with the carton in which she kept their personal papers on the floor between his feet, pawing through the meager records of their lives. His hair was flopping over his face as he hunched over. It made him look sweet and vulnerable, but when he looked up at her, with his neck stretched and his eyes wide in exaggerated surprise and pleasure, with a grin stretching his mouth, showing those horrible temporary false teeth, he looked a hundred.

"Is this my lucky day?" he asked.

"Only if you got the winner in the third at Hollywood Park."

"Fachrissake, here I'm trying to show you how happy I am to see you and you got to crack wise with me."

"What are you looking for?" she asked, not wanting to get into the tangle of misunderstandings, recriminations, hidden meanings, false readings and apologies which were his stock in trade.

"I was looking for my insurance policy."

"Your insurance policy? You mean the one I keep the payments up on?"

"What's that supposed to mean? That supposed to mean you own the policy? I got nothing to say about a policy on my own life? When you say you keep the payments up you mean like you keep the payments up on the gas and electric, right? Like you used to pay the rent, right? You're not saying it was *all* your money paid these bills. Just that you did the bookkeeping, right?"

"Mostly my money. Your money went for football pools and the track."

He got to his feet like he was ready to go three rounds.

"But you don't really mean you paid all the bills around here?"

"I don't want to argue," she said, feeling her feet getting sucked into the quicksand of his argument. "What do you want the policy for?"

"I want to see can I take a loan out on it."

"You can't."

"You mean you'll try and stop me?"

"I mean you can't because it isn't that kind of policy."

"What kind of policy is it?"

"The kind you can't get a loan on." She laughed.

"That's a nasty laugh," he said.

"I was thinking, one way of looking at it, you're so far gone you're ready to bet your life on a goddam horse."

"I guess you're right," he said, looking deeply hurt. "I'm ready to bet my life. But not on a horse."

"Baseball, football, basketball? What's the season?"

"It's not for that kind of bet," he said solemnly, doing his mourner-at-the-grave act.

She stood there staring at him, curious about what the routine was all leading up to, what lie he'd come up with now, but unwilling to play straight man and feed him the lines that would make it look like she was screwing the information out of him against his will.

He stared back, making his eyes go wet like a pleading dog's, a little smile on his face as though he envied somebody like Lisa who didn't know—pray God would never know—the kind of pain and trouble he was suffering.

He could always wait it out longer than she could.

"That Pachoulo still threatening to kill you after what he already did?" she finally asked.

"Oh, that's still out there waiting."

"I'm not going to ask Panama to talk to him again," she warned.

"I'm not asking."

"So, what is it? What the hell is it this time?"

"Maggie," he said.

"What?"

"My mother's got a cancer. It's very bad."

"Jesus, Mary and Joseph," she said, the brief appeal of her childhood forming on her lips without her knowing.

"She needs an operation. Even then . . ."

"That's what you want to borrow money on the policy for?"

"She's going to die," he said. "I know she's going to die."

He lifted his arms from his side in a helpless, longing gesture that made her want to hold him and try to give him some comfort.

The tears were running down his cheeks and he turned his head away as though he didn't want her to see them and be moved by them.

He's getting to be a better actor in his old age, she thought sardonically and was immediately ashamed of the thought. Not even Billy Ray would lie about his mother's death to gain an edge. Would he? She heard a sob and realized it had escaped from herself. He looked at her with the wet snail tracks on his cheeks running into his ruined mouth.

She went to him and hugged him. They sank down on the couch and she held his head against her breasts while he cried his heart out. She knew it was real. For once in his life he wasn't laying down a con. He was hurting for somebody else.

She unbuttoned her blouse.

She lay there feeling a little bit like Mother Teresa, a little bit like a cheat, a little bit like a victim and a little bit like a fool.

"This doesn't mean I'm back," she whispered.

"I know that. It was a kindness," he whispered back.

She couldn't help wondering what screenplay he'd lifted that line out of. "I can't help you with the money you need for Maggie's operation, either."

"I wasn't expecting you to."

They lay there for a while feeling a sweet melancholy like honey coating the nettles of their sorrows.

"What are you going to do?" she finally asked.

"If anything happened to me, would you give my mother the money she needs out of the insurance?"

"What are you talking about?"

"I'm talking about I'll go over to see Pachoulo. Tell the guinea fuck what I think of him and that he can go scratch for the three bones I owe him."

"Are you crazy? He'd have you killed."

"That's the whole idea," he said.

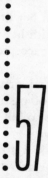

When Ana's grandfather had first taken to bed in the back room which looked down onto a skinny garden and the brick wall of the back of the apartment house on the next block, he'd asked her—a child of eight—how the sky looked over toward the Brooklyn Bridge. Later he asked her if the vine was still growing along the back fence where he'd planted it the year before. Then if the cat was rattling the lid of the garbage can just below the window. Then why the birds weren't coming to the feeder on the windowsill.

One day he asked why the dust balls were gathering in the corner of the room. The next day, and until the day he died, he was concerned only with the bed from the pillow to the blanket covering his toes, the reach of his arms, the distance from plate to mouth, the track of his tears from eye to chin.

When he died the room and the apartment didn't seem much more silent than it had before. His had always been a silent house.

When they sat *shiva,* relatives and friends even mourned softly, almost silently, moaning under their breaths, remembering the number tattooed on the wrist of the old man.

Years later, Ana asked her father, when he was close to death, why theirs had always been such a silent house and her father had said, "That's how your grandfather survived the camps and your grandmother did not. She complained and drew attention to herself. He pretended to be a mouse and sat in corners without saying a word."

She wanted to say that she could almost understand that, but couldn't understand why, after coming to America, her grandfather, father and mother had continued to make themselves small and silent and unseen. But by that time, she herself had been infected with silence and a taste for solitude and shadows.

She'd openly displayed boldness and courage only twice in her life. Once when she'd accepted the invitation of an aunt to live with her in Hollywood, in the Fairfax District, and again when she'd accepted Benny Checks for a husband.

He'd been a revelation and a wonder to her, so loud and open, laughing most of the time, loving her like she was made of pastry, scheming big schemes. Foolish and not too bright, but always so full of life and noise. Now he sat in the rocking chair by the window.

Just the other day he'd broken the silence of a week and asked if the tulip tree at the end of the block was blooming. The next he asked if the roses by the fence needed feeding.

Sometimes, at dusk, she sat in the corner while he rocked in his chair, hardly aware that she was sitting there. Sometimes his mouth fell open and saliva dribbled from the corners.

There was a bruise on his arm, left from the beating and the bites of the dog, that looked like a number tattooed in his skin.

58

"Sit down Mr. Nadeau," Fitzsimmons said very politely as the lawyer came through the door of his Rampart Street office, but he didn't rise to shake his hand.

Fitzsimmons believed there was nothing so upsetting as a well-calculated mixture of signals, the courteous gesture turned into one of subtle contempt.

They were alone in the room, and Nadeau was supposed to wonder what that was all about, too. It was meant to give him hope that there might be a chance to cut a deal.

At least that was supposed to be the way it worked, but Nadeau was sitting there looking very smug, very sure of himself.

"You're a lawyer, Mr. Nadeau."

"Yes, Mr. Fitzsimmons."

"Then, as you're an officer of the court, I'm sure I'll have no difficulty obtaining your cooperation."

"That would be dependent upon the circumstances."

"How's that?"

"If I'm to cooperate in any matter that would endanger or infringe upon the rights of any client of mine I would, of course, have to exercise the lawyer-client rule of confidentiality."

"A client like who for instance?" Fitzsimmons asked.

"I was offering a hypothetical."

"Are you saying you have no client or are not under retainer to any client who might conceivably come under the scrutiny of the commission which I have been asked to administer?"

"I'm saying if I have such a client it would be unknown to me."

"That's remarkable."

"In what way remarkable?"

"Remarkable that you should be unaware that a client of yours, one Puffy Pachoulo, is a known criminal with a long history of arrests and indictments."

"I have a client by the name of Alfonso Pachoulo—"

"Alfonso. Is that your name, too? Is Al short for Alfonso?"

"I'm not Italian. It's short for Allan."

"I thought we had a little coincidence there," Fitzsimmons said, smiling unctuously. "You were saying?"

"Alfonso Pachoulo has had some misunderstandings with the law but he's never been taken to trial, let alone convicted."

"When he was a boy. He was placed in Juvenile Hall more than once."

"The result of a broken home," Nadeau said and waved a hand in dismissal.

"I see. So he's basically your everyday misunderstood good citizen?"

"I'd say that describes him to the letter of the law."

"But not the spirit?"

"Mr. Prosecutor, why don't we get down to the nitty?"

"We know that Pachoulo's a loan shark and an extortionist. He's probably also done murder or ordered murder done."

"I don't know any of that."

"We know that he's currently setting up a bust-out operation using the Doohan Porsche dealership in North Hollywood as the bucket."

"I don't know any of that."

"We know that he set the Doohans up by sucking them into a construction project of the Nicoletti brothers."

"I don't know any of that," Nadeau said again with insulting monotony. "I was asked, however, to frame two documents concerning a legitimate enterprise."

"Two documents?"

"Yes."

"Will you tell me at least what they were, or do I have to call the grand jury and serve you with a subpoena?"

"A simple promissory note and a hold harmless."

"Hold harmless from what?"

"I don't know the details of the agreement between Mr. Pachoulo and the Doohan brothers."

"A hold harmless indicates that one party intends to engage in activities that could endanger the other party or parties."

"I don't know any of that."

"All right, let's get to the nitty like you say. We want to know the exact day the scam is supposed to go down. We want to be there to witness it."

"If you think my client is engaged or means to be engaged in an illegal act, stake it out."

"That wouldn't do the job and you know it. We need somebody to give us the word. We want you to be that somebody."

"What reason would I have for breaking the confidence of a client and putting him into jeopardy on the mere say-so of a special prosecutor brought in to stir his finger in the mud, make some headlines and convince the citizens that something's being done about the flood of crime that's drowning the town when nothing's really being done?"

"That sounded like a speech, counselor."

Nadeau stood up. "I think you'll have to look somewhere else."

"We'll gather you up along with the rest of the garbage," Fitzsimmons said.

"I don't think so," Nadeau replied. "I think you'll keep your hands off me and I think you'll keep your hands off Pachoulo."

"You seem pretty sure of that," Fitzsimmons said, getting to his feet.

"I'm as sure of that as I am of the fact that you've been fucking my wife," Nadeau said.

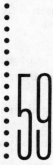

59

Iggie Deetch was stripping the assets of Doohan Porsche like a gang of locusts in a field of corn, selling off service contracts to other dealers for fifty cents on the dollar, inviting confidential offers on the lease and unloading cars below cost to a number of happy gonnifs, juicemen, pimps and murderers.

In a flurry of paper he had doubled up the order for new vehicles before paying off the indebtedness on the old, ensuring promptness of delivery and few questions asked by sweetening the cash surety by twenty percent. In a slow market the importer was only too happy to send motor arks loaded with new Porsches to a dealer who was clearing them out as fast as they could get them in.

But so far it was all small potatoes. The big score would take place when there were forty, fifty luxury cars over and above regular inventory, forty large a pop, sitting out there on the blacktop underneath the banners like a pack of greyhounds.

Forty by forty was one million six hundred thousand, fifty by forty a nice even two million. Even discounting them out, Pachoulo stood to make nine hundred thousand dollars on a one-hundred-thousand–dollar investment, because it was only the first hundred that had ever left his hands. The Nicolettis never saw the next two hundred and fifty, though the Doohans never knew that.

Iggie Deetch and Sam's Man were on the phones lining up salesmen from as far away as Portland, Las Vegas and Tucson who could sell two or three cars behind their employers' backs and nobody the wiser.

When the cars were gathered and the deals cut, when the captive Doohans had signed all the papers for this and that because if they dared do anything else they'd been warned they'd get a couple of peas each in their heads, Iggie Deetch did a buck and wing down to the courthouse with Nadeau and filed papers of bankruptcy.

They could go looking for the missing cars, the service contracts, the furniture for that matter, and they'd find nothing but the skeleton and three Irishmen with a story.

Pachoulo and Nadeau were outside the showroom wearing their topcoats. "Whattaya call that stuff on your collar?" Pachoulo asked Nadeau.

"Karakul," Nadeau said.

"What's that?"

"Lamb."

"I think I'll get me mink."

"Billy says he's going over to see Pachoulo," Lisa said in the middle of supper.

"I hope he's going over to pay him off. Otherwise Pachoulo's going to kill him," Heath replied.

"That's what Billy says he wants."

Heath stopped with a forkful of corned beef hash halfway to his mouth. After a long silence he said, "You believe him?"

"Billy's mother's got a cancer. She's going in for an operation. It's going to cost plenty. Also there's the nursing care she's going to need afterwards. If she comes through it alive."

"I'm sorry for her." He finished putting the food into his mouth.

"Billy's at the end of his rope. I think he's finally realized he's got to face growing up. It's terrible it took something like this to make him see, but I really think it woke him up," Lisa said.

"So his idea of growing up is to get killed?"

"I think he just meant he was ready to face up to Pachoulo."

"Face up," Heath repeated.

"He wants to spit in Pachoulo's soup, make him mad enough to kill him."

"What the hell for?"

"For the insurance policy I've got on his life."

"He means to deliberately get himself murdered so he can pay for his mother's operation and her nurses?"

"That's what he says. He made me promise to give the insurance money to his mother."

"When did you find out about all this?"

"Billy told me."

"I figured that out already. I didn't ask who, I asked when."

"I went over for some clothes the other day and he was there looking for the insurance policy."

"What day was this?"

"The other day."

"How come you didn't mention it?"

"Well, I didn't know if it was true. You know you can never be sure that Billy isn't making up a story to get your sympathy."

"I mean how come you didn't mention going over to get some clothes?"

"I didn't see any reason to bring it up."

"Oh. So did he?"

"Did he what? Get my sympathy?"

"Fuck you."

She dropped her fork on her plate and turned away sharply.

"If you're going to talk like that . . ."

"When did you finally believe he was telling the truth?"

"I called up Maggie and asked her if she was going to have any operation."

"I'll bet she loved that."

"You know, I think she did. I think she was happy that I cared enough to call. She said she knew that things hadn't always been too good between us, but if she came through the operation all right, she hoped we could get along better."

"Now that you're not living with her son."

"I suppose that's part of it. Some mothers are that way about their sons."

"So after you talked to his mother, what then?"

"What then?"

"Did you see Billy again?"

"I went over to tell him I was sorry I didn't completely believe him the first time he told me. It was the least I could do."

"And what was the most you could do? Fuck him again?"

She felt the tears flooding up behind her eyes, carried on waves of remorse and anger.

"If I did, it was because the fucking I was getting here was pretty grudging," she yelled.

"I don't want a fight," he said.

"I didn't go to bed with Billy," she lied. "Why would I want to do that?"

"So what do you want me to do?"

"I was thinking maybe you could have a talk with Billy. Tell him it wouldn't be very smart to get himself killed. Or go tell Pachoulo what Billy means to do. Warn him off."

He looked at her evenly across the table. "Maybe it would be smart."

"That's what I thought."

"I mean if Billy got himself killed."

"That's a terrible thing to say."

"You're right," he said, getting up. "Look, I have to go."

"How long is this working nights going to last?"

"Don't start that again, just like last time. That was one of the reasons you gave for leaving me the last time. You planning to do it again?"

"I just wanted to know. The way you've been acting the last couple of nights I'm afraid something's going to happen."

"Like what?"

"Like I don't know. I remember when I lived with you before, I could always tell when something was going down. Remember?"

"So you got two men to worry about. Me and Billy."

"Oh, Jesus, don't hammer me for caring a little bit about Billy. What do you expect me to do? After all, he was my husband."

He went to her, bent over and took her face in his hands.

"You take it easy. You watch a little television, have some cocoa maybe, go to bed early. Get some rest. I'll be all right. Billy's going to be all right, too. After tonight, tomorrow night—soon—maybe we don't have to worry about Pachoulo anymore."

"I didn't go to bed with Billy," she said.

"I heard you," he said.

After he was out the door, she thought, He heard me but he didn't say he believed me.

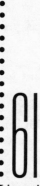

Lisa tried to watch the television like Panama had said to do, but she kept thinking about how something was building up and something was going to happen and if Billy took it into his head to go baiting Pachoulo tonight he could maybe end up right in the middle of it and who knows what would happen to him. He couldn't take care of himself. Maybe it wasn't his fault, the way his mother had spoiled him all his life, but he was as helpless as a baby about most things, no matter how he strutted around acting like a big man.

Finally she put on her coat and shoes, grabbed her pocketbook and went over to the court bungalow.

When Billy opened the door, his face brightened up right away and a sly look came into his eyes, as though he'd been sure that once they started making love again Lisa would want more of it.

He almost asked her if she wasn't getting any from that macho stud cop with the dirty hat but he wasn't that sure of himself. Later on, when she was back home for keeps, he'd grind her a little about it. Now he'd keep on playing the lost, grateful child.

"Jesus, I'm glad you came over, Lisa," he said. "I've been sitting here all by myself feeling lonely as hell."

She glanced past him into the living room and saw the racing form spread out on the coffee table but she didn't say anything.

"Well, I came over because I was afraid you might've already gone to see Pachoulo."

He thought he caught an edge to her voice like she was worried on the one hand that he'd already gone and got himself killed but, seeing him standing there, was disdainful toward him and laughing at herself, as though she should have known he was just making himself out to be a big man. That he never intended to do any such thing.

"I was just clearing up some business. You know, the tag ends. I was going to have a drink and then . . ."

She pushed past him, not even letting him finish what he was going to say.

"Let me have your coat," he said.

"No thanks, I'm not staying," she said. "I just came to see if you were serious about this business of getting yourself—"

"Would you care?"

She sat down on the sagging couch with her purse on her knees like the Avon lady. "—killed. Of course I'd care. You think I want to see you dead?"

"I don't know what else to do. I don't know where else to turn."

She was staring at him, trying to read his eyes, trying to convince herself all over again that he really meant to do it, even though she didn't really want him to do it. Because if he really meant to do it maybe he wasn't such a weak sister after all. Maybe he had some real balls.

"It's a crazy idea," she finally said, not having come to any conclusion. "Maybe he wouldn't even kill you. Maybe he'd just have you beat up worse than before."

"That's a thought," he said, sitting down in the chair across the table from her.

Speaking of crazy, she thought, this was crazy, sitting here talking about whether it was a good idea to go pester the animals so you'd maybe get killed when, truth was, Billy had probably just made it up to play on her sympathies. If he really meant to do it what was he doing checking the racing form? Going to lay a bet from heaven or wherever?

"Well, I came to tell you not to do anything foolish. You'll only get yourself into more trouble."

He laughed in a rush as though he didn't want to but couldn't help himself. As though it struck him funny to talk about more trouble when he was about to take the leap.

"I mean you go over to see Pachoulo he might not even be there. He might be in jail."

If she'd been paying attention, she'd have seen his ears perk up, but she was too busy doing him the favor, just in case he wasn't lying about getting himself killed.

"How's that?" he asked.

"It looks to me like the cops got something on him and are ready to come down on him. I'd just as soon you weren't there when it happened."

He went over and sat next to her and tried to take her hands, but she wouldn't let go of her purse.

"That mean what I think it means about the way you feel about us?" he asked.

"The way I feel about us is the same way I felt the day I walked out the door," she said, standing up quickly. "That hasn't changed."

"Even after—"

"Don't punish me for having a kind heart," she said.

"Whatever you say, Lisa."

He followed her to the door.

"So you'll stay away from Pachoulo?"

"Whatever you say."

62

Heath and Missy were playing at being lovers in the stakeout car down the street from the Porsche dealership. Every once in a while, if anybody looked their way, they'd pretend to be necking. Once Missy caught his mouth with her mouth as though it were an accident and Heath went with it. She backed off, feeling bad for a minute about teasing him that way when he was in the middle of this thing with the lady he used to live with and was living with again.

Across the street the limousine arrived stuffed with Machado and four gamooshes they hadn't seen before that night. They were probably just pickups hired for the night to shift the cars off the lot. They'd been cleaning it out for the last five hours.

After the first couple of trips Heath had gotten on the radio and told Becker what was going down and Becker had sent out Kelly and Monk to tail one of the drivers to wherever they were going and reported back that the Porsches were being ferried to a garage over in Burbank.

Mandingo and Poke Kopcha were staked out over at Benito's Restaurant, where Pachoulo, Sam's Man, Nadeau and Iggie Deetch were having a late, late supper.

Fitzsimmons had been informed. At least Becker said he'd called it in not once but three times. But nothing was happening.

The drivers piled out of the car and went to move four more.

After another fifteen minutes, a car pulled up behind them. Heath and Missy pretended to kiss as somebody got out without turning out the headlights.

"Somebody called the cops," Heath said.

A figure loomed up on the driver's side and tapped on the window. Heath turned around ready to roll down the window and identify himself. Becker stood there grinning sheepishly as if he thought they'd really been going at it.

"Sorry to interrupt," he said when the window was down.

"You didn' in'errupt nothin'. We was jus' makin' believe," Missy said.

"You everybody?" Heath asked.

"What do you mean 'everybody'?"

"They're stripping the goddam inventory over there. We going to move in on those fuckers or not?"

"I put the calls in to Fitzsimmons."

"He get them?"

"Choola told me they were right on it."

"Right on fucking what?" Heath asked.

"Right on getting Fitzsimmons."

"Where the hell they looking for him?"

Becker shrugged and looked worried.

"You know what I think?" Heath said. "What I think is that Fitzsimmons is out fucking that thousand-dollar hooker and can't be reached."

"They say they're doing what they can."

"So let's say they don't find the white-haired sonofabitch while all this is going down. Can't Choola take over? Can't somebody take over?"

"This isn't just an ordinary everyday bust," Becker said. "There's larger ramifications."

"Let them ram their ramifications up their asses," Heath raged softly. "We been fucking around for months, eight squads of the best, and this is the best thing we come up with. If it was your everyday stakeout we'd be in there catching that fuck Pachoulo with all these cars and asking him what the fuck he thinks he's doing. We'd be kicking ass and making points. Instead Missy and me are sitting around playing kissy-face while Pachoulo moves a couple of million dollars' worth of cars to a chop shop and who knows what's the next destination?"

Becker still stood there bent over, his head tilted so he could look inside the car, his hands in his pockets, like your favorite uncle half drunk and playing pocket pool.

The radio squawked. "You there, Panama?" Mandingo asked.

Heath grabbed the handset. "Yeah, I'm here."

"Guess who just walked into Benito's?"

"I got no time for games, for chrissake."

"Hey, hey, hey, Billy Ray just walked in."

"Sonofabitch, I didn't think he'd go through with it."

"Go through with what?" Becker and Mandingo said at the same time.

"We got to get the hell over there," Heath said, tossing the mike into Missy's lap and kicking over the engine. "Lisa's husband is looking to get himself killed."

"Jesus Christ, hold on," Becker said. "Let's do this by the book."

"You do it by the fucking book," Heath shouted as he peeled out from the curb.

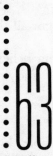

"Will you look at this?" Iggie Deetch said as Billy Ray came strolling into Benito's flashing a smile as though nothing wrong had ever happened between them.

"Hey, hey, hey, it's Billy Ray," Sam's Man said.

"I like your new teeth," Pachoulo said. "I like the way your nose looks, too."

"It gives you character," Iggie Deetch said.

Pachoulo nodded. "You was maybe too good-looking before, you know what I mean? Nowadays the movie fans like a little ugly. Maybe we done you a favor. Maybe we turned your career around for you."

"You going to ask me to sit down? You going to offer me a glass of wine?" Ray said.

There was a thin line of sweat on his upper lip and he looked a little pale. He thought he had a hand of cards but he couldn't really be sure that Pachoulo would want to play.

"I don't know should I do that until I know what you come to see me about. You come to pay me some money?"

"I got no money. After the face-lift you give me I got even less money. I got no money, I got no wife and I got no job."

"Oh?"

"My dentist's taking all the cash I ain't got, my wife walked out on me for another guy and I got fired because I tried to make what you done to me look like an accident so I could keep my health insurance."

Pachoulo's eyes had gone flat like a lizard's, the way they did before he ordered violence.

"I don't want to hear any more. I don't want to start crying, make my tie all soggy. I try to give you a break a hundred times, now you want me to give you my blessing? I ain't the pope. I don't hear confessions. What do you think you're worth to me, Billy Ray?"

"Well, how about you give me a job and let me work it off?"

"I don't need an asshole with a habit working for me. I got all the assholes I need."

Sam's Man grinned and Iggie Deetch said, "Hey," making believe that he was offended. Pachoulo smiled and patted his hand, enjoying his own little joke.

"So what do I need with you, Billy Ray?"

"Maybe I can do you some good."

"Maybe you can do me some good I use you for an example. You know what I mean? I have Carmine here put a pea in your head, all the other gonnifs on the street hear about it and they know when you try to fuck with Puffy Pachoulo you get what's coming."

"I think I could do you more good as an ear."

"You think I ain't got enough ears, like I ain't got enough assholes, I need more ears?"

"You maybe need my ears."

"How's that?"

"Because I hear things your ears don't hear."

"Like what do you hear?"

"Like I hear the cops from the special commission are about to come down on your ass."

"When did you hear that?"

"Half an hour ago."

"Where you hear it?"

"From my wife. I told you. She's sleeping with a cop."

"What cop?"

"Panama Heath."

"Sonofabitch," Pachoulo said.

Heath had nearly taken off his foot, speeding off that way. Becker stood there for a minute, then he ran back to his car and called for a cruiser from Valley Division to come over to the Doohan dealership and squat on it.

"What's going on?" Monk's voice asked over the radio.

"Panama went haring over to Benito's because Billy Ray walked in there."

"What the hell's that all about?"

"Panama said Ray was trying to get himself killed."

"Goddammit," Monk exploded. "Goddammit to hell. I knew the minute I saw them in the movie house that pussy was going to get Panama's ass in hot water."

"I'm going over there. You stay where you are—"

"Like hell," Monk broke in. "We're on our way. I got to be where my partner is if the stupid sonofabitch's going to bust in on Pachoulo."

"You stay the fuck where you are," Becker yelled back, completely losing his cool.

"I don't hear you," Monk said.

"Oh, goddammit," Becker complained to himself. He called Valley and asked for another car over at Pachoulo's garage, then he peeled off from the curb even faster than Heath had done.

"You break any more traffic laws, I gonna bust you, Panama," Missy said.

"Don't talk to me when I'm driving, you'll get us killed," he said, his hands tight on the wheel, his upper body hunched forward so he could get closer to the windshield and judge the angles better.

"What's the big hurry? That asshole husban' of your girlfrien' goin' to walk into his own funeral, tha's good for you."

"No, it's not good for me."

"What's the matter, your lady be mad at you, you don' save her husban's ass?"

"I'll be mad at myself. I don't want that sonofabitch Billy Ray to get himself killed. I want him alive so Lisa can go the fuck back to him."

Missy leaned back against the cushions.

"Hey, Panama," she said, "step on the gas."

Billy Ray stood there feeling the sweat run off the back of his neck down his collar and inside his shirt along his ribs.

Iggie Deetch and Sam's Man were looking at Pachoulo while Pachoulo thought. It took a long time. Finally he took out a sparkling white handkerchief and delicately covered his mouth while he coughed.

"When's this gonna happen?"

"It could be happening right now," Ray replied. "I got what I could. I couldn't get any more without my ex starts thinking about what she's doing and shuts her mouth."

Machado noisily came in just then, giving the glad hand to the waiters and the busboys, even to some of the customers he didn't know.

"All done," he said. "All safe and sound. All snug in their beds."

"Where's the drivers?"

"I paid them off and sent them home. What's the matter?"

"We got to move the cars again."

"How many?"

"All of them."

"Back to the Doohans'?"

"Out of the state. We scatter them out along the roads going east and south. We spread out, then everybody goes to Mexico."

"That's a very big job. It'll take my drivers maybe two, three weeks to move them all."

"It's got to be done tonight. Right this minute."

"I don't see how."

"I see how," Billy Ray said.

They all looked at him. He grinned as he plucked a small address book out of his pocket, sure of himself again, powerful in the belief that, say what you wanted to say, Billy Ray always landed on his feet with a ten-spot riding on the long shot that today of all days was going to cross the finish line a winner.

"I got here the names and numbers of half the full-time and part-time cabbies in town. How many you need?"

Pachoulo looked at Machado.

"There's forty-six automobiles," Machado said.

"I drive one, you drive one," Billy Ray said. "Anybody else drive one?"

"I'm not driving one," Machado said.

"You're driving one, I say you're driving one," Pachoulo corrected him.

"So that makes it forty-four drivers we need," Ray said. "I don't know can I get that many on such short notice."

"You get me what you can. I take a hundred off what you owe me for every wheel you get over to Burbank."

"Show me a phone," Billy Ray said, "and give me the address."

Pachoulo got to his feet, excited now, pointing fingers like he was a general.

"You go with Billy Ray, Carmine. Make sure these cabbies know where they're supposed to go. Give them good directions, they shouldn't get lost."

"These are hacks, Puffy," Ray declared. "You don't got to worry. They're like fucking homing pigeons. What do I tell them you're going to pay?"

"Tell them three hundred and expenses."

I'll tell them two and pocket the hundred, Billy Ray thought.

Sam's Man struggled to his feet, telling Sam to stay, and lumbered off after Billy Ray to start the phoning.

"Iggie, I want you to grab another phone. Call up Dolores the Hook down to Tijuana and Pistol Molera in Mexicali. While you're at it get Show Low Aldama down in Nogales. Tell them we'll be moving a lot of prime beasts across the border the next day or two."

He spun around on Machado. "Get on your horse over to Burbank. See the tanks is full. Iggie, hold it. You go with Manny. Make your calls from the garage. I want you should be there to decide which Porsche goes where after you find out how many each one of the shon-nikers'll take. See the pink slips go with the right cars. And keep good books."

"Christ, Puffy, you don't got to say that to me," Iggie Deetch said. "Don't I always keep good books?"

"Get the fuck outta here and don't ask me for a gold star on your fucking report card until this fucking situation is over with."

Iggie Deetch went flying after Machado, who was already out the door.

Pachoulo sat down, feeling like a general who had just launched an invasion.

Sam drooled on Pachoulo's foot.

"Hey," Pachoulo said.

Sam lifted his head.

Pachoulo, pleased with himself, reached down and patted the dog's huge head.

"That's okay, Sam, you can go ahead and spit on my sock if you want to."

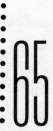

It was not a smooth operation. By the time Heath and Missy got to Benito's and walked in with Mandingo and Kopcha, Billy Ray and Sam's Man were sitting in the booth with Pachoulo having a breather and a glass of wine before Ray went over to the garage in Burbank.

But, of course, they didn't know that. And they didn't know that Ray had already scared up twenty-five cabbies, some of them turning their vehicles in to the garage so they could take advantage of this chance for a vacation in Ol' Meh-hee-co. They didn't know that Ray was ready to go over to Burbank to give them their expenses before they took off and start making calls again to scare up the other twenty-one that were needed. Worse came to worse, Sam's Man could take a car and even Pachoulo might get behind a wheel. Whatever Porsches were left over could be stashed in the alleys and back lots until they could be picked up and transported across the border.

So Heath busted in on the run, ready to risk himself and Missy if he had to, if that's what it would take to save Billy Ray's worthless life, and stood there, a sickly grin like custard all over his face, when he saw the three of them sitting there as friendly as three puppies in a barrel.

Mandingo and Kopcha peeled off, one going to the rest rooms and the other to the kitchen, making a show of it because they were feeling pretty foolish, too.

"Well, look who's here," Pachoulo said. "I don't think I know the lady."

"You do anythin' funny, you'll know the lady quick," Missy said, making a lot of bluster for no reason she could explain, except she was feeling just as foolish as Panama looked.

"What the fuck's going on?" Heath demanded, trying to cover his ass. "We got a call."

"What kind of a call did you get?" Pachoulo asked.

"We got a call that somebody was getting murdered, or was about to be murdered, here."

"Here in Benito's?"

"That's right."

"They was maybe making a joke about the food. Some people say it could kill you."

Sam's Man and Billy Ray laughed when Pachoulo laughed.

"See? Like that," Pachoulo said. "It's a joke. Somebody was playing a joke on you."

"You all right, Billy Ray?"

"Why wouldn't I be all right?"

"Because not long ago this asshole here had the shit beat out of you because you owed him a couple of bones and couldn't pay up. Now you going to tell me you're lovers?"

"We reached a . . . a . . ."

"An accommodation," Billy supplied.

"That's what we reached," Pachoulo said. "Billy Ray's working for me now."

Heath's eyebrows went up.

"That's right, Panama," Billy Ray said.

"Billy Ray's a man what has got talents which are very valuable to me," Pachoulo went on expansively.

"That's right," Ray said, grinning, his false teeth looking like chalk in the half-light.

"I think your lady got a big mouth," Missy murmured in Heath's ear.

Mandingo and Kopcha came wandering back, their hands in their pockets, as though they were just passing through.

"You want some spaghetti, some tortellini?" Pachoulo asked. "How about some cannelloni, maybe some spumoni?"

Kopcha looked receptive. Why not sit down and have a little something, it shouldn't be a total loss, his expression clearly said. Missy could see what was going through his head and gave him a dirty look.

"I don' wan' to get sick," Missy said.

"Hey, little lady, I was only kidding about the food not being good."

"I was thinkin' abou' the company."

"So, you don't want anything," Pachoulo said, his eyes and voice going flat, "maybe you'll let me and my friends enjoy our wine in peace."

"That's fair," Mandingo growled, making it sound like one more word out of Pachoulo and he'd break his head.

"We'll leave you alone," Heath said. "But we'll be resting our feet outside for a while."

"You can sleep on the curb for all I care," Pachoulo said.

When they got outside, Becker was just pulling up. He was so angry he jumped out of the car without setting the handbrake. The car started to roll back down the grade as he walked toward Heath and Missy with his finger out ready to give them hell.

"Your vehicle's getting away on you," Mandingo said.

"Oh, shit," Becker shouted, and started running for his car just as Kelly and Monk came cutting around the corner and plowed into the rear end of it, which was now on the wrong side of the street.

They were starting to draw a crowd. Any hour of the day or night you can draw a crowd if there's an accident or some kind of trouble. People were coming out of their apartments, hoping to see some action better than they were getting on television.

"What's going on?" somebody asked.

"I think that big black dude called that white man with the red face a honky cocksucker and the white man called him a nigger mother-fucker," somebody volunteered.

"That's how trouble always starts," a woman commented.

Kelly and Kopcha were pushing from behind as Becker tried to steer his car toward the curb and read everybody the riot act for leaving their assignments without permission at the same time.

Monk was yelling that the accident wasn't his fault. What the fuck was Becker's car doing on the wrong side of the street in the first place, he wanted to know.

Heath and Missy were just standing there.

"What's with the Chicana twist?" somebody asked.

"She's a hooker," a woman said. "You can tell."

"That guy in the hat her pimp?"

"Who the hell else would wear a hat like that?"

The radios in all three cars started squawking at once.

A woman dressed in a black dress with a white collar and cuffs and a little round hat with a white brim made her way through the crowd. Some of the night birds stepped out of the way politely and called her sister.

"What'd he say? What'd he say?" Becker asked anybody. He reached inside his car for the microphone. "Who the hell is this?" he shouted.

A calm voice came back, flattened even more by the effect of the shortwave band. "This is Officers Irvine and Wyzsynski out of North Valley. We're staked out by a garage on Alameda and Olive Avenue Park in Burbank. Somebody's driving out a whole bunch of brand-new Porsches. Is that what we're supposed to be watching?"

Heath turned around facing the entrance to Benito's.

Ana Checks went into the restaurant.

"Let's go back inside Benito's and have a little cannelloni, a little spumoni," Heath suggested.

"Why the hell not?" Missy agreed.

When they walked through the door, the few customers who hadn't already left to avoid the trouble they saw coming when the three men and a girl had busted in ten minutes ago, or gone outside to find out what the shouting was all about, were parking themselves as far away from the woman dressed like a modern nun as they could get.

Her back was to Heath and Missy, and they couldn't see the gun in her hand, which was pointed right at Pachoulo's head.

But they could see how still Pachoulo was sitting and the smarmy smile on his face. And they could see Billy Ray's face, which was now as white as his teeth.

"Somethin' not so good," Missy murmured.

"Don't panic," Heath murmured back.

"Min' your own business," Missy said. "I'm driftin' left."

Only Sam, asleep on Pachoulo's foot, and Sam's Man seemed comfortable. Sam's Man wasn't even looking at the woman. He was toying with a plate of cannelloni with the fork in his right hand.

"Mrs. Checks—" Pachoulo started to say.

"Chempenovsky," Ana said.

Sam's Man moved the fork to his left hand and kept on chewing and looking at his plate.

"Mrs. Chempenovsky," Pachoulo said, "I was just about to call Benny and tell him I need a partner in my loan business. I'm moving into other things, you understand, and I could use a good man like Benny."

"Benny isn't a good man, anymore. He isn't even a human being anymore."

Sam's Man slipped his right hand inside his coat as though he was going to scratch himself under his arm.

Missy slipped her service revolver out of her purse and Heath got his from his hip.

"Benny has no mind anymore," Ana said. "He's in a place where they keep people like animals until they die."

Sam's Man pulled out his gun.

Missy had the best shot and she took it. Heath fired, too.

Sam's Man looked surprised to feel a pea behind his ear and another in his throat. His face settled slowly toward his plate but never got there because his belly was too big and he couldn't bend in the middle.

Ana Checks flinched but didn't turn around.

Only Billy Ray was close enough to hear what she said when she pulled the trigger and blew Pachoulo's face away.

"First you made Benny crawl like a dog in front of his wife and then you took his brain away" is what she said.

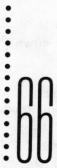

Becker was very upset.

"Pissed off," Kelly said. "I never seen Becker pissed off."

"Wha's he pissed off about?" Missy said, her thigh pressing against Heath's thigh, happy that he wasn't going to get up any minute and say he had to go home.

"Whattaya mean what's he pissed off about?" Kopcha said. "He blames Fitzsimmons for not being where he was supposed to be. Not sending out the authority. Not having a flood of cops all over those goddam Porsches. You know how many of those goddam forty-thousand-dollar Porsches can't be found?"

"How many?"

"Thirteen, fourteen."

"Those cabbies heard wha' happen to Pachoulo, they say, 'Fuck Meh-hee-co. Who's goin' to know?'"

"There's some happy asshole hacks driving around out there in forty-thousand-dollar cars," Kelly said.

"That's why Becker's pissed off," Kopcha said.

"It could have been worse," Heath said.

"And it could have been better," Kopcha said.

"Quiet down," Mandingo said.

Becker was through the door and walking down the aisle toward the booth where they were gathered around coffee and burgers and beers.

"Hey, he don' look mad," Missy remarked.

"How would you like it, you all went on overtime?" Becker said.

He was grinning from ear to ear.

"How much overtime?" Monk asked.

"Maybe it takes an hour, maybe it takes two hours. Fitzsimmons is scarfing that expensive lady again."

"Can we go over to Brentwood and make a bust?" Kelly asked.

"He ain't in Brentwood. He's in a hot-pillow motel just down the road in Studio City."

"Who told you that?"

"Piscaroon. He's making a hobby out of tailing Fitzsimmons."

"What's he doing in a hot-pillow motel in Studio City, the money he's got?" Kopcha wanted to know.

"Maybe he wan' it down an' dirty tonight," Missy suggested.

"So, whoever wants to come with me better stand up," Becker said.

They all followed him out.

They took two squad cars down Ventura to the curve in the road where half a dozen sex-rated motels stood side by side. Becker, driving the lead car, pulled into the one called West Rest and parked.

They all got out as a tall drink of water wandered up looking like he was going to tap Becker for his loose change.

"I'm going to owe you one for this, Piscaroon," Becker said.

"I heard you had an interest."

"Which one?"

"Number seven. You want to have a look, go have a look. The drapes don't make it all the way across. There's a three-inch gap on the left-hand side of the big window."

Becker started walking toward the motel. The rest of the squad started to follow. He turned around and waved them off.

"For God's sake," he whispered, "you want to warn him there's a herd of elephants coming?"

They waited until he went over to number seven, crouched down and peeked through the gap in the drapes.

He came back with a look of wonder and amusement on his face.

"What's going on? What's going on?" everybody was whispering.

He handed Kelly a five-dollar bill. "Go across the street to the liquor store and buy a jar of maraschino cherries."

Becker stood there saying nothing, his hands in his pockets, rising up and down on his toes, a grin on his face, until Kelly came back with the bottle of cherries.

Becker took the lid off and looked around at his cops, then he put the bottle out toward Missy and said, "You do it. Pick one."

"Do what?" Missy asked while she plucked a big red cherry out by its stem.

"You'll see. Be quiet now until Man kicks in the door."

"You want me to kick in a door without a warrant?" Mandingo said.

"Don't you worry."

They reached the door to number seven and piled up behind it, giving Mandingo enough room to pull back his twelve and a half, on a leg like a railroad-engine piston, and let it go.

Bam!

The door flew open and they all piled in to see Fitzsimmons, bare-naked, down on his knees eating whipped cream off Helena Nadeau's belly.

Missy went over and dropped the cherry right in the center.

"Hey, whatsamatter wi' you? You don' know how to make a sundae right?"

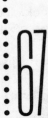

The Old Time Movie House was showing ten chapters of *The Perils of Pauline*.

Eddie "Panama" Heath sat in the next-to-last row with his knees up on the back of the seat in front of him.

Monk came in and sat down next to him.

"Good to be back," he said.

"Watch the picture," Heath replied.

"I hated it out there in the Valley. All you got is Ventura Boulevard going west, then turning north to nowhere."

Heath only grunted this time, knowing that there was no way of shutting Monk up when he wanted to talk.

"That fucker Fitzsimmons is taking all the credit for closing out a very large loan shark and putting Manny Machado and Iggie Deetch on trial for usury, extortion, assault and battery and other assorted mayhem."

"So, that's okay. Becker got a piece of him."

"You're right. You know who was the lady with her ass in the air?"

"Allan Nadeau's wife, Helena."

"How do you know that?"

"I hear what you hear from the same place you hear it."

"So what do you think?"

"What do I think about what?"

"What do you think about what I hear this Nadeau is going to charge Fitzsimmons with urging Mrs. Nadeau into prostitution?"

"I think Fitzsimmons maybe blew his chance to be president."

"In a manner of speaking," Monk said, laughing through his nose.

"Don't spray me, goddammit," Heath complained.

"You got a wild hair up your patootie?"

"I'm disgusted. They're bringing Ana Checks up on murder charges."

"That won't go anywhere. They'll have a hearing to clear the books. You and Missy'll testify she was only protecting herself and that'll be that."

"She shouldn't even have to go through the goddam bother."

"You hear how is Benny?"

"There's no there there in Benny's head. Look at that, will you?"

On the screen the grainy print showed Pauline struggling with the villain in the cockpit of a small airplane. In the long shot the little plane waggled its wings and bucked through stormy skies.

"You can tell that's a model," Monk said. "Special effects. That's one thing they do better now. What about Billy Ray?" he went on as though one remark had something to do with the other.

"His mother died on the table."

"Too bad."

"He's spreading a lot of money around."

"Oh, that so?"

"Says it came from the little bit of insurance his mother had."

"What do you say?"

"I say he copped a couple of those Porsches."

"Hey, hey, hey, that Billy Ray."

"Five'll get you fifty he's tapped out before the next track season's over," Heath said.

Heath and Monk watched the model plane crash into the waves.

"It bother you?" Monk asked.

"Does what bother me?"

"Does it bother you Lisa went back with her old man?"

"No, it don't bother me. It figured."

"I knew it figured, but I didn't know you knew it figured."

"Sure, I knew it figured."

The chapter ended and the next one began right away, the titles glowing up there like handwriting on some ancient wall.

"How about you and Missy?" Monk asked.

"I thought you didn't like her."

"I didn't like her as a cop. I never said I didn't like her as a person."

"That's good, because her and me are a possibility."

The titles were over and Pauline was struggling with the villain in the cockpit again. The airplane was diving toward the sea. Only this time she got her hands on the yoke at the last split second and pulled it up. The undercarriage of the model plane kicked up some spray but the plane didn't crash into the sea at all.

"That's a fucking cheat," Monk said.

"It's all a fucking cheat, don't you know that yet?"

AG4U